Ehrhor
Ehrhorn, Larry,
Four months in Brighton Park :
growing up in the sixties
$12.99   on1044740017

WITHDRAWN

3 4028 09435 2888
HARRIS COUNTY PUBLIC LIBRARY

EVIEWS.

...iched, a neat trick..."

Ehrhorn pulls it off beautifully and tenderly..."
- Kirkus Reivews

The story was great!" – Sherrie Warner
(Indie Book Reviews)

"**A literary treat** that had me captivated from the first to the last page." Jenna Brewster -- Indie book Reviews.

". . . a great job of bring(ing) in a fresh voice to this genre."
- Karen Matthews – (***Reader, Barnes & Noble reviews***)

"Ehrhorn's writing is fantastic... *I wanted more."* – Megan Kind (*Indie Book Reviews*)

". . . funny, *witty*, sweet, and sexy, but also deals with real issues that teens -- and adults face."
Layla Messing – **(Reader, Barnes & Noble reviews)**

Definitely a moving story that I'll remember and would recommend to others." Cody Bingham – *(Goodreads)*

"I liked the unpredictable feeling of this book."
Sherri Warner – *(Goodreads)*

Four Months in Brighton Park:

Growing up in the Sixties

A novel by Larry Ehrhorn

Copyright © 2017 by Larry Ehrhorn
All rights reserved. No part of this book may be reproduced or transmitted in any form or by any means, electronic or mechanical, including photocopying, recording or by any information storage and retrieval system without permission in writing from the publisher.

Publisher: Madijean Press | Madison, WI
ISBN: 978-0-692-92846-2
Library of Congress Control Number: 2017915977

Title: Four Months in Brighton Park | Larry Ehrhorn
Author: Larry Ehrhorn
Digital distribution | Madijean Press, 2017
Paperback | Madijean Press, 2017

DEDICATION

To my wife Becky
and my son Larry,

who always make me feel good.

CHAPTER 1

Swedarsky and Others

Life might not have been so bad if I hadn't had all those pimples covering my face, but I did, and so my existence was a lot rougher than most students at Talbot High in 1965. I wasn't sure I had surface flesh until I was eighteen. Not the combined efforts of Clearasil ointment and gallons of Bonne Bell cleansing lotion could curb the facial assault. To compound my facial humiliation, I, Kelly Elliott, the kid with the two first names, also had to cope with the school lummox. Almost every day I'd just be standing quietly at my locker, minding my own business, and Swedarsky would yell, "Hey, Elliott! It looks like your face caught on fire and somebody tried to put it out with an ice pick!" Then everyone would snicker like a bunch of jackasses. At first I'd try to picture them all with donkey heads, their mouths open, braying. It gave me a chance to secretly laugh back, but I gave up that practice for Lent.

What bothered me the most was that no matter how many times they had heard the cretin yell his clichés at me, they'd still roar like he had just told the funniest goddamn joke in the world. Of course, Swedarsky made sure that he always bellowed his witticisms during the peak of passing periods or after school when everyone in the school and South America was gathered. That son-of-a-bitch made life more miserable than it already was, and there was nothing I could do about it. Swedarsky may have had the I.Q. of an elm tree, but he was big. I mean, it doesn't take the most intelligent individual in the world to play football and to crush someone's skull, especially since Swedarsky weighed

225 pounds and I was a runty 130.

It was a Friday afternoon in March when my life took a decisive change in its monotonous and often degrading course. A split-second decision altered the attitudes of those around me and propelled me down a path for which I felt unprepared. During the next few months this one reaction perpetuated another, and I was hurled along, caught in the wave of affairs that carried me through adolescence. It was like the tumbling domino effect – nothing could deter the progression once it had begun.

That particular Friday I was in a good mood, standing at my locker, deciding what books I would need for the weekend. The relatively early arrival of the Chicago spring, which meant that temperatures often rose above freezing, had begun to put everyone in a more positive mood, as sporadic relief from the winter onslaught began to appear. Instead of piles of pure white snow, we started to see gray piles of dirty slush, which, though ugly, people took as a good sign. There was a home basketball game that night against Morton East, our most hated rival, and I had just earned a "B+" on Tuesday's exam in Bates' world lit. class, my most difficult course. In addition, on a fluke I had tossed in the winning basket during phy ed class. All of those minor victories to preface two days of warming freedom. Nothing was going to spoil one of my rare, buoyant moods.

"Hey, Elliott! I heard your car battery blew up and you caught a face full of battery acid. Tough break!"

There were the same braying jackass responses from my senior classmates. In a spirited moment of courage I thought I'd try a little bravado. I had just learned the word *bravado* in English class that day and felt inspired by our discussion of *The Old Man and the Sea* and Santiago's survival against "the great fish." Later that day I learned to realize the b.s. that was involved in trying to be a martyr. None of the literary heroes (Natty Bumppo, Billy Budd, etc.) had had a face full of pimples or had to deal with the likes of Joe Swedarsky.

I looked up the hall at the bastard and tried a sneer I had seen the Crusher use on professional wrestling. With my bottom teeth extended (very painful!), eyes squinted, and the stoicism needed to endure at least a broken nose, I waited for silence. When I could sense that my change of temperament had at least stupefied the crowd into a hush, I gave Swedarsky my best life-parting shot – I defiantly stuck-up my middle finger.

"Up yours, fat ass!" I growled.

Christ! I didn't realize someone that large could move so fast. I had figured that I could easily outrun him on crutches should the need arise, but before I was able to blink, he had me by the shirt collar, pinned against a locker, with my feet barely touching the floor. It was a natural instinct to kick my suspended feet, but I was afraid I would hit his shin and irritate him enough to kill me. His impression of the Crusher was far more realistic than mine.

Tension in his voice cut my throat. "Whatch you say to me, fairy?"

That question gave me a fair and reasonable option – I could either apologize and be arrested for attempted suicide, hoping that the governor would grant me a pardon, or I could repeat myself and painfully end a rather unfruitful life at the age of seventeen. I quickly decided that telling Swedarsky "Up yours!" would hardly qualify me for martyrdom, and that death in my situation would definitely be painful and in vain.

My voice sounded like an adolescent Mickey Mouse. "I, I didn't mean it. Really! It's just that I wish you'd stop picking on me all the time. That's all."

Being raised a liberal Catholic, I quickly began to swing my beliefs to the right and prayed like Saint Peter. My prayers' immediate effect was astounding – running down the hall came a Savior, sent from God Almighty. Mr. Shipstead, the physical education teacher and Swedarsksky's football and wrestling coach, stomped up to the scene of the murder-in-progress. All I could think of was Mrs. Peterson's drama class and her definition of *deux-ex-machina.*

"All right, men. What seems to be the trouble here?"

He didn't even tell the lummox to let me loose. Christ! Anybody with glass eyes could see what the trouble was. David and Goliath were at it again. Only this time the little guy hadn't even loaded his sling.

Swedarsky maintained his iron grip and smiled like the *Mona Lisa.* "Nothing, Mr. Shipstead, sir."

That "sir" really got me. Usually, it was "Old Shithead made me run ten extra laps for being ten minutes late for practice." I thought, "Someday that fat bastard/teacher will catch syph and everybody'll know where he got it from."

There were rumors that Shipstead stuck it to the librarian, Fern Winegarden, after school hours. Supposedly the only blind spot from the library entrance was between the shelves that housed the rarely used books on philosophy and religion, where Bill Haack reported that they had once disappeared for an entire study hall. Stories spread all over school about how Shipstead pumped Winegarden right between Rousseau and Norman Vincent Peale.

Swedarsky prattled on. "As everyone here will support, sir, Elliott here just said something that we don't mind for the locker room but is offensive in the hallways."

Smokes! That line of drivel was getting a bit difficult to absorb. I wished that Swedarsky was holding me off the ground just to keep the bullshit from devouring my shoes.

"Well, what about it, Elliott?"

Shipstead always sides with his "boys," no matter how wrong they might be. He could have witnessed his entire football team pummel an eighty-year-old woman, snatch her purse, and Shipstead would testify that she had carelessly left her purse accessible and corrupted the youths' innocence.

"Mr. Shithead, sir . . . "

"What?!"

It was out before I could stop it. Goddamn Swedarsky! Just thinking about his hypocritical behavior and I slipped with the demeaning but accurate epithet. It was a Freudian slip, but the impact would be devastating. Now Swedarsky had won, no matter what happened. He even had the gratification of hearing the moronic coach called "Shithead" to his face.

"I'm sorry, Mr. Shipstead, sir. It's just that your name is so easy to mispronounce. I could talk better if Swedarsky would loosen his grip."

Old Shithead just glared, and I felt like a fly caught in a tarantula's web. Swedarsky grinned, one of those smart-ass grins you'd like to erase with a bulldozer.

"Put him down, Joseph."

Kidding me? Joseph! What a crock! Joseph! That was as bad as Swedarsky's "sir." Joe would be an all right name for a truck driver, but to call 225 pounds of solid stupidity "Joseph" was like casting Truman Capote as Elliott Ness. It was a sacrilege, like thinking Swedarsky would marry a virgin named Mary and raise the next Messiah. What a crock! Anyway, I was glad to feel Swedarsky finally relax his grasp again. I was also surprised that I didn't feel bullshit all over my shoes.

"Now what is your problem, Elliott?"

"Well, sir, it's really no . . . ." The tension had caused my goddamn voice to crack! Christ! There's nothing like trying to defend yourself to two woolly mammoths and have your voice squeak. Everyone, including Old Shithead, started smirking behind muffled laughter. And I had no place to crawl for escape.

Swedarsky picked up the explanation. He had me buried up to the neck in sand and was now entertaining himself by kicking the squirming head.

"It's just something personal between us, Mr. Shipstead, sir. It'll be okay now. We'll settle the matter between ourselves, later!"

I didn't like his emphasis on "later." That ominous tone told me that I had best stop taking the normal bus and hire a Brinks truck to take me to and from school. Either that or hire Sonny Liston as a permanent bodyguard. Not practical.

5

Shipstead caught the gist of the remark and jumped to the rescue, though I wasn't sure whose. I sensed that he was contemplating legalized manslaughter.

"Now wait a second, Joseph. None of this after school fighting stuff. You don't need any more black marks on your record. I fought hard to get you a shot at that football scholarship next fall and you're not going to blow my reputation for coaching ball players with good sportsmanship. If you guys have an argument, we'll settle it in the usual manner."

I knew what that meant. Swedarsky grinned like the Cheshire cat. I felt my lunch of meatloaf halfway back up my throat. Shithead usually made guys "settle their differences" by lacing up the boxing gloves and headgear – ancient equipment still present from thirty years ago when boxing was a legitimate school sport—locking them in the wrestling room, and letting them "release their pent-up emotions" by pounding each other to bloody pulps, within reason, of course. With the odds of our match, the act would have been labeled as premeditated murder by any court in the land.

"I have some quick business to attend to. You two dress out and meet me in the gym in ten minutes."

God had spoken and signed my death warrant. Tramp, tramp, tramp! Down the hall went God. In my mind I could hear "Taps" being sounded from the band room. Swedarsky just stood there with that shit-eating grin.

"See you at the cemetery, gravel-face."

Tramp, tramp, tramp! Down the hall went my executioner. "Taps" had stopped. The few remaining spectators left the school, heads bowed like participants in a papal ceremony, and passed with such encouraging remarks as, "Sorry, kid," and "Too bad, Elliott."

That ten minutes had to be the longest in recorded history. I tried to pass the time by mentally singing "Wishin' and Hopin'" but it did nothing for my anxiety; the clock had ceased movement. Swedarsky just leaned against the office door, occasionally pounding a fist into his open hand, smirking. I paced nearby and studied the gym carefully, noticing cracks, colors, and banners I had never fully regarded. "State Basketball Champions – 1952." Really? I never knew that.

At 4:00 Old Shithead finally appeared, his face red and his composure flustered.

"Sorry, men. I had some work to do in the library and lost track of time."

He had also forgotten to pull up his zipper.

The fight didn't last long. If the purpose had been to "release pent-up emotions," I got the royal screws put to me. In fact, I didn't even land a punch. Swedarsky only needed to land three before Shipstead stepped in. All I could remember was a huge, red boxing glove smashing me below the left eye, so that I thought my head would rotate 360 degrees on its pivotal neck. The second punch turned it the other way. The third landed squarely on my forehead, knocking me almost unconscious. The next thing I could recall was Shithead looking down at me, pressing an icepack to my eye. I had never even raised my gloves.

"He got ya' good, Elliott. Guess ya' don't know much about boxing, but I hope you learned a lesson from this. Your eye may be black a few days, but you'll live. Remember – never pick a fight with someone bigger than you." I wondered who that wouldn't include.

My mother reacted to my black eye in her usual, calm fashion – she threatened to sue Swedarsky, his parents, old Shithead, the principal, the school board, the city of Chicago, and the Illinois State Boxing Commission, if there was such an organization. I was always her "poor boy," and anything that happened to me was a major event. As I grew older, she became more protective; I supposed that she felt me growing out of reach from her maternal hold, a transition that she could not easily accept. I was all she had, and she protected me to the point of absurdity.

For example, when I was six, Janey Thompson took me into the alley behind a garage and we pulled down our pants to see each other's "thing." I got ticked because Janey didn't have anything to look at and I did all the showing. From that day until Janey moved out of the neighborhood three years later, I'd charge Janey a nickel to see my "thing." Incidentally, Janey must have seen quite a few "things," because she quit school at sixteen to have a baby. I hadn't thought that my exposure meant so much to her, and I felt guilty to the point where I wanted to refund all of her nickels.

Mrs. Winthrop, the old bat from across the alley who kept constant surveillance of the neighborhood from her post at the kitchen window, had seen Janey and me and immediately reported the incident to my mother. Ma practically had seizures, called the cops, and told them that Janey Thompson was a sexual pervert. The cops told her to talk with Janey's mother, that they would not arrest a six-year-old for sexual solicitation. Ma chewed out Mrs. Thompson and Janey and, she forbade me to go anywhere near "that little slut."

I guess that incident was probably the major reason I was so shy with girls —it was instilled in my brain that girls would cause injury to my well-being. Unlike Pavlov's dogs, I did not salivate at the sight of female flesh until I was almost sixteen, putting me several years behind my classmates; I cringed and averted any of their casual and innocent attentions. By the time I had outgrown the fear, I was so damn ugly and insecure that no girl would ever approach me anyway. I believe psychologists professionally call it "getting screwed-up at an early age." Ironically, the only girl I ever wanted to speak to was Janey Thompson – I figured that we had no secrets between us.

I suppose my mother was over-protective because she had been cheated out of a husband, and I was her sole possession and a reminder of happier times. Six months after I was born, my father was rushed to St. Anthony's Hospital for an emergency appendectomy. When my mother went to visit him the day after the operation, he was gone. I don't mean that he had died - I mean that he had vanished. Somehow he had escaped the bureaucracy of the hospital and had completely disappeared. He hadn't signed out or left a note. He had simply disappeared from the face of the Earth as we knew it, never to be seen by either of us again. I always felt partly to blame, but at six months everything was out of my control, so I lived with mixed emotions of sympathy and bitterness. For a while I had fantasies that he was a spy and that Kruschev and the Russians had kidnapped him and were holding him in the Kremlin.

At the time of the Swedarsky altercation, my mother was 45 years old and still looked good. Every two weeks I would be sent to Walgreen's for a bottle of Clairol Autumn Amber #12. I could hear her struggle into her girdle every morning as she prepared to spend a day in the steno pool of Levin's Insurance Company downtown. Rarely missing a day in five years, she rode the orange el line twenty minutes and earned a livable wage – enough to pay the rent for the bottom of a two-flat in the Brighton Park district of Chicago. While Lyndon Johnson was waging his "war on poverty," we were trying to survive the "battle of the status quo."

Brighton Park was a "changing but safe" neighborhood on Chicago's southwest side. Settled mostly by Polish, Irish, and Lithuanian immigrants, the housing was mostly two or three floors, weathered brick dwellings with almost no yards. Talbot High School was a simple eight block walk or bus ride down Archer, the main drag through Brighton Park. Within four blocks of our apartment, we had ample businesses, including an A & P grocery store, a theatre, two banks, Simec's Polish bakery (home of the best Kolachke in the world, including Warsaw). Further down Archer toward Damen there were locally owned independent stores – Anthony's shoes (if you've got feet, we've got your size), Kiniski's clothing, Pat's Appliances (everything from Philco TV sets to Whirlpools). All the stores had banks of bright, fluorescent lights hanging from the ceilings, creating a bright yet sterile atmosphere. Rumors of a new Sears store were frequently spread.

Naturally, no neighborhood would be complete without its local teen "hang-out" -- Birdie's for ice cream after the movie, and Huck Finn Donuts, which not only had the best doughnuts in the city but was the only neighborhood late-night diner with a juke box and standard red vinyl booths. If there were teen hang-outs, then there also had to be adult "hang-outs." Mickey's Irish seemed to be the most popular. Ma took me there occasionally for their Friday night fish fry, which I thought was a real treat. The other bar, which I would probably have to wait until I turned 21 to visit, was Archer's Corner, a rather dark bar with blackened windows. Also, Paco's, Brighton Park's first Mexican restaurant, had just opened. I liked Brighton Park – it was self-sufficient, safe, developing, becoming.

Of course, what would any neighborhood be without its cornerstone – the church. My mother and I attended the Five Martyrs Catholic Church every Christmas Eve, Easter, and an occasional guilt Sunday. Not that I grew up heathen. When I was a child, Ma would take me to 9:30 mass every Sunday, the single mother determined to raise her son the right way. I was seven when I realized just how important the role of the church was to her.

We were having a lasagna supper when I thought I would lighten the evening with a joke I had heard but did not understand. Jerry had told it to me after school, and I laughed along with Jerry, having no idea what the joke meant.

"Hey, Ma. Do you know what happened to Helena Rubenstein?"

She shook her head "no." I started to chuckle before I gave the punch line, trying to build up to the humorous reaction.

"Max Factor."

Smack! She slammed the table so hard that her plate fell to the floor. My chuckle turned to fear as I put up my arm in reflex to defend myself from what I was sure was an imminent slap, something my mother had never done to me. Instead, she tightly gripped my arm, pulled me up, and hauled me out the back door.

"It's a joke, Ma," I tried to explain.

"No, it's not!"

Her grip never loosening, she walked/dragged me the six blocks to the church. I was terrified – both of my mother and the anticipation of going to hell – why else would she haul me to church, but to try to save my poor, lost soul?

"Sit there and don't you move!" she commanded as she used both hands to pin my shoulders to the back pew. "I'm going to find Father Pavlis."

The stern-looking Lithuanian (I wasn't sure what that meant, but I had a hunch that Lithuanian was a country in ancient times) priest stood by the front altar. Even he seemed a bit intimidated as Ma marched up to him; it was scary to think that even a priest would back away from the look on her face.

She was talking animatedly with her hands, even making the sign of the cross at one point, but I could not hear a word. Father's face changed from patient to shocked, back to normal, and I thought I detected a little smile at the end. He put his hands on Ma's shoulders, then gently sat her in the front pew and walked back to me. With a reputation as a strict priest, he didn't seem as horrifying as I had anticipated, especially after Ma's tirade.

"Kelly, follow me, please. I need to talk with you in my office."

We spent the next half hour surrounded by Jesus, Mary, God, and more holy relics than the Vatican possessed (maybe not). There was also a framed picture of a golden retriever on his desk. I put my hands flat on my thighs, feet flat on the floor, and never moved.

He explained about bad, sinful words, without listing any specifics, that should never be used at risk of spending eternity in the burning, painful fires of hell. I wasn't sure which was the bad word –· "Max" or "Factor." I was still confused, but didn't want to drag out the reprimand with questions. Clarity be damned!

My mother was still in the front pew, probably having spent the entire time praying for my soul. Her gentle smile was back in its place. She pulled me to her in a crushing hug and said, "I'm sorry, Kelly. I'm so sorry," and broke into tears, squeezing me harder as she cried.

Now I was confused. What was she sorry for? I was the one who had to see the priest. She thanked Father Pavlis, gently shook his hand, and led me out the front door.

Instead of retracing our steps home, Ma put a hand on my back and we headed toward Damen Avenue, away from home. Still trying to understand what had happened the past hour, I silently followed the lead. We walked twenty minutes in silence; I could hear an occasional sniffle but did not look up.

The lights grew brighter as Huck Finn's Donuts came into view. I smiled as we waited for the green light to allow us to safely cross the street. About once a month, my mother took me for a cherry doughnut and a coke, while she had black coffee and a French doughnut. No special reason – just a monthly celebration of the passing of another month. Even when I reached high school age, I still loved our monthly outing.

Ma pushed me inside and I looked for an empty table. There was one near the front, but Ma told me to wait a minute, and she spoke to Anita, one of our favorite waitresses. Anita nodded her head, held up a finger to wait a second, tore off a check, and gave it to a group of four at a booth. They promptly got up and went to pay. Anita made out a clean order slip and ran it back to the kitchen, then started to stack the dirty dishes into an empty gray plastic container and waved us over. I beamed, almost giddy, as for the first time we sat in a "booth-for-four only," with all its glorious room and privacy.

"Don't we need four people, Ma?" I asked, forgetting all the previous adversity.

"Normally, yes, but I asked Anita if we could have it tonight for a special occasion."

"What special occasion? Your birthday is in October and mine is in July."

She smiled, thought for a second, and seemed embarrassed not to have a clear answer. Instead she changed course.

"Did Father Pavlis explain things to you, Kelly?"

"I guess so. Something about using bad words and not burning in he . . .eternal fires. He seemed nice about it for a priest."

Anita came to the table with two hot fudge sundaes, piled high with whipped cream, wafer cookies, and a cherry on top.

"Enjoy," Anita said with a Spanish accent that seemed to add to the enjoyment and surprise.

I was dumbfounded. I had seen sundaes go past our table many times but the cost had seemed too high in my world. Still not sure what was happening, I wondered if I used more bad words and got a hot fudge sundae every time, if the flames of hell just might not be worth the risk.

I waited for Ma to give me the sign that the sundae was really all mine and nodded for her to go first. She spooned the cherry and whipped cream off the top, licked her lips, then waited for me. I tried to copy her, but wasn't quite as skillful or graceful.

"Eat it, don't wear it, Kelly," she joked as she wiped whipped cream off my nose.

After a minute of gorging, I just had to ask.

"Ma, I listened to Father Pavlis, but to be honest, I'm still not sure what I said that was wrong."

"Father did not give you a list of the words that might offend?"

"No."

She pondered again. "Well, as you get older, Kelly, you'll hear more and more of these words. You'll know them when you hear them because kids will giggle and tease with them. As you get older, they'll be used in anger and in dirty jokes. I want you to promise me that you'll try not to follow the crowd and use them too much, okay? I know it will become almost impossible not to use curse words but give a try, Kelly. You'll be more sophisticated and well-liked. It's important that people like you, Kelly."

"Sure, Ma. I don't want to spend the after-life in you-know-where."

That brought a wide smile to her face as she devoured more of her sundae. There was an awkward silence as we ate but something still puzzled me. "Ma, why were you so mad at me? I just thought it was a joke that Jerry told me. I didn't know there was anything wrong with it. I thought you were going to hit me. I was really scared, Ma." My voice had cracked at the end, as some tears started to form.

Again, her waterworks started and she hugged me tightly. After a minute, she regained control.

"I'm so sorry, Kelly. No child should ever be afraid of his mother. I would never hit my son. I just lost my temper and didn't think of how you would react. To be completely honest, you reminded me of someone for a few seconds."

I thought that an odd reply. "Really? Who?"

"Your father."

"My father?" I never knew him, of course, and she never spoke of him.

Again, she was silent as she considered saying more. "I wasn't going to tell you about him until you were much older, but it looks like the opportunity has been forced. Your father could be a wonderful man, but he had emotional problems. He worked at a printing company, but it was mostly simple, lower-level work. He could never seem to climb the next step, and after three years he realized that he would never become a master printer, maybe not even an apprentice. He was a hard worker, just not overly educated or naturally intelligent. He always said that the smartest thing he ever did was to marry me."

I smiled, curious about who this man, my father, was. I was willing to listen all night. "So what happened? How come he never came back from the hospital?"

Another long wait as she stared into my eyes, and I

wondered if she was debating whether to tell me any more.

Finally, "I told him not to."

She let it sink into my tiny, seven-year-old mind.

"Why?" just curious, not angry.

My mother put her hand over mine and explained. "Kelly, he wasn't a happy man, and I tried but didn't seem able to help him. When he realized that his life wasn't going the way that he wanted, he would start hanging out at the bars after work. Drinking with friends would help numb his mind to his failures. The only good thing he felt he had ever done besides marrying me was to father his son. Unfortunately, that just wasn't enough for him. He wanted a son who would be proud of the old man, and he never felt he could achieve it."

"But I wasn't that hard to raise, was I? Look at what you've done by yourself."

"Yes, Kelly, but there's more. Some nights he came home drunk and he had a sadistic smirk on his face. At first he would just grab and pinch me, trying to be playful, but I think he knew that he was hurting me. Then he'd start swearing and calling me nasty names, until one night he finally hit me, hurting me so bad that I ached for days. Finally I decided that the next time he started to call me names, I wouldn't wait for the beating and I would grab you out of your crib and take the next train to your Aunt Amy's.

"One night he was very late and I watched for him out the front window. I saw him staggering up the walk, yelling obscenities, more drunk than usual, and he terrified me. I got a butcher's knife and when he came through the door, I showed him the knife and my contorted face. He backed down the stoop and tripped down the stairs, falling hard enough on his head to not be able to get up again. I had reached my breaking point, Kelly. I had to protect us, so I called the police, who had gotten to know him from too many prior calls, and the ambulance took him to St. Anthony's, where he remained a couple days.

"A lady police officer helped me write a letter telling him

not to come back and that I had to worry about my son, too. The officer had a judge submit an order to stay clear of us. I expected a phone call or some reply. What I got was a one-page letter, apologizing to the end of the world. But he never said that he wanted to try again. Instead, he wished me the best always and asked me to please try to raise our son better than he would. He was going to Tennessee, where an uncle could get him a job at an auto-assembly plant."

"Have you ever talked to him again?"

"No, Kelly. I swear to you. We haven't contacted each other since then. We divorced, but it was all handled through lawyers. I never asked him for anything, so here we are, eating hot fudge sundaes at Huck Finn's Donut Shop in Chicago."

"Wow, Ma! How come you never told me all this before?"

"Kelly, you're only seven years old and shouldn't ever have to think about such things. I was waiting for a more appropriate time when you were older, but I guess this is it. I want you to think about your future; when all those girls start to chase you, and they will, treat them like you treat your own mother. Okay, Kelly?"

After that story I would have promised her the moon. "Sure, Ma. I think I'm done with my ice cream. Thanks for the sundae. Can we go home now?"

We walked home in silence, but I had one more question.

"Ma, can I ask you one more thing?"

"Of course, Kelly, what is it?"

"What was my father's name?"

She looked straight ahead and smiled. "His name was Kelly."

CHAPTER 2

Baldy Smith and the Scholarship

Because it was the only home I had known, I was comfortable with the working-class appearance of our apartment. Ma kept it clean and comfortable, but as I grew more educated, I couldn't help comparing it to a set from a Tennessee Williams' play. We only had one bedroom, so I slept on the front room sofa, a faded deep blue corduroy piece with hand towels covering the worn arms that left rib marks on me. Always wanting the best for her poor boy, Ma bought me a used desk and put it in her bedroom, which she let me use as my own study until 10:00, when she generally went to bed. Occasionally, if I had lots of homework, she would just shut the bedroom door and sleep on the couch, instructing me not to wake her until it was time for her to get ready for work.

I guess it wasn't easy raising me by herself, but I didn't appreciate that fact until I was on my own. Her major goal in life was my college education – an achievement not only for myself, but to give her something to brag about to her co-workers in the office. It was her fantasy, and I had no say in the matter. Ma always meant well; it's just that sometimes she'd tend to over-react to normal teen situations, like the bit with Swedarsky. It was just another happening in my life of catastrophic events, with my mother playing the role of the United Nations Relief Fund.

After I had finally calmed her to a level of mild hysteria, which was comparable to putting out the Chicago fire with spit, we managed to sit down and eat supper. I could see that she was still steaming, planning some scheme to get even with the culprits who had hurt me. She'd keep getting up and glancing out the kitchen window, as though the mysterious, definitive answer was waiting on the window sill. I finally decided to change the subject.

"Are you doing anything special this weekend, Ma?"

A positive reaction! "Oh, I'm glad you said something. I almost forgot in the confusion. Do you think you could spend the night at Jerry's? Dan Phillips called this afternoon. He'll be coming in late this evening and would like to sleep on the couch. And with him on the couch, I hate to see you sleep on the floor. Hotel rooms are so expensive, even though the airlines partially pay for some third-rate dump out near O'Hare airport. I told him that I thought it would be okay. Do you think Jerry would mind?"

The old lady was going to get laid again. I didn't mind really. I guess she was old enough and entitled to her "fun," but I hated the façade she put on. I knew where Dan Phillips would spend the night, but it was difficult to accept the scene with my own mother as one of the leading participants. This wasn't a good time with Janey Thompson – this was my mother! Still, a loyal son's duty.

"No, I don't think Jerry would mind. We're going to the basketball game, so ..."

"With that eye?"

She enunciated each syllable, probably thinking that I couldn't hear well with a black eye. "You're going to the basketball game with that eye?"

It would have been easy to reply, "No, I thought I'd leave my eye here. Soak it in some Epsom salts overnight," but I knew that I had better not antagonize an already delicate situation. She did want me out of the house, so I did have some leverage. One upsmanship was one of our favorite games.

"Okay, Ma. You're right. I'll stay home tonight. I won't mind sleeping on the floor."

Expecting a smart-ass reply, she was thrown off-balance. "Well, as long as it doesn't hurt, I suppose you can go. But be

18

careful. I would like to see Dan."

Dan! Dan Phillips! He was another draftee for my "Top Ten Asshole List," along with Shipstead, Swedarsky, and others. Christ, I hated that son-of-a-bitch! He was a goddamn pilot who flew all over hell and probably had a girl in every city, making each woman feel that she was the "only one." Buck-toothed hypocrite! He was always making crude comments about his cockpit and his Phillips head screwdriver. Ma would always giggle like the young Shirley Temple and try to hush him so that I wouldn't hear, but I always heard. He made me want to vomit.

Dan Phillips was the kind of moron you'd see in an old movie or comic strip, where the loser grease ball was trying to make it with the impressed-by-the-older-guy teeny bopper, but her kid brother was always hanging around, so the greaser would give the kid a quarter "to go to the movies." Phillips was not only like that character – he was that character. The bastard would whip a buck at me with a, "Here, kid. Get lost in the movies for a couple hours." I'd look at Ma in hopes that she'd ask me to stay, but she'd always nod affirmatively, while that simple-minded prick would leer with that beaver-like grin of his. I'd always storm out for a few hours, slamming the door behind me, having too much pride to look like a pimp for my own mother to accept the proffered bill. Too bad—I could have retired at eighteen.

Phillips and I had a mutual hatred toward each other. I hated him because I knew that the only reason he came over was to mess around with my mother, and he knew that I knew it. The major problem was that he also knew I'd do whatever she wanted, which usually meant getting lost for a couple of hours or for the entire night. I guess it was his smugness that made the situation even more unbearable. One time I faked stomach cramps and Ma made me lie on the couch for the afternoon, while Phillips paced the kitchen like a frustrated stud during mating season.

Whenever Phillips was around I used to sulk and fantasize about his plane getting hijacked to Cuba, where he'd rot in some nasty Castro prison camp, the toy of Spanish-speaking homosexuals. Not wanting innocent people to suffer, I would sometimes curb my imagination and substitute the hijacking for catching a good dose of the clap so that he would have to spend the rest of his life in some asylum getting genital warts scraped off his Phillips head screwdriver, instead of being retired to the stud farm. I really despised Dan Phillips.

That evening Ma and I ate some oven-baked frozen chicken. She usually only cooked a complete meal on Sunday afternoons. During the week we always ate something frozen, warm-and-serve, or take-away. Progress had made cooking so simple – warm something in the oven for thirty minutes and it was ready to eat. She wouldn't even fry hamburgers from scratch – I was usually sent to White Castle. With her schedule, I never resented my diet. Actually, it was a teenager's dream.

It was usually the period after supper that I hated the most. Deadening silence would fill the kitchen and expand to a tension, creating a vacuum waiting release. Once the major duty of feeding her son had been accomplished, Ma seemed to experience a change of life. Although it was nice to know that someone else's life centered on my well-being, it was a real strain trying to deal with the post-supper blues. A psychiatrist would probably have analyzed the period after supper as a time that had been special between my parents, and she harbored latent resentment about my father's absence. I didn't know what it was – all I knew was that I had to deal with her ambivalent moods.

Ma would always find a point of conflict upon which to build her super-bitch persona. It might have been my treatment of Dan Phillips, a poor grade, my possibility of attaining a college scholarship, or the fact that my shoes were scuffed. These incidents would sometimes turn into minor shouting matches, until I found the wisdom to quickly excuse myself, vanish for an hour, and hope the mood would be gone upon my return. This happened about two school nights a week.

One night after a severe argument about my whereabouts on a certain Friday night, I went to the public library to look-up "menopause." For some odd reason Mr. Curtis, the health teacher, had briefly touched on the subject during my sophomore year. Ma had all the symptoms, and I tried to be more understanding, but her moods seemed contrary to the elements of nature, because she would only become extremely unpleasant from 6:30 to 7:30. I wished that the mood would strike her for a solid week, in order to flush it out of her system; then I could have coped. The situation had gone on for almost a full year, and I still was never sure what the next problem would be, but it drove me to the brink of insanity.

"Have you heard about your scholarship yet, Kelly?"

"No, Ma. Nothing yet."

Like a shot from a howitzer. "Well, what is taking so long? You'll be out of school in four months. For God's sake, I don't know what the matter is with that school of yours. Did you see Mr. Smith today?"

Baldy Smith was my guidance counselor. He supported the theory that those who cannot teach go into guidance counseling. He was another asshole I couldn't stand. From everything I've said so far, you probably think that I was the most critical little punk ever born. I wasn't really. It's just that at the age of seventeen, when I really wanted to decide things for myself, getting help if needed, it seemed that I was surrounded by nothing but unlikeable cretins. Not just cretins that I could brush aside without problem, but imbeciles like Baldy Smith, who played a major role in my life.

Baldy Smith, not Kelly Elliott, decided what classes I would take, at what ability level I would best learn, what I would do after graduation, and even how I would finance my future. All those decisions were based on a single standardized test that I had taken in eighth grade. For a day and a half we had all been crammed into an auditorium, given lapboards, and forced to fill-in an infinite amount of tiny spaces with a #2 lead pencil. Results of the achievement test would determine our futures. If someone had misread a couple of questions or dozed off from sheer tedium, his/her whole life could have been altered. Instead of being a veterinarian, one might be guided to agricultural classes to become a farmer. Rather than an architect, an erroneous answer might steer the student to waste management.

Professional guidance counselor Baldy Smith would take three minutes with each student, turning over an egg timer once the student had been seated, and translate the test scores like a fortune teller. "Three more right on Section G and you could have been in the accounting program. As it stands, I believe industrial education would best suit your abilities." At least no one qualified low enough to be a guidance counselor. Christ! The average teenager needed Green Beret combat training to survive.

Despite my vows to remain coolly subjective toward Ma's probing taunts, Swedarsky and Phillips had put me in an equally sensitive mood. "No, Ma. I didn't go to see that asshole today."

"What did you say?"

That was twice in one day that Freud had usurped my mind and forced me to speak honestly. Truth can be a very damaging characteristic to the inattentive mind.

"I'm sorry, Ma. It just slipped out. That Smith is just a pimp. That's all." "Pimp" was the most current it's-not-enough-to-get-into-serious-trouble slang in teenage vernacular. Everyone used it, but I doubt if half understood its literal meaning.

"That's no excuse for such language in this household. Who do you hang around with at that school, anyway? I never hear Jerry talk like that."

That statement was enough to make me hurl my lunch, again. Jerry Hogan was my best friend, but he had everyone snowballed. When Stevenson wrote *Dr. Jekyll and Mr. Hyde*, he created the prototype of Jerry Hogan. Around adults he was the epitome of decorum; to his classmates he was just a sometimes likeable buffoon. For example, one day each year the two of us would hold the National Gross Day Contest. All day long, usually during the midst of a typically dull summer, we would try to out-gross each other. I had won it the first year, but Jerry had been unstoppable the past three years. Last year's winner was "Do you think if you took old lady Winegarden's panties after Shipstead had done her in the library, and threw them straight up, that they would stick to the ceiling? Ever check the ceiling when you walk in, Kelly?" So much for Jerry Hogan and his candidacy for sainthood.

"Anyway, Ma. I didn't see Mr. Smith today. He said he'd call me into his office when he got word of the scholarship, but that may not be for a while yet. There's nothing we can do but wait. Okay?"

She had cooled. "Well, he is a busy man with all those seniors about to graduate. Perhaps the scholarships just aren't important to him like they are to the rest of us. You have to keep pestering him if you want to find out anything. After all, that's an important scholarship you're up for."

As usual, the b.s. overwhelmed me. It had been a bad day, and I was rolling like a runaway garbage truck.

"Shit! I mean 'shoot,' Ma. It's not that big of a deal. It's only worth $300 a year. That's a drop in the bucket compared to the total cost. Besides, you make it sound like such an honor. It's not. The state gives them out on a lottery system. All I had to do was finish in the upper half of my class and lie that I was interested in teaching. I didn't do a thing to earn it. This isn't a Rhodes Scholarship or anything like it. There isn't even any honor in winning. It's all luck!"

As soon as I had said it, I could see her lower lip quiver, and I realized that my temper had over-stepped its practicality again. We had gone over the scholarship conversation at least ten times, but she still took pride in her "poor boy," and I had deliberately hurt her feelings. I guess at the age of seventeen, I was one of those assholes that I hated

23

so much.

All that my mother wanted to do was see her son succeed and to have some bragging rights to her co-workers about how her son had won a scholarship and was going to college to become a teacher or doctor or lawyer. I guess everyone has a fantasy that keeps him going from day to day but then I just didn't have the sympathy or comprehension of my mother's needs. I was the kid who didn't believe that a fantasy should interfere with the realities of life. I, Kelly Elliott, who practically survived on fantasies. I used to spend hours dreaming of Laura LeDuc, the senior cheerleader captain, and of the wonderful life we could have together. Of course, she didn't even know I was alive, but what was the harm? I believed that fantasies were like certain crimes – the only ones that should be prosecuted were those that conflicted with the rights of other people. I was a profound little bastard.

Stubbornly, lashing out at an unreal enemy, I had tarnished Ma's major fantasy, and that selfishness always made me feel bad, until the next time I did it. Playing her game wouldn't have hurt me. Her eyes gleamed when I mentioned teaching math (my favorite subject), but that was b.s. too. I couldn't stand teaching a bunch of jerks like Swedarsky or Jerry Hogan or myself. But I had teased her with it during one of my lighter moods, and I should have had the decency to feed her what she wanted. It wouldn't have cost me a thing, but I could be a destructive little brat when I got the rare opportunity.

Ma just sat there and stared at me, very hurt. Not just average off-the-street hurt, but the kind of hurt that worked from the inside like a cancer. Then she delivered the coup-de-grace – her eyes became glassy and in another minute the inevitable tear would swell in the corner of her eye and wind its way down her cheek. She knew how to deliver a knock-out punch better than Swedarsky. It was time to depart – I had overstayed my welcome. For once I was grateful that Dan Phillips would soon be there. I couldn't deal with a sensitive mother.

"I gotta go, Ma. I'll be late for the game."

I stood, grabbed my jacket from the back of the chair, and kissed her on the cheek. She sat frozen. Damn her, anyway!

"See you tomorrow, Ma. Have a nice time tonight." I left the apartment just as the tear began to roll down her cheek. I hated it when she did that! It just wasn't fair!

CHAPTER 3

Laura LeDuc and the Talbot High Cheerleaders

Despite Ma's best effort to laden me with guilt, I was determined to enjoy myself at the basketball game. Before picking up Jerry, I stopped at the convenient, cramped corner store elegantly named "The Beer Depot," to buy a newspaper. Since the movies generally changed every Friday, I always bought the paper to see what movies were playing and where. It was a real treat; I loved movies and usually spent a lot of time going to various theatres on the weekend, especially if my mother was "busy."

The store's owner was affectionately called "Little Joey" because he had lost most of both legs in World War II, and his artificial limbs had been poorly fitted, making him just over five feet tall. He blamed the "goddamn government" for being too cheap with its veteran rehabilitation program. Most of the time the legs hurt him so much that he chose not to use them, so he sat on a high stool behind the counter, his detached legs within reach. He hated it when a customer would ask him for something from the delicatessen case, forcing him to refit the artificial legs and painfully hobble to get a pickle out of the tub or slice a half-pound of Black Forest ham. Joey liked me because I gave him the idea to buy a new stool with big casters on it, so he wouldn't have to get up and could just glide to the deli case. I even spent a Saturday helping him install some railings behind the counters so that he could push and pull himself. I guess I liked Little Joey because he was handicapped, too. I suppose he was the closest thing to a father that I had – he was non-judgmental and listened to me, just telling me to "keep your head on straight." I think he sincerely liked me because I was courteous and never tried to shoplift or buy cigarettes and stuff. There was an invisible bond between us.

Little Joey tried to act tough and ornery all the time because his war injury had forced him into it. He made enough money to get by, but he was bitter enough to realize that he would never get anywhere else in the world and that the rest of his years would be spent behind the counter, selling slices of salami and making change.

I picked-up a copy of the *Chicago Tribune* from the diminishing stack in front of the counter. The usual groups of perverts were present, browsing the girlie magazines and nudging their friends with a "look at that shot." A recent subtle change was a small influx of gay boys hanging around the store, checking out the muscle-building magazines. If there was only one guy ogling, it would not take long before another "muscle builder" was looking over his shoulder. After a few minutes of whispered exchanges and muted laughter, the two would put down the magazine and leave, smiling and waving at Little Joey, who would glare at them in an attempt to make them feel as uncomfortable as possible, in hopes that they would never return.

"God, I hate that hustling going on in my store. Why don't they go to a bar or someplace else? Neighborhood stores don't need behavior like that."

I nodded in agreement with Little Joey, even though I really didn't care, but my fond memories of getting penny candy from the jars at Little Joey's Beer Depot were pretty much terminated.

"Christ! What happened to your eye, kid?"

Joey had a low, raspy voice, like a character from a stereotypical gangster flick. It was good he sounded that way though – it helped fend off the maggots.

"I got in a fight at school. It doesn't hurt or anything. I never knew what hit me."

He nodded, understanding. "I bet he was bigger than you, wasn't he?"

I nodded affirmatively, reading his mind.

"I knew it. That's the way it is with the big guys. The only ones they can beat up are the smaller ones. Did you at least get in one good punch?"

Joey was hopeful. Somebody had to even the scores for the underdogs.

"Yeah, I got one in. I think I broke his nose," I lied. No sense in shattering everyone's fantasies in one night.

"That's good, kid. Stand up to those bullies. Just don't get yourself killed doing it. You know what I mean, kid?"

I had known Little Joey for a long as I could remember, and I wondered if he even knew my name. He always called me "kid," but I didn't mind it coming from him. He didn't mean it in a sarcastic way ·· "kid" was just a semi-affectionate term with a nice ring to it, like Kid Galahad.

"Sure, Joey. I know what you mean. I won't do anything stupid."

I paid for the *Tribune* and glanced over the movie listings. An all-night Marx Brothers festival was playing at the neighborhood Brighton Theatre, and I made a quick mental note.

"Well, I'll see ya', Joey. Take it easy."

"Sure, kid. No other options. And remember, keep your nose clean." He never smiled, but he meant to.

It was 7:30 by the time I had half-run the four blocks to Jerry's. We usually walked the eight blocks to the school, especially to the night games. We made our own game of it. Even though we were both runts, our school jackets made the old people cower when they saw us. Anybody from Talbot High was labeled as a brutal gang member capable of killing random victims for their gold fillings and causing all sorts of mayhem. Girls with school jackets were generally viewed as sluts who sold it to anyone for five bucks and gave green stamps. The rest of the students were viewed as drug addicts who sold marijuana or worse to kids at the Tick-Tock Nursery School. If not a hoodlum or drug dealer, the other students comprised the two percent of unfortunates who couldn't afford to pull enough strings to get transferred to one of the city's "better" schools. They were only partially correct. I didn't know if all Chicago high schools had the same stereotypes or not, but Jerry and I were harmless, still enjoying strangers' mistaken reactions.

It was a brisk March night, the kind where spring isn't quite sure if it's time for its grand or intermittent appearance. The snow had mostly melted, but freezing temperatures caused a thin coating of ice to form on the walks with hidden pockets of ice. More snow was predicted for that evening.

On my way to Jerry's house I saw an old man walking a man-eating German shepherd. Damn dog looked like it would enjoy tearing out my throat and gnawing at the cartilage. It was sniffing a lawn where some other mutt had left a pile. Then it lifted its leg and peed on it. I immediately thought of Baldy Smith and Swedarsky.

Jerry was sitting on his stoop, smoking a fag. His parents didn't know that he smoked or at least did not acknowledge the fact. Whenever he was out of the house, he smoked like a fiend to make up for lost time. I was sure he'd die of lung cancer by the age of twenty, but he didn't.

"Hey, man, how ya' doin'? Wanna square?"

It was his standard greeting. Although Jerry had been my best friend since he had moved to Chicago during the middle of third grade, he had more irritating habits than the population of China. One of them was, "Hey, man, how ya' doin'? Wanna square?" I guess it was his way of being cool, but I really hated it. He'd even greet me that way in the school cafeteria. I had been tempted on many occasions to check the back of his neck to see if there was a ring to pull, to make the Chatty Jerry Hogan doll say one of eight different phrases. Only Jerry's recording was stuck on "Hey, man, how ya' doin'? Wanna square?" He made me sick sometimes; he was my best friend.

I took the "square" and lit up. Bel-Air. He smoked Bel-Air! No teenage, defiant hoodlum from Talbot High smoked Bel-

Air. Jerry was saving the goddamn coupons, hoping to save enough to get a Stan Smith tennis racket. Christ – how fruity could one person be? Schemansky and the real grease balls of Talbot High School smoked non-filtered Camels or Chesterfields. They were cool!

Smoking didn't really appeal to me, but I sometimes did it because it was expected. Whenever I tried to inhale, I'd cough my fool head off and look like a real wimp. So I learned to just take the smoke into my mouth, try to hold it there long enough to give the appearance that I had swallowed it, and blew it out through extremely puckered lips. I would drop my face down and turn it away so that nobody could see that the smoke didn't come out in a neat, narrow stream, but more of a cloud. The whole pattern gave the appearance that smoking cigarettes changed my neck to rubber, as though each puff disintegrated the top section of my spine. I don't know if anyone was wise to me or not, but if they were, they at least had the decency not to let on. They were probably laughing their faces off on the inside or doing the same thing I was. My greatest fear was that someone would ask me to exhale through my nose, but I had been lucky in that regard. Anyway, mostly I just held the stupid thing to look cool.

"Christ, Elliott! Look at that eye! Swedarsky really let ya' have it. I'm surprised you're still alive. Why didn't he kill ya'?"

It was one of Jerry's typically inane questions, but he never meant any question as rhetorical.

"Because it's illegal! Besides, old Shithead was there to stop him."

Jerry was excited. "Did you really call him Shithead to his face? And did you really give Swedarsky the finger and tell him 'Up yours'?"

Hearing about my humiliating accomplishments from someone else, even if it only was Jerry, made them seem more real and important, and I began to enjoy the mild notoriety. Then the oddity of his question struck me.

"How did you know?"

The whole affair had happened after school, and not many people had witnessed the incident. Word must have spread, but how far? Was I famous?

"Christ, Elliott. Everyone on the bus was talking about it. Hammerschmidt came running out on the lawn telling everyone that you had told off Swedarsky and that he was killing you in the hallway. A bunch of us ran in, but Principal Schwarz, the asshole, wouldn't let us up the stairs. I hung around until 4:00 when Shipstead came out of the library and chased us out; you never showed. What happened?"

I couldn't help but feel a lift in my normally vanquished morale as I related the story to Jerry. I was elated by the idea that people who had never heard of me were now talking about me and how I had stood up to Swedarsky. Even Jerry had labeled me as a "minor celebrity," and I felt that the beating I had survived had been of merit. I thought, "Maybe some of the girls will even talk to me. Maybe even Laura LeDuc." But, as usual, I was moving too fast. Still, I lifted my head like a rooster about to crow. Telling off Swedarsky, calling the coach "Shithead" to his face, and living to attend a basketball game a few hours later was no minor achievement. Certainly martyrdom could not be totally out of the question! I quickened my pace, suddenly eager to reach my former hell.

We arrived as the teams were finishing their warm-ups. Instead of hanging my head to hide my pimples, I held my head high and proud, wondering how many people would recognize my merit badge, knowing who I was. It seemed that a few more people than normal were glancing my way. Once I thought I could see three football letter winners pointing at me, and I definitely heard someone say, "That's him, huh? He's lucky Swedarsky didn't tear his head off." It was the best I had felt since showing my thing to Janey Thompson.

Jerry and I took our usual front row seats in the bleachers. Nobody else wanted to sit too close to the action, fearing that it might show that they had school spirit – a

31

social taboo. The front row was sarcastically referred to as "rhiney row," but Jerry and I always sat there, not because we could see the game better, but because of the exquisite view afforded of the cheerleaders.

Talbot High School cheerleaders were an institution in the city of Chicago. To become a Talbot High cheerleader was to gain immortality. Once on the squad, any and all problems of normal female adolescence ceased to exist. Those elite could have as many friends as desired while being very selective, even snubbing certain persons without being labeled "stuck-up." Talbot High cheerleaders could buy a date book the size of an almanac, fill it, and never date the same guy twice for the rest of their long, prosperous lives.

For a Talbot High cheerleader, academia was no problem, except for that rare teacher, like old maid Powers, who hated any pretty girl and really hated cheerleaders. It took no Einsteinian brain to analyze her mind. Even if a cheerleader was stuck with a hag like old maid Powers, she could usually flirt her way through the guidance personnel, especially Baldy Smith, and get her schedule changed to all the horny, male teachers, like Bates. Then the goddess would merely sit back, smile, and cross her legs until she could catch the teacher's eye and enjoy watching him quickly seek shelter behind his desk or put a heavy book on his lap. Legend was that Bates once lifted the entire unedited version of the *Oxford Dictionary*, but, of course, the story never had any eye witnesses and the legend had never been proven. Not to the best of my knowledge, anyway.

In the event of any lab work, like chemistry or biology, a Talbot High cheerleader only had to select some unsuspecting male and he would do all the dirty work – dissection, touching something slimy, cleaning, while she sat idle, appeared fascinated, and complimented him on his manly skills. Obtaining a sperm specimen for the microscope would have been the easiest task of all. I remember one time in sophomore biology when we had to draw our own blood and type it. Judy Carter, a cheerleader, talked Pete Ohlert, loser, into drawing his own blood a second time after his initial specimen had clotted. She didn't want to stick "that awful thing" into herself. Everyone wondered if Pete got to stick his awful thing into her, but he was such a wimp that he would have fainted at the suggestion. To be one of the select twelve (of 3,500 students) was the closest thing to being a Rockefeller; riches abounded.

Becoming a cheerleader was no easily obtained goal; there were strict requirements. Every girl had to be extremely pretty or cute – no dogs allowed! Those "uglies" who did work up enough nerve to attend try-outs were humiliated for their lack of skills and generally laughed off the stage. Another classic rumor told that all the homely rejects turned to drugs and prostitution from the humiliation, but I didn't believe it.

Besides extreme beauty, there were other stringent, preliminary requirements, such as long hair and perfect legs that were willing to be exhibited brazenly. These superficial guidelines were written by the girls themselves. They also created the 36B rule. Girls with less than a 36B chest measurement could forget about joining. They had to make the letters "THS" protrude from their sweaters like gargoyles. If all three letters could be read from one side, the girl was considered too flat and was disqualified. Other schools definitely noticed the mammary magnitude of our squad and respectfully renamed the letters of "THS" to "Tits High School," in which the cheerleaders took much pride.

During my junior year Carol McKeller, one of their own, somehow offended the cheerleader clique (reason never learned by those outside the sisterhood) and refused to quit. Principal Schwarz, acting on an anonymous tip, found a half bottle of wine and a baggie full of marijuana in her locker. School rules dictated that she be immediately expelled from the cheerleading squad, and no one came to her defense.

Looking back I am able to see the extremely sexist views of those high school years in Chicago, but when teens are entering their awareness of so much at one time, avoiding sex and the growing attitudes about sex is like abstaining from alcohol during Prohibition – it couldn't be done, nor was there much desire to do so by either sex. It was a new and exciting facet of life.

In spite of all the politicking to make the cheerleading squad, a system comparable to Mayor Daley's city government appointees, a minor miracle did occur. A black sheep got mixed in with the flock and somehow survived. In the years to come, the Madonna of Talbot became another legend and hope grew for all females as they heard of how a small town girl from southern Illinois became a THS cheerleader, retained her purity (everyone had thought), and been made captain of the squad, a title to outclass Miss Nude Universe.

Her name was Laura LeDuc, and everyone took an immediate liking to her. At first she was the stereotypical goody-two-shoes, except not to the extent of being obnoxious or an obvious brown-noser. She had the shiniest and silkiest shoulder-length blonde hair, which would sway from side to side as she sashayed though the halls. Her aqua blue eyes and petite upturned nose complemented a sincere and warm smile.

Besides her angelic face, Laura LeDuc had a body that caused countless fantasies among the male population, teachers included. She didn't flaunt her figure like some girls – everything was natural. Everyone in school knew who was real and who was enhanced. Al Eveland used to kid Debby Rafer about her overnight expansion. He'd yell, "Quick, Debby. I gotta sneeze. Give me some Kleenex from the left one!" Laura was real and perfect, and at seventeen I, and probably every guy in the class of '65, fell insanely in love.

Laura always wore dresses to school, which was a refreshing change after the administration had eased the dress code. The other girls didn't resent her for it – they used her as a representative when they needed to express the feminine viewpoint. If it seems that I have over-extended myself in creating this Madonna of my puberty, I can only add that the spirit of the young Laura LeDuc had to be experienced to be comprehended. As Mrs. Fosland used to say in general science, "The concept of infinity is beyond the comprehension of the human brain." That is what I used to feel about Laura LeDuc until . . .

She had transferred into Talbot High in mid-November of our junior year. Laura had an innocence about her that indicated sincerity, not hypocrisy. Even though she was the most stunning girl in the school, she would play on others' perceived weaknesses to gain their confidence and trust. For example, she was the only one to competently handle Patty Baker.

Before Laura had moved in, Patty was known as "Boobs Baker." Other girls had challenged her for the title, but nobody could compete with the dimensions of Patty's chest. Patty was not shy about flaunting her curves. What Patty did not have which Laura did was a very small waist, which caused Patty to lose her unofficial title. That dethroning fueled further conflict, including malicious rumors that Laura was rather loose during lunchtime, if anyone had a few bucks to spare.

In spite of all this adversity, Laura retained her poise, refusing to acknowledge the rumors or stooping to Patty's level. Laura usually searched for the best qualities in people, complimenting someone on her gymnastic skills, his ability to quickly solve a trigonometry problem, or various comments about clothing, hair styles, etc. She knew how to work a crowd.

Laura's greatest conquest was over Patty Baker, which was like closing a lobotomy with a band-aid. Mrs. Springstead, the girls' gym teacher, sensed the rivalry between the girls and paired them as a badminton team in a phy ed tournament, hoping their difficulties would be put aside for the sake of teamwork. Not all teachers were complete morons. Patty carried the team with her power, but Laura had a drop shot that was usually unreturnable. Throughout their match they complemented each other perfectly, and soon words of praise were exchanged. Together they were unstoppable and eventually won the school title, nothing major but important. All animosity was eradicated during the three-week tournament, and soon they became something close to friends. Patty even confessed to creating lies about Laura's lunchtime activities. Thus, Laura LeDuc added another head to her collection. Given the chance, I think Laura might have been able to persuade Swedarsky into becoming a priest.

Laura had been at THS for two months when Carol McKellar, the victim of snobbery and non-conformity, was framed and kicked off the team. Thoreau and Emerson would have loved her nonconformist courage, but they weren't in charge of the cheerleading squad. During Christmas break it was discovered that Carol McKellar was about four months pregnant. She had been dating a college freshman, the father of the child. Despite her growing condition, she decided to graduate, and everyone made jokes about her delivering during graduation ceremonies, which would have been one hell of a lot more interesting than the standard "road of life" speech by the valedictorian. She did deliver at seven months; the baby died and Carol was broken physically and spiritually. Everyone who made jokes about her "dropping her load" at graduation felt shitty.

After Carol's exit, Laura decided to try out for the squad's vacancy. By that time she had made so many friends that even the incumbent cheerleaders wanted her on the team, figuring that she would not only add looks to the team, but also some sophistication. So Laura became a Talbot High cheerleader, did not conform, and rose to the top. And I fell more in love with her every day.

Jerry and I had all the breaks that night at the basketball game. Laura LeDuc was stationed directly in front of us. Whenever she was off the floor, she would kneel before us like a queen before her king, only showing her back to the king. I watched the entire game with glassy eyes. Occasionally when she came off the floor she would brush against us and excuse herself. It was enough to melt a seventeen-year-old boy with pimples and a black eye into a pool of butter.

One time she came off the floor and knelt so close to me that her perfect ass hovered a mere inch over my shoes. Hell, I could have acquired the worst leg cramp in the world, but Chicago would have turned Republican before I would have moved my foot a millimeter. Jerry kept giving me the sign to goose her and even whispered that it was a once-in-a-lifetime chance to make close, personal contact.

The basketball game was taking its usual course – we were getting killed, and our crowd was riding the referees. I never knew what referees earned to call our games, but it could not have been enough. I was sure that their life insurance companies labeled them as "high risk" and charged an extra $5,000 a year in premiums.

On that particular night the game was a real blow-out, and the crowd began chanting, "Club! Club!" This generally made the experienced refs tremulous, but the crowd was not suggesting that the zebras should be clubbed. Rather, they were yelling for the coach to put in Jimmy Pularski, the twelfth man, who was affectionately known as "Club." Unfortunately, he didn't get that name from the power in his fists, but because he was so uncoordinated that everyone was convinced that he had two club feet. He stood 6'8" but lacked that part of the brain that controlled all of his motor skills.

Whenever the outcome was hopeless, the spectators began yelling, "Club! Club! Club!" until the coach conceded and put him in the game. Then everyone would laugh and cheer for him as he clumped his way up and down the court, his arms flailing like those of a demented octopus.

His only basket that year had come on a court-length pass that he was able to lay in when the other nine players were at the far end of the court. Club had tripped getting back on defense, so he had stayed under the offensive basket. Jackson rebounded a missed Cougar shot and threw a bullet to Club, which he put in – after the buzzer. The crowd went wild with elation that their "freak" had made a basket. Then it noticed one referee crossing his arms emphatically with the "no good" signal. I remember four people getting onto the court before the other ref, an experienced veteran of Talbot High games, sensed the butchering of an innocent human being and overruled the initial call, avoiding a riot and saving a life. The gymnasium shook with joy and everyone went home happy. Again, the crowd was calling for Club, and a time-out had been called.

Laura LeDuc finally raised her gorgeous rear end from the vicinity of the dead meat I called my feet. I tried to regain the circulation by rotating the anesthetized feet, but it did no good. They were dead and I felt like Club.

Unfortunately, Laura had taken the floor to lead the crowd in the school song. Ordinarily I would have been pleased, except that everyone was supposed to stand. Having lost both feet, I felt that rising for the fight song was an unjust demand. Yet, I had to try, at least to show Laura that I was sincerely interested in school loyalty. It was a lot of b.s., but for the woman I loved . . . Everyone was up and singing when I made my big move. Wham! Down I went crashing my tailbone on the bleachers. "Christ, Elliott! You all right?"

Jerry seemed honestly concerned. He must have assumed that Swedarsky's thrashing was still affecting me.

"Yeah. My legs are asleep, that's all."

Jerry's concern was quickly replaced with laughter. Being in front of everyone, I had been clearly seen and more than likely would become the butt of many jokes for the next few weeks. My tailbone smarted and my feet began to feel like ten billion pins were sticking into them. Everything was normal for me.

As the teams took the floor, the crowd became manic. Club was in! If he scored during the remaining eighty-two seconds, Talbot High would have a statistical loss but a moral victory. Even I averted my attention from Laura LeDuc and concentrated on Club. It was the only excitement available for the fans of a losing team.

Two exchanges up and down the floor brought no results

for Club. He merely lumbered like an advertisement for uncoordinated athletes. Then it happened – my life began to end.

Koenig threw a wild cross-court pass to Club, who, because of his slowness in getting back on the rebound, was at the guard position. The pass floated through Club's outstretched paws, and he backed up to get it. Laura LeDuc foresaw the calamity, scooted out of the way, and I had Club in my lap.

Having 230 pounds of Club land in my lap was like trying to catch hundred pound weights dropped from the top of the Prudential Building. Again, my back was slammed into the empty bleachers behind me. My legs joined my almost revived feet in their death throes. After only two runs up the court, Club was sweating and smelling like the city's trash during a hot, summer sanitation workers' strike. The entire situation was gross and humiliating as I tried to catch my breath with that uncoordinated idiot on my lap. He was so stupid that he sat there until another player, who I couldn't see, pulled him back onto the floor. For his valiant efforts, he was applauded. I felt worse than when Swedarsky had kayoed me. Then heaven entered my blurred vision.

"Are you all right?" she asked.

I turned my head to see to whom my angelic Laura was speaking. Seeing no one else, I assumed it was me. The pain had stopped. I had to be dead, but at least I went the right direction after dying.

Again she spoke. "Are you all right? Getting hit by Swedarsky and Club in the same day is a bit much. Remind me not to walk in a lightning storm with you. Are you going to be okay?"

Laura LeDuc knew who I was! She knew that I had taken Swedarsky's best shot and survived to have Club pulverize every bone in my 130 pound body. My celestial thoughts were disrupted by a sharp elbow in my ribs – Jerry was trying to return me to Earth.

"Me?" Clever comeback!

"Yes. Are you all right?"

My mind ran wild with delirious thoughts of grandeur. She had demanded the center court cheerleading position so that she could be near the new unsung hero. It was her way to capitalize on some glory. She was probably hoping I'd even ask her out during the next week, before the novelty of my heroics had worn off. After all, she had spoken to me first! I imagined that she'd probably brag to all her friends about how Kelly Elliott may not have looked great from the outside, but had a beautiful inside, unafraid to stick up for his beliefs. Another thought spiked my heart – maybe we'd start going steady, and eventually we'd get married. Christ, when all the pimples vanished, I would probably be the ugly duckling to swan cycle incarnate.

The fantasizing took all of ten seconds, but I realized that I had better say something impressive to charm her. I had to show that I had some sophistication. I had even read Philip Roth! Something had to be said to keep the conversation alive, leading to a long and permanent relationship.

My mind became a whirlwind of words. "Yes, I'm fine, thank you. Have you read *Goodbye, Columbus*?" Too dull! "Fine, thank you. Would you like to go out next weekend?" Too fast, too bold. "Yes, I'm okay, thank you. I was just enjoying your cheerleading. You do it so well." That was it! Then she'd blush, have to respond with a thank you and I would come back with, "There's no need to thank me. I've noticed that you do so many things well." Then another thank you and Wham! – the ball would be rolling. I would be polite, witty, urbane, and absolutely charming. Irresistible!

I peered into those soft eyes and actually felt my heart pound, just like the characters in the *True Confessions* magazines that Ma always read. Slowly I felt the words climb up my throat and begin to form on my lips, ready to begin my new life with the goddess before me.

Then it happened! I farted! Not just a silent gas passing attack that could be blamed on someone else, but a quaking fart that would make all the disaster annals as the Great

Chicago Fart, alphabetically before the Great Chicago Fire. At the very least it would be entered in the *Guinness Book of World Records* as the loudest fart ever witnessed at a public sporting event.

I felt my face redden, my mouth close, and my embarrassment overwhelm me. What does one say to any girl after farting? Not only was the sound loud enough to vibrate the walls, but the odor began to permeate the gym, seemingly causing a mass evacuation. Of course, the game had ended, but at the time I felt sure that the game had been called for unsportsmanlike conduct by a fan. I could see people wrinkle their noses as they passed, and a few laughed, presumably at me. In front of me stooped Venus.

My well-planned words never got past my lips. Laura gave an abrupt shake of her head and moved back to the floor for a closing cheer, but I could tell that her heart wasn't in it. She may have been dizzy. I simply wanted to die. I was trying to wish a sharp pain in my chest that would lead to a heart attack. Then I could keel over and an ambulance would rescue me, abating the fart humiliation. Later I would get tons of sympathy cards, and I would have my last feeling of ecstasy before I died, the victim of a fatal fart.

Jerry abruptly broke in. "Christ, Elliott! I'll meet ya' at the usual corner." Even my best friend deserted me, leaving me alone to bask in my disaster.

I didn't know what to do. My imagination had enlarged the calamity tenfold. Probably only five people had heard it, but one of them had been Laura LeDuc! I began to wish that an explosion would cave in the walls of the gym so that everybody would be so overwhelmed fighting for their own lives that a fart would not even register on their memories.

With only one alternative I made a quick exit through a rear fire door. I left the arena where twice in one day I had experienced unlimited humiliation. In spite of the fact that I had lost the fight with Swedarsky, at least I had gained some notoriety to the point where the most beautiful girl in the world had recognized me. With one fart I had blown it all, literally! Conversation of our fight would be replaced with my untimed catastrophe. On top of it all, Laura LeDuc would never speak to me again, and even if she did, I would never be able to face her. How could anyone face a girl whose first and only attempt at social contact was an appalling disaster?

Despite the forecast, light snow was falling lightly over the city, just giving the streets enough of a coating to make them slick for unconcerned and inattentive drivers, and enough to make foot traffic acrobatic. I trudged along Archer Avenue, leaving my shuffling, ski-like tracks on the sidewalk behind me, slowly making my way to the box office at the rapidly deteriorating Brighton Theatre. I paid a dollar for the all night Marx Brothers film festival. Inside, it was warm and possible to find a seat among its 1,500 in which I could sleep safely for the night.

Jorge, the doorman, ticket taker, and concession counter vendor greeted me warmly as he expertly tore my ticket into two equal pieces, handing me my return stub. I didn't spend too many full nights there, but he had started to recognize me as a semi-regular and wasn't concerned about the city curfew of 1:00 a.m. on weekends. He seemed as tired as I was.

I asked him where Walter, the former man-at-the-door, was and Jorge informed me that the seventy-year-old man had died shortly after Thanksgiving. Judging Jorge's age to be around sixty, I figured this job was the final stop for some people. One warm summer night last year, the kind that Chicagoans cherish as an opportunity to walk safely in the right neighborhoods, I saw Jorge running a hot dog stand over on Damen. Recognizing me from the theatre, he said, "Hello" and gave me a hot dog with the works.

We talked a few minutes, since I thought it rude to just take the dog and run. It turned out that Jorge actually had three jobs, the third being a counter man at Paco's, the first Mexican restaurant to open in Brighton Park. I thought I'd try the place for lunch once, but I felt uncomfortable, because almost all the patrons I could see from the front window were

Hispanic. After finishing my dog, I slowly walked away, feeling sorry for old Jorge, but he sure didn't seem unhappy.

I was usually at the Brighton Theatre about once a month since Dan Phillips had come into my mother's life. I wasn't about to ask my best friend if I could spend the night at his house so the old lady could "entertain" her boyfriend. Teens were quick to recognize reality in awkward situations and thrived on the notoriety in spreading the stories.

The theatre was old but still functional, though patron numbers were dwindling since the renovated Atlantis Theatre opened. When the Brighton first opened, in 1919, there was a twinkling-light ceiling to make it seem like you were watching a movie "under the stars," as the marquee proudly stated. Unfortunately, forty years later with only minimal maintenance, about half the stars had burned out and nobody had replaced them. In an attempt to draw more customers, the Brighton began running all-night movie marathons, from Roger Corman horror films to John Wayne western/war pictures on weekends. Therefore, the Brighton Theatre became temporary sanctuary for society's nightly cast-outs.

Curiosity seekers might come to check for the ghosts of two teenage girls, who in the 1950s, mysteriously disappeared on the way to the Brighton to see an Elvis film. Their murdered bodies were found a month later by the side of a rural road. Still, rumors spread and more people claimed to have seen their ghosts sitting in the fourth row.

Other than the curious, all species of society were represented. In the back row an old prostitute was making change for limited service. A couple of rows in front of her and her clientele sat an unshaven derelict who tried to nonchalantly watch her action, his burnt-out brain digesting what it could. Throughout the dark auditorium, bloated lips emitted loud snores from various slumping figures. They were the fortunate ones with enough money for a night's shelter. Occasionally life stirred in the form of a bottle being lifted to a decayed mouth.

I took a seat near the right front, on the aisle, the same I usually took. The extra room allowed me to extend my legs, a more comfortable position for sleeping. Each of the individuals had an unofficial seat. Jorge would make an hourly round, but I never saw him do or say anything to anyone.

On the silver screen Harpo Marx was leaning against a wall. A policeman asked him if he was holding up that wall. Voiceless, Harpo could only nod "yes" vigorously. The policemen told Harpo to move on and when he did, the entire structure fell down around them.

A few snickers could be heard from the dark auditorium. Those still conscious thought it funny. Everyone failed to notice the seventeen-year-old boy, alone, except for the self-pitying tears which were quietly and steadily flowing from my eyes. It wasn't the first time. Everyone there had earned the right to cry – it was their reason for being there. Outside the snow covered my footprints and wiped out all traces that I had ever been there.

CHAPTER 4

An Afternoon with the Mummies

Saturday afternoon I took the el train to the Loop, then called home to see when the "coast would be clear." The entire time I was talking to Ma, I could tell that Phillips was playing "grab ass" or something equally disgusting, because she giggled half the time and agreed to everything I said, including plans to expose myself to some children at the Lincoln Park petting zoo. She did have enough presence to ask for one more favor – Dan had been fortunate enough to catch an 8:00 a.m. flight back to New York on Sunday, so she wondered if one more night at Jerry's was too much to ask. Listening to her voice reminded me of our last conversation and the nasty way I had ridiculed her scholarship hopes for me. I saw her tears as I left the apartment, so I was ready to atone by granting her the second night with Dan Phillips.

She made her standard invitation for Sunday – a trip to suburban Wheaton to visit her sister, my aunt Amy. Ma made the same trip every Sunday, catching the 11:30 Northwestern from track six. About four times a year I went with her, but suburbia, two house dogs, and two younger cousins were tough to handle at any age, in any state of mind. I was in a restless stage, and watching a Bears game with my bratty cousins was torturous, like babysitting for Brats Anonymous, if there was such a group. So I usually spent Sunday afternoons alone, too, but I really didn't mind. I was used to being a loner and found my company the most enjoyable of anyone I knew.

Like my mother during her post-supper blue periods, I tended to have schizophrenic traits with a few sides to me.

The side most people saw and knew was the one that I didn't like -- awkwardly polite and passive. Another, known only to me and the many other personalities I assumed, was the side that appeared when I was alone. Without the presence and pressure of a peer group, I enjoyed enough finesse, self-confidence, and bravado to do almost anything. Should a conflict occur, I could muster enough courage and poise to cope satisfactorily, like some kind of a comic book super-hero. Put someone of my own age group near me, someone whose criticism mattered to me, and I had all the "cool" of a Club.

What child behaviorists had labeled the "age of confusion" was exactly that – a time of trying to conform to society while exhibiting individual characteristics. Therefore, I would spend half my time ridiculing people and institutions that were more secure than I was, just to try to feel superior to them. I guess the reason I liked myself at all was that I was the only one who had complete access to and understanding of everything I was and hoped to be.

The day was spent trying to forget about the recent embarrassments and tragedies. It was a common cycle for me. With six dollars in my pocket, I sat in the downtown Greyhound Bus Terminal (one of my favorite people-watching places), and planned the day. Chicago was still a brisk day with the usual biting wind off Lake Michigan. I needed a dollar for sleeping at the Brighton Theatre and two dollars for food, so my entertainment budget was low. The day had to be spent on free amusements —window shopping, hotel lobbies, and museums.

One of the worst places in the world to go on a Saturday afternoon was the Museum of Science and Industry. It was as though all the demons of hell were released to desecrate any place of culture. A place of great, potential education was transformed into one extensive battleground – the domesticated vs. the feral orphans, the sane vs. the diabolically insane. Because there was no admission charge, every parent in the city sent their kids there; guards became nothing more than uniformed babysitters. Rules called for

46

mandatory parental supervision, but once inside, the parents would give their kids a few bucks for lunch and tell them to meet them at the front door in three hours. Instantly, those imps would turn into hyper-active banshees, pushing all the buttons that would activate a moving display, then running off to another display, oblivious to the purpose of the exhibit they had just set in motion. Cries of, "Get away from there, you kids! Where are your parents?" and "That's not a toy!" resounded off the high, arched ceilings. The guards' rebukes would be answered with piercing shrieks and the clumping of winter boots in frenzied retreat. The only exhibits safe from their attacks were those without moving parts. No kid wants to waste time reading about the four chambers of the heart.

When I was their age, I had acted the same way until one day a guard straightened me up by telling me that if I misbehaved again, he would lock me up with the mummies. Even though the mummies were not in the Museum of Science and Industry, as I discovered several years later, it was enough to scare the hell out of a seven-year-old kid. I was always mindful of my actions after that warning. In spite of the Saturday bedlam, the museum was to be my activity for the day, and my goal was to try to enjoy it.

I arrived about 1:30 and the chaos seemed to have reached every corner of the building. In the entrance hall were the most astounding eye-catchers —the display of World War I and World War II fighter planes suspended from the ceiling.

"How did they get those airplanes in here and hung up on the roof like that?"

It was the same moronic question I had heard from every little kid upon his first visit to the museum. Even I had said it. I turned to the sound of the voice and saw a typical, runny-nosed boy, dressed in standard blue nylon ski jacket, red stocking cap, and idiot-mittens, holding the hand of a woman who shared his puzzlement. She was engrossed in a conversation with her husband, studying the museum floor plan, so I kindly took the initiative to answer the kid in a whisper.

"They catch them in these giant spider webs when they fly through, and only their skeletons are in the planes now. Wanna see?"

The kid's eyes grew and his face became taut. I took the expression as my cue to exit down the Hall of Nutrition, hearing "I don't want to stay here any more. Can we go home now?" In the hall was a farm exhibit, complete with eggs hatching in an incubator. People would gather and watch the chicks try to peck themselves free of their shells. Some people would bet on which eggs would crack next. It was a life-threatening chore, but the chicks always made it.

One of my favorite exhibits was the Whispering Chambers. There were two acrylic curves set sixty feet apart, their concave sides facing each other. One person stood in each, back toward his partner, and whispered. The other person could hear as clearly as if it had been shouted. I always wondered why science hadn't improved on the original so that people's thoughts would be echoed like shouts. Then everyone would know the thoughts of everyone else, and people would be more cautious of their musings. People would become more wary of their actions, too. For example, if some little brat pushed a display button and ran down the hall, he could be bombarded with, "Hey, you little cretin. Drop dead!" or "Someone tear that little brat's heart out!" It seemed that people could always think a good game, but they didn't move the pieces very often.

I always enjoyed creating mental dialogues between the people in the whispering chamber. Some middle-aged guy is on one end, and a young, blonde knock-out was in the other. They were whispering, "Hello, can you hear me?" back and forth like most morons did. With a thought chamber, the dialogue would have been more exciting, "Hey, sweetheart. How'd you like to take a 'ride'?" Response, "I would love to 'take a ride,' but not with you. They should lock you up overnight with the mummies." Anyway, it was fun to watch the people, especially if I created their conversations.

Set off in the corner of the museum was my absolute favorite exhibit – The Street of Yesteryear. Because it was located in an obscure basement corner, and because it had no moving parts, the Street of Yesteryear generally escaped the savage onslaught of the infantile hordes.

Had I the choice, I suppose the Street of Yesteryear would be the place in which I would have most wanted to spend the rest of my life. It was a block of Gay '90s era, complete with cobblestones, gas lamps, hitching posts besides horse-drawn milk wagons and quaint store fronts. Between the Power and Light Company and the *Youngstown Gazette* stood the sole house – it was white frame with a knee high, white picket fence surrounding an abbreviated front yard. The most gratifying part was the wax figures that could be seen through the windows. In the kitchen were the parents, turning the crank of an old-fashioned ice cream maker. The mother was a beautiful woman with excited eyes, while the handsome father, complete with handlebar moustache, stood beaming over her shoulder, sharing something undefinable with his wife. In the living room were the brother and sister, intently involved in a checker game. The girl was about ten, but the boy was my age, and I envied him, even if he was made of wax. It was a family, happy to be there without the sound of a television or the bickering over money or other trivia. I was envious, but I suppose that those wax figures had a whole different set of troubles.

Breaking my trance, I eased my way up the rest of the street. Tinkling old piano music from the nickelodeon grabbed my ears and pulled me to the box office window. The theatre was empty. Harold Lloyd was in one of his usual fixes, hanging from the ledge of a building, alternately letting go of each hand in order to measure the twenty stories to the ground. Once he gave the appearance of letting go with both hands, but he still didn't fall. Finally, he let go, hit an awning, and trampolined to a safe landing. Harold Lloyd was tops in my book.

I had covered most of the museum in three hours. It had

probably been my twentieth trip, but I never tired of it. I even visited the health exhibits, which had bottled babies in their various stages of development, and I was always hypnotized by the maturation process.

With only a half hour until closing time, I made my way to the Hall of Mathematics. One display explained centrifugal force. Upon pushing a button, a one-inch ball bearing would be released and very gradually work its way down a funnel, until it disappeared with a rapid vibration and a final clunk down the middle. Then the button could be pressed again, and the process would repeat itself. It was a hypnotic display, and everyone wanted to push the button once – it emitted a feeling of power, even if it lasted only one minute. The crowd watched in silence, as though participating in a church service.

When I arrived at the exhibit, there was only one person there. Unfortunately, it was the little brat I had scared at the front door when I told him about the skeletons in the airplanes. He still hadn't blown his nose, and he was one of the grossest little mental cases I had even seen. If he had been my kid, I would have tied him in a gunny sack and tossed him into the middle of Lake Michigan, Chicago-style.

The ball bearing was about two thirds of the way down the funnel. I could tell the kid recognized me – he kept a close watch on me as I circled the display. When I smiled at him, he quickly averted his attention to the steel ball, then continued his surveillance of me. Still, his hand hovered over that display button – he was not about to relinquish his rights to anyone, especially me.

Sproooong! The bearing disappeared down the center of the funnel. Thunk! The little bastard hit the start button and the bearing reappeared for another sixty-second journey. I continued to circle the display, arms behind my back like an ice skater, and glared at the demon in an attempt to make him nervous. Like I said, the machine gave its user a sense of power, and this was a battle of wills between the two of us. Nobody else was within sight; I decided to give him one last chance.

Sproooong! Clunk! The ball disappeared and our eyes locked as his hand readied to hit the start button. I was about to dare him to hit it and hesitated. I was not one to be reckoned with, at least not to a six-year-old snotty-nosed kid. Thunk! The bastard did it again. I wanted to choke the little jerk but decided on a more permanent remedy, one that had been used and proven effective on me years ago. Smiling sadistically, I stood next to the kid, whose eyes were locked on the orbital path of the ball bearing. I spoke nicely to him.

"Hey, kid. Do you know what a mummy is?"

He glanced at me over that crusty nose and nodded affirmatively.

"What?" I asked to assure that he really did know.

He spoke slowly, wary of who I was and what I might do. "It's someone who's dead that they wrap all up in bandages."

Success! The twerp was mine! "That's right. Have you seen the mummies they have in the basement?"

He seemed puzzled. I couldn't believe that he knew they were in the other museum. Kids were too gullible.

Hesitantly, a little fear in his voice, he replied, "Yeah, but I don't like 'em much. They scare me."

The kid seemed to be the mirror image of me at the age of six – scared as hell of mummies. Of course, at the age of six I would have at least had the manners to wipe my nose on the back of my jacket sleeve. That kid was hopeless.

I could visibly see terror spread across his face. For a fleeting moment I felt a slight pang of guilt, but I knew that I was doing this for the good of the museum and the kid's maturation process. At least, I think that's why I did what I did. Every kid should grow up fearful of something, just to keep him in line. To this day I think if Ma told me that she'd lock me up with the mummies if she caught me with drugs, I would have become a priest. Sensibility over-rode my temporary guilt. He was awaiting my answer with trepidation.

I still spoke gently, letting the words carry the impact. "If the guard sees you press that button one more time, he's going to take you downstairs to the mummy room, turn off all the lights, and lock you in overnight. How's that grab you, kid?"

Apparently it did not grab him at all well. His eyes began to glaze over as his face became contorted in an attempt to stifle a scream. It did no good.

"Ahhhhh!" Christ! I bet the centrifugal force ball jumped its orbit. People appeared from nowhere and looked at me as the brat darted down the hall. Everyone stared at me as though I were a child molester.

"He turned around and found out that I wasn't his brother. I guess he's lost. Poor little guy. The guards will help him."

Reading the crowd, I could see that my bluff had been temporarily accepted. They began to disperse with derogatory comments about parents who leave their children unattended. I was on their side – a kid like that needed to be supervised every minute.

Clunk! The ball had ended its descent, and the machine was all mine. Feeling a minor victory, I began the process again. The circular motion had an entrancing and soothing effect, and I felt content, my troubles of Friday retreating to an obscure part of my memory.

Suddenly I felt a firm grasp on my shoulder, like the iron claw the Baron used on All-Star Wrestling. I turned and saw the biggest and meanest psychopath in the world! He was the kind of guy who had a five o'clock shadow immediately after shaving. If I had offered him a dollar to torture his sick grandmother, he would have asked, "For how long?"

"This the punk, Mickey?" boomed a voice from the depths of hell.

I looked down and saw the snot-nosed reject, his face stained with tears. He nodded his head, not realizing the similarity of his affirmation to the Black Hand Kiss of Death. I figured the kid usually only nodded because his old man had torn out his tongue to keep the kid from crying in his crib.

"So, you like scaring little kids, huh, punk?"

Numbness was seizing my shoulder, and I wondered how much abuse my body could take before dying. Surely the arms were sacrificed – a picture of a seventeen-year-old boy with an empty coat sleeve painted itself in my mind.

"Well, punk! I'm talking to you!"

"Ah, no, sir. I don't like scaring little kids." I wondered where all those people who had so quickly appeared to rescue snot-nose had gone. They must have been swallowed up in the vortex of the centrifugal force display.

"Did you or did you not tell my kid that you were going to lock him up with the mummies and that the airplanes all had dead bodies in them?"

That little bastard had a good memory for a little bastard. I realized that it would not be easier to bluff a Mafia hitman than to bluff Conan the Barbarian, but I had to try to survive.

"Ah, no. Not exactly, sir." I was stooping to Swedarsky's tactics, but I had to fight any way I could.

He tightened his grip. "You calling my kid a liar?"

It was time to lay it on thick. I wished I had worn glasses. He might have shown some mercy to a skinny, pimple-faced kid wearing glasses. Of course, he might have chosen to grind them into my eyes. I was suddenly glad that I didn't have glasses.

"Oh, no, sir. I'm sure that a fine little boy like that, cute as the devil with that little ski jacket and. . ."

"Cut the bullshit, kid, before I donate your body to the museum."

It was an excellent idea – cut the bullshit!

"Well, sir, it's just that I think he misunderstood me, sir. I could see that he was lost, and I suggested that he might find his MOMMY downstairs." It wasn't bad for a dying person.

Out of nowhere Mickey found his tongue again. "Uh, uh, Dad. He said if I pressed that button again that the guard would lock me downstairs with the mummies and turn off all the lights."

The most sadistic grin of all time spread over the big bastard's face. He knew he had me, and all he had to do was decide how far to torture his victim. I could not reason with the ogre. I had to use my only superior physical skill - speed. One more well-placed bluff to loosen his grip, and I might escape alive.

"Careful, Mickey. You'll fall . . ."

The mammoth turned his head, relaxed his grip, and I chopped at his arm to free myself. I must have been some sight running down the hall, one arm pumping like an oil rig drill, while the other hung lifelessly at my side. I felt I had made a clean break until I heard a muted roar behind me.

"I'll kill that little dickhead!"

Down the steps, two at a time. It hadn't occurred to me that the son-of-a-bitch would give full pursuit, but he did, and I felt my heart trying to pound its way out of my chest.

Near tragedy befell me when I tripped on the bottom two steps. The hunter must have been closer than I had thought, because he tripped over me and crashed to the marble floor, sliding out of my reach. His claw darted out and half-grasped my wrist, driving me to drastic measures. I spit on his hand, causing a repulsive reflexive retreat. It was a gross gesture, but nobody could have saved me but myself.

Finding my feet, I was up and running, forgetting the fact that I could scarcely breathe. Again I could hear the ominous sounds of pursuit, only this time the muffled mutterings were echoing off all the walls.

"I'll tear that mother's heart out and make him eat it." Somehow, I believed him. At least it wasn't broccoli.

I accepted the fact that the simian would pursue me forty days at full speed across the Sahara Desert. What I needed was a coup-de-grace — something to definitively end his pursuit.

Finally the exit doors were in sight. Because it was only five minutes to closing time, the area in front of the exit doors was blocked solidly with people, preparing for the colder outdoors. It would be impossible to exit without slowing down, and then Mickey's paternal assassin would take me for slaughter. My life would be over. Even the threat of possible imprisonment would not deter the madman from his goal.

A janitor was mopping the floor near the back of the souvenir stand. The floor glistened and I knew it was my only hope. After spitting on the creature/father's hand, I was more desperate than ever. Feeling sure-footed in my sneakers, I raced across the wet area, like a half-back tip-toeing the last ten yards for the touchdown.

Thunk! It had worked. Cyclops had lost his footing and fallen on his tailbone. Without hesitation I darted through the crowd, rudely pushing people aside, and escaped through the front doors.

I don't remember ever slowing down. Never looking back, I raced block after block down Lake Shore Drive, finally arriving at a corner the same time as a downtown bus. I stumbled on, deposited my quarter, and collapsed in the back seat. Instinctively, I checked out the rear window for signs of pursuit. It appeared I was safe. I had pulled off a caper, a death-defying adventure. Unfortunately, I probably would never tell anyone, because nobody would believe it. I had no witnesses to the deed. I had my head nearly taken off by Swedarksy – the entire school, even Laura LeDuc had known it within three hours. I had farted at a basketball game, and the entire school was there to testify. I had outfoxed a Mafia hitman, and I was the only witness. Peer pressure neutered every decent achievement I had, but I guess that was part of my growing up.

CHAPTER 5

The Striptease and the Swan Hotel

The National Title Insurance Company flashed the time at me – 5:17. It was time to eat, then plan the rest of the evening. My afternoon activities would be difficult to surpass, or so I thought at the time.

Getting off the bus at Michigan and Van Buren, I walked two blocks to Jake's, my favorite seventeen-cent greasy hamburger stand. I would always order three hamburgers, fries, and a chocolate malt – the all-American meal. What pimples? Fear of fatal communicable diseases forbade me to look behind the counter. Jerry told me that he once saw a cook drop a frozen patty on the floor and nonchalantly pick it up and toss it onto the grill. I didn't care – it tasted good.

One of my favorite places to eat Jake's "gourmet steak burgers" was in one of the city's classiest hotels – the Palmer House on State Street. I don't mean the Boulevard Room, Trader Vic's, or any of the other expensive dining rooms in it. My favorite spot by choice and necessity was on the second floor. The cavernous lobby was filled with plush couches, leather chairs (easy for clean-up), and enough space so that I was hidden from the front desk, making it easier to relax and not be observed as some vagrant. Where else could one eat horsemeat while surrounded by the chic décor and clientele that the Palmer House attracted?

I would often spend time in the lobby, just getting warm and watching people. If the adventuresome spirit grasped me, I would pull minor pranks on the social elite. One of my best was to stand in front of the ladies' room, tucking in my shirt, as though I had just come out. Often a woman lost in thought would see me in front of the door and automatically enter the other door—the men's room. It usually caused considerable embarrassment, and there was nothing the authorities could legally do to me.

My usual "table for one" in the center of the depot-like lobby was open. From there I could see everyone, yet I was reasonably safe from the scrutiny of the busy desk clerks. Four couches formed a square. Three sofas were occupied, but the one that would allow me to have my back to the desk clerks was vacant. I sat, put my greasy bag on a corner table, and spread my banquet on my lap.

To my immediate right was a middle-aged, matronly, upper-crust woman, dressed for dinner in one of those rooms that I could not afford. She peered at me through thick lenses, and I figured that she would be an easy mark to fluster. Taking a long sip on my malt, I prepared a stunning belch.

The only definite positive notoriety I received throughout school concerned my belching technique. I was a great belcher, especially with a malted milk for fuel. I was able to load my lungs with air and slowly work it out. Jerry and I would always rate our burps on a scale of one to ten, five being average. I would always erupt with an eight and often hit a nine. It was an unwritten rule that nobody could achieve a ten unless it caused serious structural damage. My fart had probably been a ten.

Out of the corner of my eyes, I could see the nosy, rich bitch watching me, wondering why I was looking upward as though in prayer, while I continued taking deep gulps of air. I opened my mouth and it emerged – an eight! Tremendous! The best factor to aid resonant belching in the lobby of the Palmer House was the high ceiling – it was an acoustical phenomenon that amplified the initial effort by three times. Of course, the clothes of the surrounding people always absorbed some of the impact. I often wondered how many people realized that their clothing absorbed the burping sound and consequently felt dirty.

Looking at the woman I could see an open mouth the size of Carlsbad Caverns. I spoke sedately, as though it was the natural manner in which to react.

"Excuse me, ma'am. I know what I just did was extremely rude, but I have a digestive condition which causes me to emit disgraceful sounds. But as long as it's out, on a scale of one to ten, five being average, how would you rate that last eruption? Please remember that people's clothing, including that heavy mink you're wearing, partially muffle the sound, so allowances should be made."

She huffed and rose quickly, embarrassed not only by such crudeness, but also by being addressed by its creator. As I had calculated, she was snooty. Still, she wanted me to learn a lesson.

"Hasn't anyone taught you any manners?"

"No, ma'am. I'm an orphan. All the kids at the orphanage rate our unintentional burps. I did apologize and explained my condition."

"Oh!" and she stomped off, heading for the elevators. I had no doubt that she was going to change her mink.

From the others in my elite square I received only a couple of headshakes and one stifled laugh. Deciding that they were not the kind of people to fluster so easily, I continued eating my gourmet meal without interruption.

Even though Ma wasn't there, I felt like I should go into a post-supper depression. It must have been Pavlov's stimulus-response reflex, because as soon as I had finished eating, I felt bitchy as hell. I sat staring into space, waiting for someone to tell me to move along, so that I could snap off his head.

As I sat there, thinking back on the day, I judged it a success. I had enjoyed myself at the museum. I had outsmarted and outrun a trained killer, elevating myself to a James Bond figure, or, in my case, a figurine. I had successfully insulted a society matron who probably trampled kids like me as a way of life. Most important, I felt that I had had some impact on the lives of a few people. Even if the people had only been a six-year-old kid, his father, and a rich woman, I had left an impression on each of their lives, even if just for a short time.

It was 7:30 by the time I returned to Earth. I felt better and used the marble-walled bathroom, then nonchalantly walked to the telephone bank, found a dime, and called Jerry.

"Christ, Elliott! Where the hell you been? I been trying to get in touch with you all day. Some wise ass keeps answering your phone and tells me you're out molesting girl scouts. Who the hell was that – your uncle or something?"

Good old Dan Phillips, fooling around with my mother. I didn't even have a living uncle.

"Yeah, it was my uncle. He's staying over for the weekend."

"No offense, Elliott, but he sounds like a real jerk."

I didn't like Jerry calling my uncle a jerk, but I let it go.

"He's just weird, Jer. That's why I haven't been home all day."

"I don't blame ya. Anyway, you got anything planned for tonight?"

Something was in his voice that I didn't trust.

"No. I thought I'd call you to see what's up."

His voice became softer, as though he were about to reveal a secret of the universe or that he was afraid of being overheard.

"Listen carefully. I have to talk soft because the old lady just came out of the can. I got this sensational idea we just gotta try."

Already I didn't like it. The word "try" implied possible failure, something for which I was not in the mood. The day had been good to me, and I saw no logic in ruining my minor conquests.

"Where are you now?"

"I just had dinner at the Palmer House."

"Come on, Elliott. Don't bull . . . kid me. Where are you?"

"I'm in the Loop. I went to the museum, then grabbed

some greasy burgers for supper."

"Jake's? Heaven. Anyway, can you meet me at the corner of State and Van Buren in an hour?"

Trying to think of what was located at that corner, I could only recall a pawnshop and a Greek restaurant. Jerry had something uncouth in mind, but I had no other plans.

"Yeah, I can be there. Why? What's up?"

"Good. I'll see you there about 8:15." Click!

The son-of-a-bitch had left me hanging. Nobody had a mind like Jerry's, so there was no use trying to outguess him. I was resigned to forty-five minutes of devising credible excuses in the eventuality that I was totally averse to his plans.

By 8:10 I had walked four blocks down State Street to Van Buren. Overhead the el train rattled, making conversation and thought impossible. It was getting chilly and people hurried to their destinations. The Prudential Building had registered thirty-three degrees, and I hoped that Jerry would not be too late.

State and Van Buren was the southeastern corner of the Loop and was not the classiest part of downtown. Most of the sex shops, strip shows, pawnshops, and arcades were located there, and my curiosity grew as I waited for Jerry.

From the corner I could see a blinking neon sign for the Swan Hotel—a name quite incongruous with the hordes of dirty, city pigeons and their massive droppings décor. The dilapidated, five-story Swan was two steps above a dollar-a-day flophouse, but still drew a few non-suspecting tourists who were attracted to its Loop location. The sputtering blue neon swan figure helped make the hotel's façade a little intriguing and I thought I'd like to spend a night there some time just for the adventure.

Looking south I could see the bright, flashing marquee of the Follies Theatre, the city's oldest burlesque house. Belle Starr and her twin 44's were beckoning from the brightly lit marquee. Some of the guys at school had bragged about their excursions there, but I never believed them. Minimum age for entrance was eighteen, and most of the guys who did the bragging looked closer to eight. Then it hit me like a Swedarsky punch – the Follies was Jerry's plan!

Standing agape, my awe was interrupted by a "Hey, man, wanna square?" from the top of the el platform stairs. He had his standard shit-eating grin on his face.

I ignored the greeting in my panic. "Christ, Jerry. We can't get in there and you know it."

He was pleased that I had figured out his master plan. My appalled expression was worth the spoiled surprise.

"Yes, we can! Lots of guys at school have got in. Even Ralph Jacobsen, and he looks like a middle school geek. You only have to be eighteen, and we can pass for a year. Besides, all they can do is tell us to get lost. But, God! If we get in, think! Belle Starr and her twin 44's! Christ, Elliott, I bet you never even saw a real pair, have ya'? Think of twin 44's!"

For once my subconscious told me that he did make sense. People aren't arrested for just trying to get into a strip show. And he was right. I really hadn't seen a real pair in my life. Pictures didn't count. And to start with twin 44's! The son-of-a-bitch made sense for once, but the risk still scared me. Who knows how the ticket seller would react?

"All right, let's go."

So it was proclaimed – the night that Jerry Hogan and Kelly Elliott would attempt to see their first strip tease. Another step into Manhood! A step towards the never ending search for maturity! An opportunity to become school celebrities. The world was waiting! Man, was I scared!

We walked in silence toward the Follies. The pawn shop windows, displaying everything from army jackets to guitars, were barred for the night. The doors to the adult book stores were frosted and bore signs, "No one under 18 admitted." My nervousness increased. Stopping ten yards from the Follies marquee, Jerry laid out our strategies.

"Now listen. I look older than you. With all your pimples and stuff, you look like a young kid." Encouragement was not one of Jerry's virtues. "That's why you have to buy your ticket first."

I knew I'd get screwed. He wanted to use me for a guinea pig. "Me? How do you figure? If you look so goddamn old, why don't you buy yours first? Better yet, why don't you buy both our tickets and we won't have any problems?"

Jerry was like a general – he had all the devious moves well planned and all the answers at his disposal.

"I can't do that. Christ, Elliott, guys don't buy tickets for other guys. They only buy tickets for their girls, and you hardly pass. Do you want 'em to think we're a couple of fags?"

"But why should I go first?"

He was losing patience with his disobedient private.

"Because if they let you in, they're bound to let me in. If I buy mine first and they don't let you in, then I'll be stuck alone in there. I don't want to go by myself. There's probably a bunch of perverts who'll try to grab my crotch and stuff like that."

His logic was sound. He must have spent the entire day planning the caper. I had no counter argument, and I was resigned to be the sacrificial lamb. The commander continued his strategy.

"Now, when you get there, have your money out and ready. That way you don't have to fumble around and let them get a long look at you. Besides, if you have your wallet out, it's too easy to ask for an I.D. Just keep your head down, put the money on the counter, and wait for the ticket. Don't say, 'One, please,' because she can tell you only have enough money for one, and that you must be nervous about something. Got it, so far?"

I was impressed. "Yeah, I got it."

"Good. If she asks you for some I.D., tell her you don't drive, always take the bus, and don't have any identification. If she hassles ya', just walk away. Don't argue. If you get in, just go into the auditorium and sit down. Don't go looking for popcorn or shit. Keep your face hidden and don't act suspicious. Once in, you're set. I'll be right behind you. Questions?"

"No, sir." The "sir" was another unintentional slip.

We made the final steps, Jerry nudging me like I was a pirate forced to walk the plank, glancing at the movie posters. There was also a movie – "Naked in the Jungle." A middle-aged man in a smart business suit bought his ticket, just as Jerry had instructed me, and went in.

It seemed easy – everything depended on the ticket seller. According to senior class "royalty," at all dirty movies or strip shows, there seemed to be three kinds of ticket sellers – all institutions of the American theatre.

The first was the young woman who personally didn't care who bought a ticket. She was paid by the hour, no matter who she let in. She also chewed gum like a cow. The second was the older male, generally the manager, who couldn't get enough help or was too cheap to hire someone extra. He was a tough bastard who immediately sized up the ticket buyer. He would either press the dispensing button with authority or say, "Get the hell out of here, kid" in such a commanding tone that he seemed to derive his power from Satan. The third kind was the worst – the old witch. She was a warhorse of approximately two hundred years, whose life centered on hassling kids my age. Instead of the authoritarian command of the manager, she would make her victim squirm by asking for an I.D. and drumming her fingers on the counter as though there were a thousand people in line. Then she'd tell the kid to wait while she got the manager to deal with the situation. It was enough to scare the hell out of the average thug.

My luck held true to form – we drew number three, the old bag. She was big enough to play on the line for the Bears or any professional football team. Her eyes squinted through thick glasses, challenging any unsuspecting fools who would dare to cross into her territory. I grabbed Jerry at the sight of Medusa, complete with snakes for hair.

"Christ, Jerry. We'll never get by her. Just look at her. She's almost challenging us now. It's probably Swedarsky's mother!"

"Bull, Elliot! We've come this far and we're not turning back now. Get out your two bucks and I'll be right behind ya.' Just stick to the plan."

Reluctantly, I took two of my remaining three dollars from my wallet. Taking a deep breath, I strode up to the counter and affirmatively slammed the two bucks on the counter.

"One, please." Shit! Already I had blown the procedure. At the shock of my stupidity, I erred again as I lifted my face and looked at the crone peering at me curiously. She should have been mounted atop Notre Dame.

"What?" she barked.

I gave a false smile, innocent as hell. "One, please."

She continued her scrutiny. It was a longer time than I had felt facing Laura LeDuc. I concentrated on not farting. I knew then that I really had to go to the can. I quaked as I waited for her to call the manager. It was a showdown, only I wasn't armed. Then came the surprise announcement.

"Three bucks."

I couldn't believe my ears. "Huh?"

"I said three bucks. It's a Saturday night show. You got problems, kid?"

My fake smile became sincere. Assuming I had made it past the major hurdle, I pushed my initiative.

"Oh, sure. I'm used to being here on a week night. Sorry."

'Bullshit," came the reply.

As I dug into my wallet for my last dollar, I heard her say, "Russ," to someone behind the counter. Still, she accepted my last dollar and I entered heaven - Belle Starr and her twin 44's.

Jerry was right on my heels as we made our way eight steps directly to the auditorium doors. Neither of us spoke, afraid of ruining our good fortune. A gruff voice from our right, behind the candy counter, shattered our momentary elation – we were like boys being told by a female teacher that our zippers were down.

"Hey, where you going in such a hurry?"

We hesitantly turned and looked at the man behind the

counter. Undoubtedly, he was the manager and the one that the ticket seller had called "Russ." It appeared that their scheme was to collect our three dollars, then kick us out for being under age. Two kids sneaking into a burlesque show would hardly report a dishonest manager to the police. It was a scam.

"Huh?" It was as intelligent as I could be at the time.

"Where you two BOYS going in such a rush?"

"Inside," I said. "We paid for our tickets. Just ask the lady outside."

He shook his head at our stupidity. "That's no lady, that's my mother. Then where the hell are your tickets? What do you think I'm standing here for?"

Jerry and I looked at each other with relief. This time we had cleared the final hurdle. Despite our apparent success, my knees felt weak as I gave him my ticket and he returned the stub without the flare that Jorge did at the Brighton. We did a quick about-face and hoped to reach the auditorium without additional incident.

"Hey!" Russ wasn't giving up, the jerk! We turned to face his leer. "How old are you kids?"

Jerry finally found his voice. "Us?"

Russ was pissed. "No, the forty kids behind youse."

Like fools, we looked behind us, hoping like hell to see Troop 43 of the South Side Boy Scouts. No such luck. He meant us.

"I'm nineteen. He's eighteen," lied Jerry shakily.

Russ sneered. "You wouldn't want your teeth knocked out for that lie, would ya',kid?"

The dumb bastard had me terrified. I was willing to surrender my three dollars to escape without further incident.

"Honest. We are," pleaded Jerry.

"Let's see some I.D."

We should have predicted that line. I was still dumbfounded and immobile. So close, yet so far. Jerry would not surrender.

"Well, we don't have any. We don't drive and we don't carry any I.D. But we really are old enough."

The manager played his trump card. "Maybe we should call home to verify those ages. What's your phone number, kid?"

He reached for the phone in the box office and awaited Jerry's reply.

"Our folks aren't home tonight. They're at their card club at the Johnsons'. I don't know the number. Please, mister, give us a break."

Another pregnant pause added to my complete mental collapse. I could not cope anymore. I was ready to wet my pants as he just leered at us, phone in hand.

"Hey, Ma. What do you think I should do with these two kids?"

A harsh voice quickly replied, "Oh, let them in, Russ. They just wanta see some titties." Saved by Medusa! Thank you ancient Greek gods and goddesses!

"All right. Go on in. But if I ever find out that you guys lied to me, I'll get the cops down on you so fast that you'll forget you were ever toilet-trained."

He had enjoyed his game, and without further incident, we made our way straight through the double doors and into the house of pleasure.

The Follies Theatre could easily have been condemned under every building code in the city – fire hazard, sanitation, unsound structure, exposed wires, and for fostering the perverted life styles of horny businessmen, skid row derelicts, and high school students. On each side of the narrow center aisle were four wooden flip-up seats. The aisle resembled an airplane runway – long (about a million rows) and very narrow. The only lighting was cast from some fluorescent pin-up girl pictures mounted on the peeling and cracked walls. Closer to the front the lighting improved because of the movie screen and stage lights.

According to high school folklore, Saturday night at the Follies was the rowdiest. Even the inflated three dollar admission did not deter the kinds of people who patronized the sleazy theatre. According to locker room info, at the late show one of the strippers took off everything, then strutted up the aisle and gave out inflated rubbers to a few lucky patrons. Of course, this act definitely helped fill the place with deviants, including us.

In the first four rows were nothing but sailors. It looked like a training mission from Great Lakes Naval Base. After the sailors, the crowd was pretty diverse. All races, creeds, and nationalities were represented. It was the United Nations of Perversia. I even saw a few women, and immediately assumed they were lesbians, another first in my night of earthly delights. It was creepy all right.

Jerry nudged me. "Let's try to get a place near the front so we can get a rubber."

From the size of the crowd, I figured that we'd be lucky to get two seats together. On the screen was the movie – some broad with big boobs was posing while two guys jumped all over with cameras shooting pictures. It was obviously "Naked in the Jungle," because the two photographers wore pith helmets. I couldn't quite understand why they wore them in a motel room, but I felt that I was being a bit too critical. We later found out that the movie had an alternate title – "Tarzan and Jane's Little Helpers." It turned out to be more than an hour of these five women rolling around while these weirdos came to the motel and paid them to pose. The pith helmet was a signal to be allowed in. There was no sex or even a full crotch shot. It was a major disappointment, and not only in the world of filmdom.

"Hey, kid! Get out of the way!"

I couldn't tell where the voice came from, but it sounded like Russ. Everyone there sounded like Russ. "Damn! There aren't any aisle seats left. We'll have to take those two against the wall," commanded Jerry.

We edged our way over two pairs of uncooperative knees. As we slid by, I concentrated on not farting in their faces. Jerry crashed into his seat. I wasn't as fortunate. My seat had been removed, and I slid right down to the floor. At least I had amused the surrounding customers. It was obviously not the first time they had witnessed this humiliation.

"Hey, kid. You think if you sit down there that you can amuse yourself without anyone seeing ya'?"

Another roar of approval from the cretinous crowd. Big joke! Was this also high school? Jerry and I maneuvered our way out again.

"Make up your goddamn mind," barked the end voice.

We finally found two seats near the rear of the auditorium and repeated our acrobatics. We had just sat down, and I was wedged between Jerry and a stranger I could not see. He spoke in a raspy, suspicious voice.

"Hey, kid. You're not a fag, are ya'? Because if you are and try any funny stuff, I'll break your neck."

My patience was expiring. "Christ, mister. I ain't no fag, and if I was I'd like to think I could do better than you."

My words were out before I realized what I had said. Freudian slip. Fortunately, he seemed so much in his own world that the unintentional insult seemed to go right over his head. When I realized that he wasn't going to counter with any words or a punch to the body, I relaxed, smiled, and almost laughed at my witticism. I was almost eager to use the line again at school. Maybe I could lure Swedarsky into setting me up.

I really grew to dislike the Follies Theatre. Just as Jerry and I had settled into our seats to relax and enjoy ourselves, the lights came on. The movie had ended. I noticed several people trying to cover their faces, subconsciously hiding something. Jerry and I automatically did the same. I never saw the face of the guy next to me.

"Five-minute intermission. Please feel free to patronize our concession stand in the lobby," announced a mysterious voice from the loud speakers. It sounded like Russ, of course.

The movie screen disappeared into the ceiling, and a few colored spot lights illuminated a small stage in front of a red, moth-eaten backdrop.

"I hope we get the full nudity version," whispered Jerry.

"Me, too, but I'll be happy with some nice, juicy tits."

Real man talk! What the hell was a "juicy" tit?

The five minutes only took ten to pass, the auditorium lights dimmed, and the mysterious public address voice welcomed us.

"Welcome, ladies and gentlemen, to Chicago's finest burlesque theatre. We have a titillating show in store for you, with four of the finest strip-tease artists in the country."(The word "artist" really hit me right where I cross my legs.) "So sit back and relax – if you can. Enjoy the show. And to get things rolling, let's have a big welcome for St. Louis' own Ginny Dare!"

Only the sailors clapped and whistled. Gliding onto the stage was Ginny Dare, dressed in more clothes than an Eskimo about to take a three hundred mile journey on a dogsled. She had probably been an attractive woman in her youth. I guessed her age at forty. Raven hair hung straight past her shoulders. She whipped her hair from side to side, teasingly. Her face showed wrinkles, probably signs of the hidden past of most in her profession. With all the clothes she wore, it was difficult to tell anything concerning her body. From the speakers boomed the old standard "Night Train."

"Hang onto your shorts, Elliott," Jerry panted, almost drooling. I was excited and felt increasingly aroused as she "danced."

Ginny Dare, my first ever stripper, started out very slowly, sashaying around the minute stage fully clothed. It was about as exciting as watching an oil change at the auto shop, but the anticipation increased my fever. When she got near the front edge of the stage and the lights hit her in the right way, I could see that her eyes were heavily made up with purple eye shadow. Her nose looked like it had been broken, and the bottom dropped almost straight down. It was what we called a "boxer's nose." Her mouth was sensual, partly opened, with an occasional teasing flick of her tongue. As she crisscrossed the stage, she would wiggle her ass and the sailors would respond with wolf whistles. But it was the worn look of her face that captured my attention; she looked so used and defeated.

"Take it all off, baby! Show us what you got, Ginny!" It was a class audience.

It took Ginny the entire length of "Night Train" to just peel off her gloves. I was afraid that she would leave the stage, but there was a long pause as she awaited her second number – a pulsing rumba. The second segment was better, as she took off her silver-sequined evening gown, stockings, and garter belt, and paraded around in her bra and panties. She may have been an older stripper, but she had a good body.

By the time the third and final segment had started, the audience was ready for Ginny Dare to bare all. She had her ravenous audience on a string and worked the crowd to a frenzy. Everyone was on the edge of his seat, waiting for her coup-de-grace. She kept flitting her tongue in and out like a snake, and I was mesmerized.

Finally she turned her back to us and unsnapped her top. I was so excited by then that I thought I'd split the seam in my crotch. I rested my hands in my lap to cover any obvious signs, and I knew every guy in the audience was doing the same. I was about to lay my eyes on my first real set of boobs! When she finally turned, she was wearing pasties. I was disappointed but enthralled with those two mounds of female flesh – beautiful and alluring.

"More! More!" shouted the audience.

Ginny Dare knew how to handle men. I supposed at her age it was quite a thrill to arouse a crowd of men the way she had. Again, she turned around and slowly slipped off her panties. I thought I'd die happy right then.

Again Ginny turned around. Hoping for more, the result was disappointing. Across her crotch was a sequined patch covering her playground. Still it was a great start to the show. She was talking to the sailors, teasing them like a seasoned hooker, or so I imagined. I grew a new respect for the term "artist" as applied to the female dancer.

"You men wanna see what's under here?" she taunted, pointing at her G-string. Unanimous approval. I could hardly stand the anticipation any more.

"Well, come up to my place after the show, sailors, and I'll show you plenty. But please, no more than ten at a time."

That finale brought down the house, and Ginny Dare came back for two curtain calls. It was difficult to tell whether they were applauding her strip-tease or her skill in handling a bunch of insane men. When she bowed, she bent from her waist so her two jugs were hanging like oversized Christmas tree balls, and she knew the effect she had on us all. She even turned around to bow, wiggling her fanny at the crowd. She had gotten to me – I think I instantly fell in love with my first older woman.

Jerry disrupted my fantasy. I had forgotten that Jerry was even there. In fact, I had forgotten everything but Ginny Dare. I forgot where I was for a minute.

"Shit! That wasn't so hot, Elliott. No real gritty parts. The rest of the show should be better. It's Saturday night, so I bet they put the dogs on first, just to get the audience warmed-up."

I didn't care for the way he was talking about my woman, but being the man I was, I agreed. I still felt the bulge in my pants and became increasingly aware of my need to take a leak. I thought I'd burst, but I didn't want to miss any of the action. If Jerry was right, and Ginny Dare had just been a mild warm-up, we were in for more excitement than we had ever imagined at our age.

When the applause had subsided, the announcer introduced the second stripper as Sweet Sandy Sugar, and the whole routine started over. Jerry must have been very disappointed, because Sandy's act was a duplicate to Ginny's, except not as arousing. She hadn't mastered the teasing techniques. Also, she had rolls of fat on her thighs that shook when she moved. It was somewhat gross. Her eyes stared out into space, oblivious of the crowd of hungry, screaming men.

She didn't even try to carry on a conversation with the crowd and never came back to the light and scattered applause for a curtain call. Ginny had been a tough act to follow. I wondered how I would have felt if Sandy had stripped first. There is something special to a boy about seeing his first live naked woman – the memory will probably always last. Laura LeDuc was a fantasy, too, but I would have had to watch her mature, and we probably would have had arguments and all the normal, emotional steps of an adolescent relationship. Ginny Dare had already passed those stages; she would always be first in my memories.

"And now a short ten-minute intermission before our final two acts, including headliner Belle Starr and her Twin 44's! Please feel free to make use of our concession stand in the outer lobby. Ten minutes!"

I had postponed the bathroom for as long as humanly possible. "Jerry, I gotta take a leak. Wanna go?"

He smirked and snickered. "What's the matter, Elliott? Can't take the pressure? Too much for the old gonads?" Jerry could be a real asshole at times.

"Cut the crap, Jerry. You coming or not?"

"No, not yet. Are you?"

He got a real joy out of that line, and I stumbled over the two people in the end seats. When I got to the lobby, I couldn't believe my eyes. There was a wide, disordered line of men backed up from the door to the john to the auditorium entrance. The guys at the bathroom door held it open while they waited for ones in front to finish. Everyone could look in and see two guys pissing into the urinals. It was gross and I really didn't care to go on display before that pack of perverts. I had no choice, so I impatiently waited.

As I worked my way out of the auditorium and closer to the bathroom door, I almost croaked. Directly opposite the john door was the candy counter, only Russ wasn't behind it. It was Ginny Dare! She kept an eye on the two guys taking a leak, laughing when some wise ass yelled, "Hey, Ginny. See what you do to us guys."

"You guys are so full of it anyway that I couldn't add anything," she retorted smartly.

Everyone laughed at her gamesmanship. I didn't think I'd be able to go through with it, but I was almost wetting my pants by that time. The closer I got, the more urgent grew the need.

My heart quickened as her eyes briefly locked with mine. I figured that she must have felt awkward taking off her clothes in front of a pimple-faced kid too young to care about anything but the naked female form, but that was probably part of her job.

I watched her as I stood waiting and could sense from her quiet interludes that her stage bravado was more likely as false as her painted face. She probably had to strip just to make a living, and there was nowhere else to turn at her age. Ginny Dare was really no different from most people – locked in with no place to go and even with a choice, no way to get there. For a moment I felt pity for her, but who was I to pity anyone? I guess it took the Ginny Dares of the world to effectively make kids like me think about how screwed-up life could get; there's always someone worse off. I was the real philosopher, standing in line to get to the john at a strip show.

Finally I made it to the door and looked in. There was a drunk on the floor to the left of the urinals. He was actually lying on the floor, snoring, oblivious to everything. I shyly stepped up to the urinal, mindful of the drunk a few feet from me, and unzipped. I felt half an orgasm as I relieved myself. More pleasure in life I had not experienced. I didn't care if Ginny was watching – the relief felt too good. Then I noticed the guy next to me craning his head to sneak a peek at my glory. The stream was coming out so hard that I thought I'd knock a hole in the porcelain.

"Hey, guys! Guess what Junior's got?"

I wanted to die as the laughter filled the men's room and the lobby. At least I didn't have to look Ginny Dare in the face. Concentrating hard on the Marx Brothers, I wished myself back to normalcy. Still, the piss flowed as another guy stepped up and tried to sneak a peek. I moved closer to the urinal; I couldn't run until I was finished.

Then I felt a wetness at my feet. The bottom pipe of the urinal was not completely attached and the accumulated urine was slowly draining onto the floor, meandering its way to the sleeping drunk, whose bulky winter coat absorbed it like a sponge. I could not believe that I had lowered myself to such a base level, and I felt my face flush in embarrassment and shame.

Finally finishing, I left the bathroom, almost slipping on my own urine. The drunk still snored as the piss soaked into his old gray coat sleeve. It was tempting to run for the exit, but I had lived through the worst part. Swinging wide of the incoming line, I felt a firm hand grab me by the arm. Her voice was strong but sympathetic.

"Hey, kid. Don't listen to those guys. They're just having fun with you. Just give it back to 'em. It's what I do."

Ginny Dare's face, time-worn as it was, revealed a gentle understanding and empathy. She reminded me of my mother, though I couldn't understand why. I gave her a weak smile, still feeling too embarrassed to reply or to enjoy her touch.

"This your first girlie show?"

I nodded, not having the courage to say anything, and hoping for a little pity from the person who I had pitied just minutes ago.

"Does Russ know you're here?"

Again I nodded, only half-playing the deaf mute.

"What's your name?"

"Kelly Elliott," I replied weakly. I didn't have to give her my real name, but there was an aura about her that commanded truth from me. She smiled sweetly, not that tantalizing smile she had used on stage.

"Go in and enjoy the rest of the show, Kelly. Have some fun. That's what you should be doing at your age. Forget about those guys. They probably forgot what it was like to be your age."

With a sincere smile, she turned and waited on a customer. From stripper to counselor to Rainsinettes' vendor. Quite the range of talents in Ginny Dare. Her kindness and surprising gentleness were too incongruous with her stage persona, and I pondered which was the real Ginny Dare. We each had that contrast in our personalities, and I wondered if I would ever see her again to learn more about the real woman. For a moment I flushed as I felt embarrassed at having seen her almost totally naked body and having witnessed her coarse personality. I returned to the auditorium, confused but having forgotten about the incident in the men's room.

"Christ, Elliott. Where the hell ya' been? Having fun in the can?"

Good old Jerry – he could take a state of tranquility and turn it to chaos, but Ginny Dare had already claimed my mind for the night, so I ignored my best friend.

"There was a big crowd. And . . . and . . ." I hated to tell him anything, because absolutely nothing was serious with Jerry. He had all the sensitivity of a drunken surgeon.

"Well. And what?" he persisted.

What the hell? "I was talking to Ginny Dare in the lobby."

There was a long pause, an awe-stricken face, and a "Bullshit!"

Defensively, I snarled, "Go to hell, Jerry. I did. She was selling candy at the counter."

He pondered for a moment, attempting to analyze my face and tone of voice.

"Christ, Elliott. You really did talk to her, didn't ya'?"

I nodded defiantly and hoped that he would shut up.

"Well, what did she say to ya'? Did she say she'd give ya' a private show for twenty bucks? Shit, she must have said something gross."

As with Swedarsky's insults, I felt my anger rise quickly. I wanted to pummel him into his wooden seat, but I understood his view; we weren't really so different. I gritted my teeth and spoke firmly.

"Jerry, shut up before I bust your goddamn head open."

I had never really lost my temper with him, and Jerry at least had enough common sense to know that he had intruded on some unknown territory. His eyes were wide.

"Yeah, sure Elliott. I just figured, you know. . ."

The tension had abated by the dimming of the house lights and the appearance of a man we had grown to know too well -- Russ.

"Ladies and gentlemen, before we begin the second half of our evening's spectacular entertainment, I want to introduce you to the best bargain in the city. First of all, a packet of four 5 x 7 glossy photos, one of each of our four fabulous stars. Here they are in all their glory, and I do mean in all their glory." The sleaze ball had me ticked off, but he did have my interest.

"Secondly, we have a back issue, a collector's item if you will, of *Girls! Girls! Girls!*, the magazine you won't find at your local newsstand. Forty-two pages of jokes, stories, and photos of some of the most beautiful girls in the entire world. And believe me, folks, as I stand here now, gazing at these lovely pages, there is little left to the imagination concerning the female anatomy." Jerry was on the edge of his seat as though he could see the pictures from thirty yards.

"And now comes the frosting on the cake. The delightful little joke booklet titled 'The Farmer's Daughter,' a wallet-sized copy of the raunchiest drawings and jokes to be found anywhere. Now, you may ask, 'If it's so raunchy, how can you legally sell it?' Ladies and gentlemen, you would be one hundred percent correct. We cannot sell this booklet without losing our license. This city in conjunction with federal obscenity laws, forbids the sale of this booklet I now hold in my hand. However, we can GIVE it to you!"

Jerry almost leaped up to get a closer look. The pitchman had him more hypnotized than the strippers had. At least Jerry could take Russ's wares home with him and show it off to the guys in the locker room. It was proof that we had been to the Follies.

"That's right, folks. We can't sell it to you, but we can give it to you with each purchase of a packet of four glossy photos and the collector's copy of *Girls! Girls! Girls!* This is a perfectly legal act, and in keeping with the policies of this theatre, we intend to satisfy our customers."

I knew Jerry would fall for the ruse, even if he had to skip lunches for the rest of the year.

"Now, you may ask, 'What is the purchase price of these three unique items?' One would expect to pay at least a sawbuck for this collection. But not here. Not tonight, anyway. Five dollars? Oh, no! Lower yet? You bet. Would you pay three dollars? Of course, you would. How about two-fifty? Not for our customers. No. Tonight you can have the photo packet, the magazine, and the liveliest little party book around for the unbelievable price of just two dollars!"

Russ was on a roll; he was good at his job. "You heard me right. Two dollars. This is the best deal on erotica to be found in the city of Chicago. Now, I don't know if I have enough for everyone here, but I'll start my way up the aisle and give rainchecks to those I don't get to. Please have your money ready."

Jerry had turned himself into a genuine teenage pervert, like the kind who hung out in Little Joey's store. "Christ, Elliott! Get it! Go down there before they run out!"

"I don't want them! It's just probably some big rip-off. Besides, I don't have any money."

He was shattered. Had I lost my sanity? How could I turn down such an opportunity to get the best collection of erotica in the city of Chicago? He was not to be denied. "We'll go halves on it. Okay?"

I was losing my patience again. "I just told you, Jerry, I don't have any money."

He was adamant. "You can borrow a buck off me and pay it back on Monday. Come on, Elliott. Be a sport! We'll be the hit of the senior class!"

Figuring no human way out of the situation, I reluctantly

agreed. Jerry leaped up and pulled two dollars from his wallet, keeping an eye on the progress of the salesman. I refused to go down there to get the garbage, and he impatiently waited, never taking his eyes from Russ and his "best deal in town."

Needless to say, since I was closer to the aisle, it was up to me to buy the smut. As I watched the earlier buyers, I could sense their disappointment. They'd snatch up the material, practically tearing it open in their lust, quickly page through it all, then shrug and put it aside. Despite the fact that we were near the rear of the auditorium, Russ looked in no danger of running out. I knew it was a rip-off, but Jerry was not to be denied.

As soon as our money had been exchanged for trash, Jerry tore it loose from my hands and studied it more closely than he had studied his textbooks in four years of high school. As I had suspected, we had been royally screwed. The magazine had about six pictures of T and A, and a few off-color, soft core stories. "The Farmer's Daughter" was a series of eight black and white ink drawings, about as pornographic as *The Christian Science Monitor*. Looking at the 5 x 7 glossies, I paused at Ginny Dare's. She was kneeling, giving that pseudo-sexy smile, dressed in a bikini, but I felt that I saw more of her than the deviants who surrounded me.

"Hey, Jer. You can have the rest of this crap if I can keep this picture. Okay?"

He could not disguise his foolish disappointment. "Yeah. Sure. I guess you were right. It was a rip-off. But you still owe me a buck."

The second half of the show improved slightly from the first half. Boom-Boom LaRue went through the same motions – three songs and a strip to a G-string and pasties. The only unique element of Boom-Boom's routine was the tassels – the lights went out and two phosphorescent orange tassels began to twirl, in opposite directions! They looked like egg beaters, and I was impressed with her talent to rotate her boobs in opposite directions. It wasn't even sexy – just a feat of physics that the average person couldn't do. I supposed that sometimes when her timing was a little off, they slapped together and that's why she took the name "Boom-Boom." Anyway, she got the biggest hand of the night, and even Jerry applauded her dexterity.

Belle Starr and her twin 44's was the closing act, and tension permeated the house. I had expected the same rut all over again, but it was difficult not to catch the fever. When she came on stage, we were all able to tell how she got her name. The twin 44's were her chest and waist. She was built, but she was fat – gross fat! Jerry became comatose again, becoming conscious only long enough to remind me about the inflated rubbers.

There were no inflated rubbers, but the evening was not an entire waste. When Belle Starr turned around after unsnapping her bra, she was not wearing any pasties. The mounting disappointment of the show thus far gave the act a bigger impact than it deserved. There were my first real-life set of a woman's tits, staring out at me, like two hypnotists' coins. I had to confess that they were real dandies. Everyone was agape as Belle bounded around the stage so hard that the sailors in the front row expected a lapful.

"Christ, Elliott! Have you ever seen anything like those in your life? God, wait until the guys at school hear about this. They won't believe it!"

Belle had even reached the pseudo-urbane Jerry Hogan.

"Too bad she couldn't have gone all the way, though."

Jerry would not have been content if she had smothered his head in her cleavage. "I couldn't see anything," he would have complained. I was satisfied – it had been enough excitement for one evening.

The show closed with all the girls coming out for a bow and some applause. When I saw Ginny again, I couldn't believe it was the same woman who had talked to me in the lobby. It was another person, and I was amazed that she could change so completely. Still, she acted the role that she had created, and I was glad to see her again.

Against my better judgment, Jerry and I stayed for the entire second show. I had no place to go, so I didn't really mind. Jerry was convinced that Belle Starr would pass out the inflated rubbers at the late show. She didn't. I watched Ginny with a warmer, closer feeling, trying to see through her façade. I don't know why but I didn't want her to know that I was still there. I was fascinated by Boom-Boom and Belle's studies in centrifugal force; it was even more interesting than the display at the Museum of Science and Industry. Still, I was more than ready to leave when the show finally ended.

It was 1:30 when we stepped out into the city's blustery, cold night. Except for the immediate crowd, the streets were deserted. I half-feigned a bitchy mood and told Jerry that I wanted to be alone, and that he should take the el home alone. It was easy to tell when Jerry was in one of his hyper-active moods and would be loud and obnoxious on the train, talking about Boom-Boom's tassel trick. I, or anyone in his proper mind, could hardly tolerate Jerry Hogan when he reached that state.

Jerry climbed the stairs and I awaited the bus, because it would take longer and I had just enough change in my pocket for the fare. There were only three other people on the bus, and they stared out the windows like mannequins, mechanically getting off at various stops. I apathetically joined the group – the city sometimes did that to people. It was dehumanizing.

It was the second straight night that I spent in the Brighton Theatre. Although I had no money, Jorge, the doorman, listened patiently, understood, and agreed to loan me the dollar admission charge until Monday. That made two dollars I owed on Monday – one for a place to pass the night, the other for a 5 x 7 glossy of a timeworn stripper, which I carefully carried flat in my coat pocket, being careful not to crease it.

It was the same crowd as the previous night. Only the faces changed. I took my usual seat, glancing over the crowd, trying to secure some privacy. From my pocket, I withdrew the picture and studied it, using the glare from the wide screen.

Somehow, the woman had affected a boy in a mere sixty seconds. I had the usual youthful fantasies – wondering where she was at that moment, where she lived, and if I would ever see her again. With a few kind words she had taken me from an increasingly embarrassing moment and told me how to cope and be more confident. She made it sound easy, but I wasn't sure how competent I'd be in actual practice. Still, I was grateful to Ginny Dare, but I felt bad when I saw the old hooker in the back of the auditorium and wondered how she had ended up there. Relaxing in my seat, I gently replaced the picture in my pocket and stared up at the screen but saw nothing.

CHAPTER 6

Linda Martinsen and the Traffic Ticket

Sunday I waited until noon before going home. Ma would have already taken the 11:30 train to Wheaton, and I was satisfied just to have a day to recharge my depleted body and to reflect on the turmoil that had begun on Friday.

The apartment looked like a railroad salvage depot. Clothes (men's and women's) had been piled hurriedly on the armchair. Empty beer cans and half-eaten TV chicken dinners lay scattered on the kitchen counter. It looked like Dan Phillips had had his way, again. He couldn't even take her out to dinner? Never too sure of Ma's mood upon returning from Aunt Amy's, I cleaned the entire apartment, even moving the furniture to vacuum. I tossed any men's clothes in a shopping bag and put them in Ma's closet. Making life a little easier for my mother was something I should have done more often, but it didn't come naturally.

By 2:00 I was ready to lie on the couch, watch television, and catch up on some lost sleep. It hadn't been easy sleeping in theatre seats for two nights in a row. *Casablanca* was playing on channel nine, so I was able to watch it for the millionth time without concentrating, leaving my mind free for more important matters.

I figured that Monday would be a decent day. My black eye would bring me some recognition, and people would probably admire my nerve in telling off Swedarsky. I would probably become a minor celebrity. Swedarsky had done his damage to my body, so the worst was over with him. Everything I had survived should push me up the "Maybe-he's-not-a-total-loser" scale.

Our excursion to the Follies Theatre would bring more curious notoriety to Jerry and me. Everyone would gather around to hear Jerry pompously relate our story of Belle Starr and her twin 44's. Jerry would embellish the story and I would be forced into supporting his claim to have seen full frontal nudity. Our exploits at the Follies would become well known and assure us of fleeting increased popularity. As evidence, Jerry would even bring the "Farmer's Daughter" joke book we had bought. Monday seemed destined to be a good day the more I envisioned it.

My only worry was my Friday night fart at the basketball game. It probably had not been as loud as I had imagined, but Laura LeDuc had definitely heard it. Getting back into her good graces would be a slow, tedious process, if even possible.

As usual, thoughts of Laura LeDuc triggered more fantasies. Within the next two hours, not only had I gotten into her good graces, but I had taken her to prom, given her my class ring, made it in the back seat of Muffler Mulhouse's Ford and anyplace else we could be alone, proposed, married her, had so much uninhibited sex that I was forced to cheat on her just for variety, been caught in bed with a voluptuous redhead, divorced Laura, and attempted suicide, just to see if she still had the old feelings for me. It was one hell of an afternoon, and I had done it all on the couch. I was exhausted! *Casablanca* had nothing on my romantic fantasy life.

Ma got home about 8:00, and something was wrong. She stared at me like a zombie and asked if I had eaten anything. I feigned interest in the activities of Aunt Amy and her two brats, Bradley and Tammy. Ma answered tersely, without emotion, and went to bed by 9:00.

I lay on the couch that night and could hear Ma crying in her bedroom. I wanted to go to her, but I wasn't sure how to handle her troubles or what was expected of me. It was doubtful that something tragic had happened at Aunt Amy's; the two sisters got along very well. The problem was not likely me, or she would have erupted like Krakatoa. That left one possible explanation – the son-of-a-bitch airplane pilot. He must have done or said something to hurt her feelings during the weekend. I wanted to break the bastard's neck and found it impossible to sleep as my ire grew. My only consolation came from the thought that maybe they had broken up, and that the lousy prick would never be near us again. The alarm clock said 1:50 as I drifted off into a restless night.

Ma's mood hadn't change in the morning, and we ate breakfast in relative silence. It was like a non-violent, post-supper period. I hadn't seen her like that since she had been denied a promotion at the insurance company, and I knew that I was of no benefit to her during her depression. Everything had to work its own way out. I only hoped that I wouldn't lose my poise when she needed me most.

School was better than normal, but far less than my fantastic couch scenario. My black eye brought a few stares and hushed conversation, but no one made a major issue of it. Locker room conversation about the Follies created some curiosity, but everyone seemed less interested than I had anticipated. I suppose it was considered "uncool" to be involved with someone of my menial social status, but I knew that they really wanted to hear all about our trip to see Belle Starr. Jerry had left the magazine at home, because, as he confessed later, "It was a real rip-off, and where's the buck you owe me?" Still, if we had been Swedarsky, everyone would have been perched on the edge of the benches, anxious to hear every detail about Belle Starr and her twin 44's. The words "tits" and "ass" did not have the same effect coming from my mouth, the words seemingly forced and me trying too hard to be "cool." It took someone more simian to really milk the situation.

The miracle on 34th Street occurred as I was on my way to chemistry class. I was walking with my head down, like a Chinese peasant, as was customary, when I heard a, "Hi, Kelly."

It was Laura LeDuc! She had actually said, "Hi" and called me by name.

Stunned, I did not react until she had turned the corner of the corridor. I pursued and saw her vanish into Bates' English class. Not wanting to let the opportunity to return to her social graces escape me, I went to the door and peered in. Laura sat on the far side of the room, bending over a desk, talking to some classmates. She had endless legs, and I felt myself frothing. With a little wave, I braved a "Hi-i-i-i, Laura."

Son-of-a-bitch! My voice had cracked again. I was way past puberty and could not understand my ill fate, except for the social pressure. All day long it could have cracked, but it had decided to wait until I had worked up enough nerve to say something to Laura LeDuc with a watching audience.

Laura gave a little wave as she embarrassingly looked at her classmates and shrugged her shoulders, as though she didn't know who I was. At that moment I decided to call off the prom date and possibly the wedding that I had shared with her the day before. After I had embarrassed us both, I was sure that she felt it best not to have anything to do with me, under any circumstances.

I headed for chemistry class, almost running down the hall, afraid of being late and wanting to put distance between Laura and myself. I was determined to leave behind the whole ugly scene. So my voice cracked again. At least I didn't fart again. Progress was slow in the world of Kelly Elliott.

My lab partner was already there and had already set up the day's project. Linda Martinsen was a quiet girl who wouldn't complain about having her feet cut off by a lawn mower, as long as the cutter apologized. I suppose that's why Ewald paired us up. Linda wouldn't have whined about having me as a lab partner. I would have liked a gorgeous, over-sexed blonde, like Diane Kyrk, who would repay me with feminine gratitude every time I completed the day's project and still gave her half the credit, even though she did nothing. With Linda Martinsen I was still doing most of the work but only getting a sickeningly sweet, "Thank you, Kelly," each time.

Actually, Linda Martinsen was a nice girl. She was the kind of girl I could bring home to my mother, and after Linda left, Ma would probably say, "She seems like a nice girl, Kelly." Not that I was opposed to nice girls, but with a girl like Linda it would probably be two years of steady dating before I would get much action. At seventeen the average boy craves a nymphomaniac, not someone "nice." Linda would never be like that, or so I assumed.

Linda Martinsen was an "average" high school girl. She had a small clique of friends, was polite, dressed neatly in conservative, inexpensive clothing from Sears and Goldblatts. She was a little pudgy, but certainly not fat. Unlike most of the girls in our senior class, Linda's hair was dark and short, and her mouth, which rarely smiled wide enough to show any teeth, was small and without cosmetic enhancement. She was about six inches shorter than I was and she wasn't really too bad looking – no pimples or anything. I had never made any advances toward her, because she was more aloof than I was. Besides, I never even thought of Linda as a girlfriend . She was too quiet and a date with her would be like dating an inmate of the Holy Virgin Convent. Still, I kind of liked Linda. She was consistent and sincere. Definitely one of the "nice" girls, but just not in vogue at the time.

"What do we have to do today, Linda?" I asked, impressed by her initiative to get today's work ready.

Her voice was quiet and even. "Find some unknown. I'm not sure how. Are you?"

Same old story – helpless female needing help from the unsuspecting male. It was chauvinistic, but it was also the way things were. I hoped that attitude would change some time in the future. I had carried us through the course, and I wouldn't let her down now. Besides, it made me feel useful and intelligent, even if it was only Linda Martinsen.

"No sweat, Linda. I'll do the experiment and you record

the data."

She gave her standard narrow smile in acknowledgment, and the class began. One step that Linda could handle well was the dipping of the old litmus paper. She was handicapped in every aspect of chemistry, but when it came to the standard acid-base test, Linda shined like Boom-Boom LaRue's tassels.

We had completed and recorded the results of the experiment in a half hour, leaving us twenty minute to fake business so that old man Ewald wouldn't find us "something more challenging," like a pig heart transplant. So we made small talk without flirtation, I think.

"I heard about the way you told off Joe Swedarsky. That took a lot of nerve, but I'm glad someone did it. Does your eye hurt much?"

After one hellish weekend, I finally felt the laurels being placed on my head. I looked round for additional recognition, but everyone seemed occupied in the race against the clock. I really appreciated Linda's acknowledgment – all my suffering had not been completely in vain. She hadn't said that Swedarsky had knocked my block off, or that I was an idiot to insult somebody forty times my size. She had admired my nerve.

"No, it doesn't hurt much, Linda. I just got fed up with his abusiveness to anyone smaller than him. It was no big deal." The hell it wasn't!

"Well, I think it was something. It's too bad he's so big, but I still think you did the right thing. At least you let him know what you thought about him. That's more than anyone else has done."

The girl was a saint – intelligent and appreciative. I wondered if she knew how good a verbal shot I had gotten in.

"Did you hear what I said, Linda?" I asked, a little hesitant, somewhat embarrassed.

She blushed and turned her head. "Well, yes. I did hear it, but I think everyone gets mad and uses language they shouldn't, don't you?"

Definitely a saint. I had spent twenty-five weeks in class with her and had been blind the entire time.

"Well, I don't use language like that all the time. I was almost going to use the 'F' word. It's like you said. Sometimes people get so mad that they don't think about what they're saying."

Holy shit! Was I rolling! I wanted to let her know that I had such offensive tools in my arsenal without actually proving it. The words were coming so easily and honestly that I couldn't believe myself.

Mr. Ewald's voice broke into my elation. "Okay, group. Let's clean up. The bell rings in two minutes. Put your results in the top basket before leaving."

We had already cleaned our area and had two minutes to sit. I decided right then that I liked Linda Martinsen a lot. I didn't love her the way I loved Laura LeDuc, but that mousy, sympathetic girl had a lot of qualities that I had not seriously considered. There were certainly uglier girls in the school. Linda was the kind of girl I could safely be seen with, without engendering much negative criticism. If I took her to a game, the guys without dates would secretly be jealous and wouldn't be able to say, "Who's the pig with Elliot?" On the other hand, she wasn't so pretty that they would say, "She must really be hard-up to go out with Elliott." There was a certain satisfaction in that security, and I decided that Linda would suit me very well until Laura came around.

The bell rang and the hordes filled the hallways, anxious to reach their last class of the day. Linda walked slowly, waiting for me to catch up. At least, I thought she was waiting for me.

"Where's your next class, Linda?"

She feigned surprise at my voice, but I knew better. She had the hots for me – I was gaining popularity.

"Phy ed," she replied coyly.

"Really? Well, I'm going down there, too. I'll walk you to class." She smiled at that line. Actually, my world literature class was on the opposite end of the wing, but never having walked a girl to class, I figured the tardy detention would be worth the experience.

"What on earth do you have by the girls' gym?"

That was a tough question to answer. The only rooms near the girls' gym were the cafeteria and home economics classes.

"Well, actually I have English, but I always go out the door by the gym and walk down the driveway, so I don't have to fight the crowds in the halls." Good thinking, Elliott!

We made it to the gym, and I only had two minutes to rush to Bates' English class. It felt awkward being the only guy in the corridor leading to the girls' gym, but I didn't really care. I was even stupid enough to walk her to the locker room door, amidst the scrutiny and giggles of all the other girls. With a quick, "See you later," I bolted out the exit and down the driveway in a vain attempt to make it to class on time.

Luck was not running in my favor. Swedarsky was also in the driveway, coming at me, probably sneaking a quick smoke before trying to get a peek into the girls' locker room. There was no avoiding him, as his bulk and shit-eating grin moved laterally to block my passage.

"What's the rush, pit-face? Just coming from girls' phy ed? How was your field hockey game? Did ya' have to play goalie again?"

It was no time for games. "Look, Swedarsky, I have to get to English, and I'm going to be late. Let me get by, huh?"

He was still smiling. "Sure, lady. I just wanted to congratulate you on that great fart at the basketball game on Friday. I guess I must have really knocked the insides out of ya', huh? I wasn't there to hear it, but everyone's talking about it. Christ, Elliott, you're the laughing stock of the senior class."

Good old Swedarsky. Anything to demean an already pathetic figure. The bell sounded and I knew that Bates would show me no mercy.

"Too bad, dumbass. You're late. Might have made it if you hadn't stopped to talk. Well, keep up the good farts, Elliott.

Ya' know, I bet all those pimples are air sacs that give you that extra force. See ya' soon, I hope."

He brushed by me and knocked my books from my hand. As I started to pick them up, I could only feel grateful that nobody else had witnessed the confrontation. There would be no need to save face or feel the need to seek revenge.

Bates had just finished taking attendance when I stumbled into class. Middle-aged, bi-focaled, and stern, he was Talbot High's hardest English teacher. He was not pleased at my late arrival; he would have to alter his attendance slip.

"Where have you been, Mr. Elliott?" He was a sarcastic son-of-a-bitch. I suppose that if I had been teaching for twenty years and still wore a flat top haircut, I'd have been nasty, too.

"Sorry, Mr. Bates. I forgot my book and had to go back for it. It won't happen again." Until tomorrow, I thought.

"Just to make sure, here's a little reminder," and he tore off a one-hour detention slip. It was a rule he loved to enforce.

"Now hand in your homework and take your seat," he barked sadistically.

My homework? Damn! Damn! Damn! With everything that had happened over the weekend, I had forgotten my Chaucer translation. I stumbled for words.

"Ah, it's not quite done, Mr. Bates. Could I hand it in at the end of the hour? My rough draft is hardly legible."

Bates had been teaching too long to let a half-assed excuse get by him. "Most of your work is hardly legible, Mr. Elliott. Give me your rough copy."

It was time for some real acting – I was an amateur being evaluated by a professional. I sorted through my notebook, pretending to look for the non-existent translation. The members of the class smirked, knowing, as did Bates, that I had no such paper. I tried to pull a major bluff and pulled out some chemistry notes, quickly replacing them. I had them believing for a second. My chemistry formula had hardly resembled Chaucer, but a desperate man will try anything.

"I must have left it in my other folder, sir. I'll get it right after school." I didn't believe my own naivety as I continued digging myself into a deeper hole.

"And I will mark it 'late.' You've wasted two valuable minutes of class time with this charade. Since there are thirty-two students in this class, that means you have wasted sixty-four precious minutes. I believe you owe your classmates an apology."

Bates was a master at humiliation. I would have bet that he was Swedarsky's mentor or vice-versa.

"Sorry," I mumbled and took my seat with a reddened face.

"We are on page 263 – 'The Pardoner's Tale.'"

Whoopee! I thought. All my life I had been waiting for the day we would discuss "The Pardoner's Tale." What the hell was "The Pardoner's Tale"?

As soon as I had sat down, Diane Kyrk, by far the sexiest girl in our lit class, and a definite "9," came bouncing into the room.

Bates flushed. "You're a few minutes late, Miss Kyrk. Any reason?"

She swayed her ass up to the front of the room, pressed her boobs into his arm, and whispered into his ear. Bates turned red, trying to remain professional and grinned. She had probably told him that she was having her monthly and had to replace her sanitary napkin. Girls could always fall back on that excuse, leaving male teachers no option but humble acceptance. I watched with curiosity.

He asked her for the Chaucer homework, and she again leaned into him and whispered. Bates' entire act was put on for my benefit, so that he would avoid criticism of unequal treatment. She whispered something else, and he quickly took his seat behind his desk.

"Very well, Miss Kyrk. Now please take your seat."

Diane Kyrk had scored again, and I hated her guts.

Jerry would buy a copy of *Playboy* on the fifteenth of every month from Little Joey, who kept the copies under the counter. One month there was a page on interesting statistics that said the average male has thoughts about sex nineteen times a day on average. My instincts told me that the number should well exceed nineteen, especially in high school senior boys. Bates babbled on about Chaucer, but there were better ways to pass that wasted time.

Despite my late arrival for class, the period still seemed to approach infinity. While old Bates droned on, I kept thinking about Linda Martinsen. Nobody could ever replace Laura LeDuc, but a bird in the hand was worth two in the bush. (Bates would have nailed me for using a cliché, but if the shoe fits . . .)

There I sat, a senior in high school, and I had never been on a date. I never figured any girl would vaguely like a guy with looks like mine. I had accepted celibacy until I was at least twenty. It was a fact of life. Maybe I should "man up" and ask Linda on a date. The worst that could happen was that she'd say "No." I didn't feel that Linda would say "No" and then tell others about it in order to make me feel smaller. And if she said, "Yes . . . " I'd cross that bridge when I came to it. (Sorry, Bates—not really!)

Linda had seemed sincerely friendly and interested in my life, and I had an anxiety attack waiting for the class to end as a plan formed in my mind. I grew extremely restless and crossed and uncrossed my legs a million times. I even felt stomach cramps coming on and I started to sweat, waiting for the class to end. Asking a girl out for the first time was a real bear. There was no simple way and I had no time to prepare or find a mentor to help me.

Like belches, we rated the girls in our school. I tried to occupy my mind by rating Linda. In all honesty, I would rate her as a seven. Still, I hoped the rest of the guys would rate her as an eight. Kelly Elliott with an eight would be a major accomplishment in my eyes. I hoped nobody would rate her as a six, though I could hear Swedarsky rate her a two, because she was stupid enough to go out with me. Laura LeDuc was the closest thing to a ten at our school, and we never rated anybody a ten.

My mind raced from rating systems to rehearsals of what I would say to Linda, and how I would accept her probable rejection. Either way, in twenty-two minutes I would have my answer, but the sweat and other anxious symptoms would not take leave.

After class I would race down the driveway and try to catch her in the hallway. I would walk her to her locker, then to her bus. Somewhere in that five minutes I had to "pop the question." I just prayed that the words would come as easily as our last conversation had. In fact, I literally prayed, asking God to get me through the crisis and have Linda accept my invitation. I must have been raised Catholic for a reason.

There were still seven minutes left in the period, and I honestly questioned my ability to make it through 420 more seconds. I was literally shaking inside and out, as though I had been hit with a sudden attack of the stomach flu. I just could not tolerate sitting there any longer. Bates was reading some crap in Old English, as though anyone really cared. I hoped he would choke on his tongue and class would be dismissed early. I hated Bates and Geoffrey Chaucer with a passion. I wanted to get to Linda immediately. It was unfair to make me wait.

Finally the bell sounded, ending the longest English class in recorded history. I checked the calendar on the way out, surprised that it was still March. I damned Bates and Chaucer to spend an eternity through hell like the one with which they had unjustly punished me.

I sprinted down the driveway and through the exit doors by the girls' locker room. There was no sight of Linda. I guess that I had subconsciously hoped that she would have waited for me, but, as usual, I was wrongly misled by my imagination. She had to be at her locker, and I raced up the stairs. She was putting on her jacket as I turned the corner. It was time to be nonchalant, a major feat considering my shortness of breath.

I gasped, "Hi, Linda."

She seemed genuinely surprised but not disappointed.

"Hi, Kelly. Why are you all out of breath?"

An observant woman! She caught my death throes as I leaned against a locker, trying to grasp a breath of oxygen. It hurt to talk, and I had to do so quickly.

"I, I had to run and catch Mr. Bates. I brought the wrong folder to class."

"Oh, how was your English class?"

"You know. Same thing. We talked about Chaucer."

Her face beamed. "Don't you love Chaucer? I have lit first hour, and I just love to hear Mr. Bates read some of those parts in Old English."

Another door had opened. The words would be able to flow smoothly, if I didn't choke on my own hypocrisy.

"I love Chaucer, too, and the way Mr. Bates read the prologue, I was hooked from the start. I wish I could do that." I was becoming what I would have referred to as a "real asshole."

"Yeah, I know what you mean. I have to run or I'll miss my bus. I'll see you tomorrow, Kelly," and off she walked.

I was stunned! I had waited too long for the opportunity to ask her for a date. It had been forty-two whole minutes! It was like going to the doctor – it wasn't the examination that caused the pain; it was the anguish of waiting. I couldn't bear to postpone my question any longer. I would never have been able to get myself psyched up for another attempt. I pursued and grabbed her arm.

"Ah, Linda, there was something I wanted to ask you."

"Could it wait until tomorrow? I have to catch my bus. Mr. Priegel always leaves on time."

It couldn't wait or it might not happen. "I'll walk you out to the bus. It's kind of important."

Curiosity and concern crossed her face, and I realized that she was just as scared as I was. Her female intuition must have sensed that I was about to ask her for a date, and she would be forced into a decision. As I had chauvinistically rated her and fantasized about the reactions of my classmates, so would she probably go through the same mental assessments. What would the girls say if she went out with Kelly Elliott, the pimple-faced farter? If she said, "No," she'd be forced to come up with some plausible excuse to protect my feelings. She was a kind human, but I'm sure that she had limits. The whole system of dating was just too mentally stressful. It always has been and probably always will be. It's why so many good people go dateless. The predator and the prey – offense and defense, good and evil, and no coach in the world could help evaluate all the factors to give the best result.

We got to her bus as the last of the students was boarding. It was time!

I spoke distinctly and firmly. "I was wondering if you'd like to go out Friday night. Maybe to a movie or something."

Again time seemed to slow to an inert pace. It was hard to read her face. I had backed her into a corner.

"Friday night? I think it would be all right. Could I let you know for sure tomorrow? I really have to ask my parents. They might have something planned."

Bitch! Who did she think I was, falling for a line like that? I had just spent almost an hour in hell for her, and she wanted to drag out the agony for another day. Still, she hadn't said, "No," and she even thought that it might be "all right." Maybe she was being honest. I'd have to suffer another day and hope it would be worth the anguish.

"Sure, that's fine, Linda. I'll see you in chemistry class."

Linda boarded the bus, Mr. Priegel shut the doors, and I watched her take a window seat. We waved and I felt like I was in an old movie, waving a last farewell to the girlfriend before going off to war. But I felt good. I honestly felt that Linda Martinsen would say "Yes" to Kelly Elliott.

The events that followed all seemed to construct one massive nightmare, but they seemed to compose an inescapable fate. There was no stopping the falling dominoes in my life, and I had to cope with the crises as they arose.

I stood at the bus stop feeling fairly elated about myself

and the day's events. I had asked a girl out for the first time, and she had said that she thought it would be "all right." She hadn't laughed or commented on my pimples. She had given me a hope, no matter the time and anguish involved with the waiting.

Along came Muffler Mulhouse, a classmate with whom I had once been paired to form a tennis team for gym class. It had made us a temporary unit, and Muffler never hesitated to ask me for a favor – copying homework, borrowing money, etc. What closer bond was there between people than having played tennis or badminton together in gym class?

Muffler Mulhouse also had quite a face full of pimples, making him another member of the "Clearasil Clan." He weighed well over 200 pounds; he was a slob and pretty much of an outcast. The one thing that made Muffler more socially acceptable was his car. Having a car was almost like paying dues to rise on the social ladder. Guys would ride home with him, and even get him a date if he agreed to double, so that they could use his car. They were using him, but he didn't mind. None of us at the obscurity level minded being used if it offered the opportunity to be part of the acceptable high school hierarchy. He had a whiny voice that grated one's hearing.

"Elliott! Hey, Elliott! Wait up!"

I was in too good a mood to ignore him. "What's up, Muff?"

"Glad I caught you. Wanted to ask you for a favor, if you got the time." His car entitled him to ask a favor.

"Sure, Muff. Name it. I mean, what are ex-tennis partners for?"

He was excited about something. "You know Gloria Steiner?"

I thought but could not place the name. There were two thousand students at Talbot High School.

"She's a sophomore. Short brown hair. Kind of heavy and short, but with big tits. Thompson told us about her in the locker room. Remember?"

A light came to pass. "Good time Gloria?"

"Yeah, that's the one. She's home all alone until seven, and invited me over if I take her to the Beach Boys concert at the stadium next month. You know what that means?"

I knew. Word had it that Gloria would put out for anybody in exchange for a favor. Thompson had taken her to a basketball game and for a pizza, and he claimed that she had banged him for two straight hours. She insisted on using a rubber, which she even provided. I hadn't ever seen her, but, like every guy in school, I was anxious to get into her good graces.

"So, what's the favor, Muff? Who could deny anybody a date with Gloria Steiner?"

"My old lady leaves for work at 4:30 and has to borrow my car because the old man's working overtime. I can't tell her that I'll be late because Gloria's going to show me a good time. Will ya' take my car home for me? I'll give ya' a buck, and you can catch the bus back to your place. Whadda ya' say? You owe me one. After all, who saved all those lousy lobs you made in gym class?"

I wasn't sure about anything he had said, especially the bit about the lousy lobs, but Linda had put me in a good mood, and the milk of human kindness poured through my veins. Besides, driving a car was a rare opportunity for me, even if it was Muffler's heap.

"Sure, Muff, no sweat. Where's it parked?"

He thrust the keys into my hands. "It's over in Lot C, by the shops. Thanks a lot, Elliott. I owe ya' one. I'll introduce Gloria to you. See ya' later." He was in a major hurry.

Meeting Gloria would be all right. After all, I was a semi-respectable senior. Of course, if all went well, I'd have Linda and wouldn't need Gloria. Until that moment I hadn't even thought about having sex with Linda. It was difficult to picture her naked, so I restrained my fantasies (probably thirty so far today), determined not to create an illusion which might never happen.

The red 1963 Thunderbird awaited me. I felt apprehensive of the rush hour traffic but considered the opportunity to drive a privilege. Muffler Mulhouse did not get his nickname from use of a muffler. Rather, it was the absence of one that gave him notoriety. Until our senior year he had been known as Dwight Mulhouse, but "Muffler" quickly erased his given name. He liked it more. Who could blame him? Dwight?

I started the engine and it roared. There was a feeling of power, sitting behind the thunder machine, and I assumed a dominating personality, sitting straight and tall, rather than my usual slumped posture. It was then that I noticed Laura LeDuc coming down the sidewalk. She had seen me.

When she was even with the front of the car, I shouted, "Hey, Laura!"

Obviously embarrassed by the din of the car, she waved, mouthed something, and continued walking. She had probably said, "Hi, Kelly," but I pretended she had said, "I love you, Kelly." By the time I was at the intersection of the parking lot, she was miming, "Want to go to my house and have sex all day?" Good old Laura – if only she had known.

Stopping at the sign, I noticed Laura waiting at the bus stop. Fear fought my bravado. It was a golden opportunity, and she could only decline the offer. Events had gone so well that day that I felt confident that she would accept an innocent offer for a ride. I had to chance it or I would spend my dying moments wondering if Laura LeDuc would have accepted my offer. Fate played witless tricks. Why else would Gloria Steiner offer Muffler Mulhouse afternoon gymnastics?

I lowered my voice an octave. "Would you like a ride, Laura?"

She heard my voice but none of my words. The car sounded like lunch hour in the cafeteria. Looking around for signs of anyone else, she approached me. I thought I'd wet my pants, I was so nervous.

"Did you say something?" She leaned through the window.

"Would you like a ride?"

Again, she scanned the area, probably fearful of being

seen talking to someone like me in something like Muffler's Ford.

"I'm only going to the library."

"Right on my way." It was actually out of my way far more than Linda's gym class had been on my way to English.

One final scan and she agreed. "Okay. It'll save me a crowded bus."

I could not believe my incredible fortune or the fact that everything good had started with my telling Swedarsky, "Up yours." Recognition by the prettiest girl in school, a possible date with a girl I had known for years but had never had the confidence or desire to ask out. A ride with Laura LeDuc. It was the nearest feeling to orgasm without manual assistance.

Remembering all the suave traits of Humphrey Bogart in the movies, I leaped out of the car to open her door, but I was too late – she had already gotten in. I looked a bit foolish standing there, but I quickly cast aside my minor gaffe. I started to reach inside my imaginary white dinner jacket so that I could withdraw my 14K gold cigarette case, but I soon realized that I had no vest pocket in my sweatshirt, nor did I have a 14K gold cigarette case. Nor any cigarettes.

I was so excited that I felt as though a troupe of midgets was rehearsing a trampoline act in my pants. Coincidental or not, when I climbed into the car, Laura had mercifully turned her head away. I steered with my left hand so that I was able to rest my right arm discreetly across my crotch. It was awkward, but how many guys would have envied me?

I cautiously pulled into the traffic pattern and headed toward the library. We rode in silence for a full minute, obviously feeling as uncomfortable as two people possibly could. At least with my concentration on the traffic, I was able to gracefully remove my conspicuous arm.

"Is this your car, Kelly?" she asked.

"No. It's Dwight Mulhouse's, but he asked me to drive it home for him today."

"Why?"

"Because Gloria Steiner is going to let him bang her," I thought.

"He had some business. I don't know what."

"Oh." She had accepted it. "What are you going to do after school, Kelly?"

Was she asking me if I was busy? "I don't know. Probably just go home and start some homework."

"No, I mean after graduation."

An innocent mistake - no need to lose my cool.

"I'm not sure yet. I was thinking about college." Trump card! "Maybe Yale or Princeton, but I'm not sure yet."

It had impressed her, I thought.

"Oh, have you applied yet?" she asked suspiciously.

She was pacifying me. I had better return to reality. From Ivy League to state school – tough transition. "Actually, I haven't. I only put in at Northern State. I hope to get a very big teacher's scholarship for there. My mother really wants me to be a teacher. I don't know why."

Honest enthusiasm came back at me. "Really? That's where I'm going, but I'm not sure what I'll take yet. Do you want to be a teacher?"

The ball was rolling. "I'm thinking about it. I've had so many bad teachers that I don't know how I could do much worse."

"I know what you mean. The one I really can't stand is Bates. I have him third period. I go nuts when he starts to read that Old English. He's so boring. And he undresses every girl with his eyes. He thinks he's cool, but he's not and I can't wait to get out of his class."

A match made in heaven! "I know what you mean. I can't stand him or his Chaucer babble either. It drives me right up the wall." I hoped that Linda never talked to Laura. What were the odds? In my world?

We drove in silence for a few minutes. The library was only eight more blocks. I was too scared to talk but felt I had to take some initiative.

"Laura, how did you know my name?" I was sincerely

curious. How was I viewed by the social elite?

"Cindy Jameson saw your run-in with Swedarsky after school. She pointed you out to me at the game. I never did like him. He's been trying to go out with me ever since I moved here, but he's just so crude. I can't stand to be near him, let alone date him. He keeps hounding me. I'm glad someone took him down a notch."

I was "cool" in Laura's eyes. My excitement was returning and my arm took its covering position. We pulled up to the library and I watched her get out after thanking me for the ride. I was in love. I had already known it, but that trip had absolutely confirmed it. There would never be another girl like Laura LeDuc.

Waiting to watch her go inside, I felt a twinge of pain. In front of the library stood a stud in a DePaul University letter jacket. She ran up to him, kissed him hard on the lips and they went inside. Jealousy cut through my body, but I diminished the ache by reliving our last ten minutes. Some day she'll leave college boy for me and we'll have all those mad nights of passion as I had fantasized on my living room sofa.

Because of my prior elation, I drove without really thinking about the task. Everyone has driven and suddenly awakened, unaware of the past few blocks or miles. The body acts like an automatic pilot, braking at the red lights and accelerating at the green lights. However, the one reflexive response not allowed for was coping with the yellow lights. My system was sharply jolted by the screech of the brakes as a yellow cab skidded to a stop within a few inches of Muffler Mulhouse's passenger door. An enraged voice shattered my tranquility.

"Jesus H. Christ! What ya' doin,' kid? Dontcha know that a yellow light means caution? For Christ's sake, you ran the goddamn red light, ya' little asshole! I oughta tear off your balls and make ya' eat 'em!"

I cautiously got out of the car; I had never seen such a maniacal face; he looked like an enraged psychopath. My heart was pounding, and I felt sure that the creature would slaughter me and sell my remains to Marshall's Meat Market.

I replied weakly. "Sorry, mister. I didn't see ya'."

"Didn't see me? How can ya' miss two tons of bright yellow steel? Ya' got brain damage or sometin'?"

Brain damage! It had been my exact comment when Billy Astin was seized by an epileptic fit during gym class. It was worth a try. Jerkily, I grasped my throat and started to jerk, sticking out my tongue as far as humanly possible.

I rasped, "H,h,h,h, help. I,I,I,I'm having a seizure. Do something." I crossed my eyes for added effect but decided it was too melodramatic and quickly substituted body convulsions.

The cab driver backed off, his desire to kill me mellowing to an "I don't wanna have nothin' to do with this." I knew I would be able to rely on the desire not to become involved. I hadn't lived in the city for seventeen years without getting a good street education. It was just a matter of engaging one's resources.

Knowing he couldn't completely abandon the chaos he had created, he sidled his way back toward me. "Sorry, kid. I didn't mean to rattle ya'. Just calm down. It'll pass. No harm done to the cars, and that's all that really matters." He was scared, and I wanted to laugh in his reddened face.

Deciding to let him off easy, I retracted my waving tongue and began to speak. Then I noticed a curious, gathering crowd on the corner. It seemed a shame to let such an enthusiastic audience go to waste. I was in control for a change.

My legs shot straight out like an ironing board behind the steering wheel. By then my eyes had glazed over from the tension, so I crossed them again and glared at the driver. He was stunned senseless.

"Holy shit! I better radio for help. Don't move, kid. I'll be right back."

He started for his cab, but I hit the horn to attract his attention. Reluctantly, he returned, like a man hit it in the head with a howitzer shell.

I whispered, "Wait. It'll pass. You go on. I'll be better if you get out of my sight."

The sympathetic crowd began to resemble a lynch mob as they hurled epithets at the driver. I was sure that if he had not been so frantic and burly they would have maimed him. Then I could have been on the Channel 2 Big News. He sensed the crowd's hostility and drove away in his cab, squealing his tires through the red light.

Relaxing, I slumped back into my seat and shook my head, feigning the return of sanity. After waiting for two more lights, I slowly drove off, leaving behind a captive audience. It had been another Kelly Elliott triumph – another that my peers would not believe, so I would not bother to tell them. Maybe I'll save them all up for a book some day. My false courage had gotten me through another minor crisis, and I began to wonder how to channel those talents to the most important aspects of my life – handling Swedarsky, making time with Laura LeDuc, or maybe getting a "good time" with Gloria Steiner.

Not quite as serene as I had been, I kept a closer scrutiny on the swelling traffic, which was not the only interesting view during rush hour. It was time for the office buildings to regurgitate their stores of comely feminine workers. As I stopped at another light, a redhead in a short-skirt-for-winter crossed my path. Like the proverbial black cat, she proved to be a bad omen.

Chicago women were the only kind I knew, but I was sure they were in a class of their own. In spite of the brisk winds off the lake, and the below normal forty degree temperatures, they still looked beautiful, almost flaunting themselves like proud artists at their first showings. It was a great city with some great women, most with whom I was in love.

A gust blew up the redhead's skirt, and I could almost see her complete rear, which caused me not to notice that the light had changed to green. Apparently, she had captivated more than me, because nobody honked or showed the usual signs of impatience. We allowed her to cross the street, swaying like a porch swing in a hurricane, and even took a few precious bonus seconds to allow the impact to find its final resting places in our crotches and in our hearts.

Finally, a horn four cars back, probably a woman out of view of those bakery-grade buns, began honking. I looked up and the light was turning back to yellow. We had almost missed an entire green light – an act punishable in the city of Chicago by life imprisonment. Rumor was that the city council was trying to change life imprisonment to the death sentence. I really didn't care.

As I sat musing over the red-haired temptress, another thought occurred to me – I never saw the complete package. It's not too often that you get a view like that, especially in the winter. I really wanted to know what the entire picture was. Besides, I had nothing else to do.

When the light finally turned green again, I inched my way halfway through the intersection and turned on my left-turn signal. Drivers who waited until the last second to signal created another one of Chicago drivers' major annoyances. And if I had been behind me, I would have had a fit and vigorously flicked my finger at him while pounding the steering wheel, but I was really curious about the redhead. Was she stunningly beautiful? What were her measurements? I just had to get one more look at her. The car behind me swung around to the right and over-dramatized his irritation, yelling and pointing like a madman, just the way I would have.

With a sharp turn of the wheel and a heavy foot, I screeched left up the cross street, the red hair still in sight. The swaying hair and matching ass turned suddenly into a drug store, and I cursed my unfortunate timing. I'd have to circle the block – there was no parking during rush hour.

Turning my eye away from the drug store and back to the street, I saw a bus coming at me like a whale about to engulf

Jonah. My life seemed to be over. I slammed the brakes to the floor, as did the bus. We stopped with our bumpers a half-foot apart. Two near traffic collisions within ten minutes. I felt that I was not meant to drive – ever!

As I looked up I saw the bus driver vehemently pointing at a street sign. A one-way arrow pointed in the opposite direction of my vehicle. Because I had the insatiable need to check a strange woman, I hadn't even looked at the signs. I knew then what the other angry driver behind me had been pointing at as he passed me. I felt lucky that the driver hadn't gotten out and threatened to make me eat my balls.

I put the car in reverse and looked for the quickest exit, abandoning all hopes of seeing the redhead again. It was as if Swedarsky had just given me a heart punch. My escape route was blocked by a squad car, his cherries flashing as if a ten-car pile-up on the Eden's Expressway had occurred. The bastard had me pinned in – what the hell was he advertising for? I was surprised he hadn't turned on the siren and called for back-up.

The cop sauntered up to the car in order to give me more time to increase my blood pressure. He wore dark glasses and looked like the state trooper who first saw Janet Leigh in *Psycho.* Down to business as I rolled down my window.

"License."

I fished out my wallet and unintentionally handed him my weekly lunch ticket.

I rarely used my license. It really pissed off the cop.

"What the hell is this, kid? You a comedian?"

I smiled innocently and found my driver's license. He read it for what seemed an hour. I wondered if he was trying to extend my agony or simply couldn't read. By the end of our meeting, I had deduced the latter.

Joe Friday. "You know this is a one-way street?"

No shit, dumb-ass. I was only going one way. Besides, I enjoy playing chicken with a ten-ton bus. I could fantasize a mean game.

"Yes, sir. I do now."

He looked at the rear of the car, as though he could see the noise violator. "Ever heard of a muffler, kid?"

Still meek and respectful, I replied, "It's not my car, sir. I'm just driving it home for a friend." I felt like a hypocrite; I spoke the way Swedarsky had spoken to Shipstead prior to my execution.

"Well, Mr. Elliott, I'm going to have to give you two citations – one for inattentive driving, causing you to drive the wrong way down a one-way street, and another for the absence of a muffler, a flagrant noise violation."

He was determined to stick it to me, but I had to fight.

"But it's not my car! Honest! And I didn't see the arrows or I wouldn't have turned. Can't you just give me a warning this time?"

Suddenly Joe Friday became Mr. Southern Sheriff. The dark glasses came off, and I swore he had two black holes where his eyes should have been.

"Now you listen to me, kid. I see a hundred noisemakers like this in the course of a week, and they all belong to know-it-all kids like you. Think it's real cool to wake up people in the middle of the night by racing up and down main thoroughfares through quiet neighborhoods and even hospital zones. Sick people probably die from lack of sleep and fear that a goddamn hoodlum bomb is going to drop on their beds."

Jesus Christ! He actually had me blowing-up sick people in their beds!

"Someone's going to pay for it, and you're the one who got caught. There are four arrow signs posted at that intersection and two 'Do Not Enter' signs, so don't give me any bull about not seeing the signs, or I'll tack on a few more violations, including obstruction of the law. You read me, Jack?"

The jerk had me convinced that, like Bates, he could have been Swedarsky's stepfather. I resigned myself to my fate.

"Yes, sir," and I slumped in my seat while he slowly took care of the paper work. As I stared blankly ahead, I noticed the redhead who had been the cause of all my problems. It was her fault! I could not accept the fact that I had caused my own problems. She crossed in front of my car, but her heavy, now fully buttoned winter coat would not allow me to satisfy my complete curiosity, except for her face. Sadly, she resembled my deceased Uncle Ralph.

"Here's your ticket, kid. You can pay the fine or appear in traffic court, where the judge will probably reduce your fine or even dismiss it, as you're a first-time offender. Traffic court is a week from Friday at 8:00 p.m. Don't keep the judge waiting."

Off strolled hard-ass, waving away the curious on-lookers. He was tough, all right. He had succeeded in subduing and scaring the life out of a seventeen-year-old kid with pimples.

CHAPTER 7

Trials of a First Date (The Night of the Gross Rubbers)

When Muffler Mulhouse got word about the noise violation, he was ready to tear me a new one. He called me a real "dumb ass" for not staying off the major thoroughfares during rush hour and refused to pay for the ticket. To compound his frustration, when he and Gloria had arrived at her house, Gloria's mother was there, home early with cramps. All hard-up and no place to go, he had been forced to take a crowded bus home and extinguish his passion with a cold shower, because his mother had come home early, too. I sympathized with his calamity – it was typical of something that might have happened to me. Anyway, he told me to drop dead and never talk to him again. He even thought that I should pay for a new muffler. I guess being tennis partners was not as sacred as it had once been.

Linda was absent on Tuesday, and I doubted my patience to wait for her answer until Wednesday. During lunch I decided to call her, another first, but gave up the idea when I noticed the large number of Martinsens in the Chicago directory. If I had really wanted to call her, I could have gotten her number from the office, but I became so terrified when I just picked up the phone book that I decided the anxiety of calling was worse than the anxiety of waiting. I let the germ fester for another night.

Wednesday I finally caught Linda at her locker between class periods. Walking her to sociology class, we made small talk about her absence Tuesday. I figured she had been having her monthly. Probably caught it from Gloria's mother. Wanting to appear cool and collected, I did not ask her about

Friday night, and quickly made my way to gym class. I couldn't help but think of how idiotic I had been not to ask her when I had the chance, but delicate dating decorum had to be handled tactfully and according to present social standards.

In chemistry Linda told me that she would not be able to go out Friday night because her parents were taking her to see her aunt Trudy in the hospital. That was bull! She probably didn't even have an aunt Trudy. Nobody did! I wanted to barf on her face. Then she said that she would be able to make it the next Friday, which made me decide that I wanted to barf on her aunt Trudy's face for making me go through another entire week of first-date jitters. Still, the bottom line was that Linda Martinsen was going to go out with me, and I would not have to look back on my high school days as being completely dateless, unlike one third of the graduating class. Linda had not been grossed out by my pitted face or by the fact that I had farted near Laura LeDuc in public. She honestly seemed to like something about me.

Just as I was about to scream for joy at the idea of dating someone other than Jerry Hogan, another thought smashed me in the gonads. I had to appear in traffic court a week from Friday night! I really couldn't afford the ticket. Joe Friday said that a judge might dismiss it because I was a first offender. I had to be practical. Postponing another week was unthinkable – ten days was enough anguish to make me spill my guts to the Nazis.

I leveled with Linda – told her that I had been doing Muffler Mulhouse a favor, was stopped for a noise violation, and had to go to traffic court on that particular Friday night. I discretely omitted the part about chasing a strange redhead who looked like my dead Uncle Ralph to see if she was as glamorous as I wanted her to be. I didn't think she'd care for that facet of the story, even if the guys in the locker room had elevated me to sub-socially acceptable status for getting a traffic ticket. Only Swedarsky had said that I was a real asshole, but inside I had the feeling that the epithet was his way of being half-civilized. Some people had reputations to guard and would always play the fool. To this day I cannot be with a group of ten friends and not honestly label three of them as "complete assholes." It must be a viral behavior caused by the city environment.

Linda squinted and turned her head as though searching for a solution to the awkward situation. Traffic court was not an omen of a "fun date." I suggested that she go with me to court, as the whole ordeal would probably be over in an hour, and we could go out for something to eat later. She didn't think her father would approve, so I suggested that he never really needed to know. Jesus Christ! She made me feel like the Mad Doctor of Auschwitz. She had always had a firm understanding with her father and would never lie to him about anything! That attitude forced me to wonder if I even wanted to go out with Saint Linda. Any girl who was totally honest with her father would probably never let my hand anywhere out of her sight. She'd have to tell her father! Not that I expected much on the first date, but I had hopes. When two people go out for the first time, they must have hopes that something might happen between them or they probably would never have committed themselves in the first place. I doubted if Linda and I would ever be able to have as much fun as Jerry and I had together. We wouldn't be able to sneak around the neighborhood and act cool. We'd never be able to tell gross jokes or hold belching contests. We'd never be able to experience the comradery that two guys could share. Dating Linda was a whole new game, and I just hadn't learned the rules yet.

Still, I had spent two days holding my side in agony, caused by the pains of anxiety that Linda might turn me down, so I figured the worst was over.

"What about Saturday, Linda?" I grasped.

"I'm sorry, Kelly, but Saturday is usually family fun night."

Of course it was! Playing Old Maid and eating pizza, no doubt! As sincerely as possible, I suggested that she tell her father the truth – that it wasn't even my car and that I was only trying to help a friend. She hesitantly agreed to the plan and sent me home for another night of pre-first-date cramps. I even sneaked two of my mother's Mydol tablets, figuring that a cramp was a cramp, but they didn't help.

All turned out well, as Linda's father reluctantly gave permission for her to go out with that "Elliott boy," so long as he wasn't some "hoodlum." Borrowing a thought from Groucho Marx, I thought, "No gang with any self-respect would take me as a member."

The next eight days were like a sentence on death row. No matter what happened, all I could think about was our Friday night date and the worries that accompanied it. Jerry offered to get me some rubbers from his college brother, Paul, but I thought such action might be a bit premature.

On the following Tuesday there was an all-school assembly to honor a graduate, Rodney something, who had been killed in Vietnam. Nobody there gave any indication to having heard of him, and the speaker, president of a local VFW chapter, made the guys nervous; we were already terrified of the military draft waiting for us upon graduation. At eighteen there were better things to do than die. The speaker said that it was an ironic fact of life that the young people in their prime of life were the ones who created and composed the death lists. It was still an era of few protests, and best wishes and prayers accompanied those who went to "serve with honor." By the end of the war, four of the boys in that auditorium, including Muffler Mulhouse, had been killed in Vietnam. I always regretted letting such triviality break up our casual friendship.

Anyway, none of the guys wanted to hear about Vietnam, and the girls were more concerned with the gossip of the day. (A school poll later showed that only 25% of the student body knew for sure that we were fighting on the side of the South Vietnamese. Or was it the North?) The assembly was rather raucous, with most people trying to finish homework so they would not have to take it home.

A local military recruiter droned on about the advantages of enlistment, while half the audience scribbled some homework and the other half "quietly visited" with friends. We had our priorities – the adults just were not conscious of them.

I spent the entire period alone, daydreaming about my first date, trying to decide where to take Linda after traffic court. Of course, the more I thought about it, the more apprehensive I became. I feared the judge would levy such a huge fine that I would not be able to pay it and would have to spend the night in the slammer. How would Linda get home? Her old man would never let her date an ex-con, and then I'd have to restart the whole dating procedure. I'd never be able to get to first base with her if that happened.

Prison did not thrill me, either. I'd probably get gang-raped by a bunch of over-sexed inmates, who would call me their little "chicken white meat." I'd be labeled as a "homo" for the rest of my life, and no girl would ever come near me. Everyone would snicker behind my back, and with a prison record and "homosexual activity history" clearly labeled on it, I'd never be able to get a job. I squirmed in my seat as my worries multiplied and the period dragged on. I had turned a perfectly innocent date into a life of despair.

I hadn't even told Ma yet, figuring I would be able to keep the ticket a secret, but if I was going to have enough money for the fine, I would have to confess. All of that misery because of some elusive redhead.

My nightmare was aborted by the sight of some beautiful blonde hair located across the aisle and two rows up. It was Laura LeDuc, the Madonna with a Smile. (Last semester I had completed my art appreciation class.) She was talking to another cheerleader, but there was something different about her – it was her sweater. Instead of her "THS" letter sweater, she wore a DePaul University letter sweater. The sleeves were rolled up, and it appeared to be four sizes too large for her. It meant only one thing: She was going steady with a college man. She wouldn't have been the first. Dating a college man was the ultimate status symbol amongst the elite senior girls. In my 3 ¾ years of high school, only three girls had ever worn college sweaters to school, and they had all married the sweaters' owners. I was losing Laura to some prissy college jerk. Probably that limp-wristed bastard she had kissed at the library. I would have fought Swedarsky for Laura, but there was no fighting the prestige of a college sweater.

I did a slow burn, blaming her for the tragic circumstances of my first date with Linda Martinsen. If I hadn't taken the time to drive her to the library, I would never have been in such an elated mood, neglected the oncoming taxi, which delayed me enough to arrive at the corner just in time to see the redhead, and I would never have gotten that stupid ticket. It was all her fault, and she would never know the anguish I went through for her benefit. At that moment I decided Laura LeDuc was a real bitch, even if I did love her.

When it appeared that I was about to lapse into a severe coma over all the mentally tragic events of the past thirty minutes, the band began to play "The Star Spangled Banner" and we all rose for the finale. The national anthem was followed by the Pledge of Allegiance, recited by less than half of those in attendance, and early dismissal from school – the only bright spot of an otherwise morose assembly.

Life continued despite those tragedies, and the week picked up momentum as it approached first-date Friday. In gym class Swedarsky, not wearing any protection, had slipped on a simple vault over the pommel horse, landed sideways on his testicles, and let out a shriek more piercing than the twelve o'clock whistle. I loved it when they carried him out to pack his groin in ice. Everyone called him "No Nuts Swedarsky" behind his back, and he was out of school for a week. It brought a smile to the face of every student alive, especially me.

Another rare highlight included a substitute teacher for Mr. Bates. She looked at least two hundred years old, and it appeared that the administration had simply propped up her mummified corpse behind the desk, a figurehead like the queen of England. Besides not having to listen to Bates' drivel and watch him salivate as he maneuvered for a look up the girls' skirts, the most satisfying moment was watching her give Diane Kyrk an hour's detention for being continuously late. Not able to use her body for a defense, she broke into tears, cried out that it was unfair, and stormed out of the classroom. For her exhibition she received an entire week's detention. I loved it – not as much as "No Nuts Swedarsky," but it was really great to see them finally get what they had coming.

The "piece-de-resistance" of that week occurred when Baldy Smith, the guidance counselor, pulled me out of chemistry class to notify me that I had received an Illinois State Teacher's Scholarship. It was only for $126.50 per semester, but it was enough to pay my full tuition. All I had to do was express an interest in teaching in the state of Illinois. It was no big deal, but the news almost knocked Ma on her ass when I finally said, "Yes" to her eternal evening interrogation. She got misty, hugged me, and told me that she knew I could do it. I could have reemphasized the luck involved, which would have been the truth, but I didn't want to ruin her rare happiness. Besides, it made me feel good to do something positive for her. Once in a while it was nice not to be a real prick. Not only that, but I needed her good graces in order to get some extra money for Friday night's traffic court. I was determined not to end up as some bum on skid row.

Friday night finally came, and my stomach felt like a squeezed lemon. Next to being informed that you have three hours to live, I suppose a first date is the most painful event of one's life. I could have almost sympathized with monks, priests, and nuns, who wisely escaped the potential trauma. I figured that they all had brothers and sisters, in the literal sense, who had acquainted them with the agonies involved in the first date, causing them to decide on an easy alternative – celibacy.

I never knew the crises that girls faced when dating, but I felt sure they had an easier time. The pangs experienced by the average boy could not have been equaled by the Marquis De Sade in his prime.

The only definite of our date, where to go, had already been settled by one of "Chicago's finest." Transportation posed my next obstacle. I felt that a bus would be too tacky; I couldn't afford taxis, and the only person I knew with a car was my former "friend," Muffler Mulhouse. Just as I had opted for the bus, fate played another of its quirks. Dan Phillips and his Phillips head screwdriver were due in for the weekend. He offered me use of his rental car in exchange for my vow not to return until Sunday. He knew I couldn't refuse the offer.

Trying to act all fatherly/best friend, he took me aside and gave me some advice – be sure to walk the girl to her door and use the flashlight from the glove box. It showed that you cared about her safety and the extra gesture would really impress her old man – always a good thing. Grateful, but still untrusting, I thanked him and pushed my leverage one more step.

I got thirty bucks from him as a "loan" for traffic court along with his promise that "the old lady will never know." I felt like a pimp selling my mother for thirty dollars and two days in a rented Chevy. I later learned to regret my decision.

My next concern was my clothes. Since I was going to traffic court, I felt that I should wear my only sport coat, a too small green blazer, with a tie. Linda's father would probably figure I had real style or that I was trying to brown nose him. A sweater and levis seemed perfect for a first date but too casual to appear before a judge. I blamed Muffler Mulhouse for the dilemma and hoped that Gloria Steiner would give him syphilis and that he would go insane – a short trip. I hoped that he'd get gang-raped by fifteen psychopathic prisoners. I hoped . . .

Anyway, I opted for the coat and tie, deciding that first impressions on parents were important, not that I really cared, but I did. If my date had been with Laura LeDuc, I would have rented a tuxedo, but a coat and tie was more than sufficient for Linda Martinsen.

Finally, I remembered that I had to stop at Little Joey's and load my pockets with breath mints. Peppermint was the only flavor that gave me enough confidence to be close. All the preparations seemed to be completed as I prepared for fiasco number one.

Jerry Hogan felt left out that Friday, but he was fairly understanding, for Jerry Hogan. He reiterated his offer to get me some rubbers from his brother Paul, but I declined politely. It was odd – I had fantasized about banging Laura and what a stud in the saddle I'd be, yet when it got right down to it, I doubted my assertiveness to even try some light petting, let alone touch all the bases with either girl. Hell, I was terrified about even kissing Linda Martinsen! It made me wonder about all the guys who bragged about doing Diane Kyrk or Gloria Steiner. I wondered if they had even kissed first. Did they slowly undress each other, like the stories in the men's magazines? Did they pet on the couch? What was the first move? Who made the first move? Did they just go to the girl's house, where she pulled him into her bedroom? That's probably what I would need to happen.

After brushing my teeth for the final time, I was ready to leave. I went to the kitchen to get the car keys from Dan Phillips. Ma was standing at the sink, and he was behind her, kissing her neck and massaging her chest. I was so pissed that I wanted to choke the son-of-a-bitch. Sex was okay except when my own mother was involved. She was giggling and seemed in a better mood than I had seen her since she had returned from Aunt Amy's two weeks ago, when I had hopefully and mistakenly assumed that she had broken up with Dan Phillips. I decided to wait a few minutes before trying again.

Five minutes later they were sitting at the kitchen table, sopping suds. I entered hesitantly – I had the feeling that Ma was expecting to make a big deal out of this first date business, and I didn't want that bastard pilot to see me fawned over. "I'm ready to go now. Can I have the car keys, please?"

Ma looked at me and seemed somewhat amazed by my appearance. She was sincerely touched – I could read it in her eyes. Dan Phillips had evaporated in our minds, and there was a moment of understanding between my mother and me. It was a moment we would never experience again, but once was enough.

She stood and hugged me, kissed my cheek, and looked at me from arm's length. I felt good inside, despite the anxieties of the evening ahead.

"You look very nice, Kelly. That must be some special girl you're all dressed up for. Do you have enough money?"

"Sure, Ma. I've got fifty, fifteen dollars. It's plenty."

Reaching for her purse, she pulled out another twenty.

"Well, here's a little extra, just in case something unexpected pops up."

I was hesitant. She really couldn't afford to give me an extra twenty. "No, Ma. Really. I don't need it."

She stood firm and pushed the extra bill into my hand. She spoke sincerely with a whisper. "I want you to have it. Please. Take it."

Then she kissed me again, her eyes misty, her smile tight; she felt proud. Maybe old Dan Phillips was doing her some good after all. Then again, maybe I had done something good for her.

The moment was shattered by the drunken slap on the table. "Here's the goddamn keys, kid. Put the keys under the floormat when you bring it back. Never know when a guy needs to make a quick escape. Don't crack it up, and if you spill something in the back seat, be sure to clean it up. And don't forget to walk her to the door. Use the flashlight in the glove compartment. Her old man will love it." He laughed like a jackass and I tried to read between the lines.

Still, everything had felt too good to let that drunken loser rattle me. I took the keys graciously, kissed Ma, and left, my worries about traffic court and Linda Martinsen increasing. Concerned for my mother, I wished Dan Phillips had been locked up over night with the mummies.

I stopped by Little Joey's for the breath mints and final approval. He gave me a mock wolf whistle and told me to behave myself and to have a good time. Joey even told me to bring her around some time, and it was reassuring to know that somebody had enough confidence in me to believe that there would be a next time.

Phillips's rental car was a red and white '61 Chevy. I had to admit that it had real class and was what the guys generally referred to as a "chick magnet." Still, back seat action was the farthest thing from my mind. Getting kissed was a more immediate concern.

I arrived at Linda's by 6:55, so I decided to park up the block, wait four minutes, then go in. Promptness always impressed the hell out of people. I was sure parents wouldn't be any different. Being early might have made it seem like I was too eager to get into Linda's pants, and being late was a sign of unreliability. For some reason, meeting Linda's old man scared the hell out of me, and I wanted to immediately impress him.

Linda lived in a nice single floor ranch house, white with green trim, a real contrast to most of the housing in Brighton Park. I took a deep breath and walked the last torturous block to the doorbell. I rang it and waited for two centuries. Finally the porch light clicked on and an old man of five hundred years answered the door. I was appalled that the decrepit being was the object of my fear and the person I most wanted to impress. Christ, he hadn't even put his teeth in his mouth! Fighting not to laugh, I forced myself to put on my best manners.

"Hello. I'm Kelly Elliott. Is Linda ready?"

He squinted at me for two hours before he raspingly responded through parched gums, "Linda? Linda's not here."

I couldn't have been hit harder if Swedarsky had jumped on my gonads with football cleats. My jaw hit the top of my shoes in disbelief. How could she have lied to me? It wasn't possible. She had seemed so sincere about going out with me.

I thought, "Swedarsky and Mulhouse must have put her up to it. That was her reason for postponing our date – Muff had told her the circumstances under which I had gotten the ticket. Mulhouse had to be responsible. I would be the laughing stock of the entire school, again. It seemed to be 'Kick Elliott in the Head Week.' I would not be able to attend school again. I would have to quit and take a GED diploma, which meant no college, a probable military draft, and being killed in some rice paddy. All for a joke by some frigid witch and two assholes!"

Apparently the old man was tired of standing there looking at some well-dressed, pimple-faced kid about to die in Vietnam.

"If you're looking for Linda Martinsen, she lives next door." He spit out the gummed words.

I felt like a death row inmate in his eleventh hour, and the warden had just called.

"Isn't this 5506 California?"

"No, son, this is 5502. You want the house next door, the one with the porch light on and Linda Martinsen in it," and he politely shut the door, mustering all his strength to get the lock over the latch.

I could not believe that one person could be so stupid! It made me wonder if I hadn't possibly caused some of my own problems. Besides, who had said that Linda was frigid?

Like a zombie I marched next door to a modest, yellow, popular, Sears-mail-order home where the porch light clearly lit up the numbers "5506." I rang the bell and awaited my fate.

No old man answered this time. It was Linda, dressed in a dark blue flowered print dress. She had even put a matching blue ribbon in her hair, and I thought that she looked cute as hell.

"I'd like you to come in and meet my parents, Kelly." It was back to the real world. It had to be worse than awaiting

St. Peter's decision at the pearly gates – heaven or hell?

"Sure, Linda, I'd like to." I also wanted to have diarrhea in the middle of watching *Gone with the Wind.*

She led me to the living room where a fire was crackling in the fireplace, curbing the chill of the cool spring night. Her father sat in an over-stuffed chair, smoking a pipe and reading the evening paper; Mrs. Martinsen sat in a chair across from him and knitted. I felt like I was participating in an episode of *Leave it to Beaver,* and I got to be Eddie Haskell.

"Dad, Mom. This is Kelly Elliott," she said quietly, as though fearful of shattering the domestic tranquility. The old man peered over the top of his paper, puffing his pipe like the magic dragon.

He spoke in a staccato pace. "Hello, Kelly. I understand you have a very interesting evening planned for my Linda. I must tell you that I really did not approve of her going out with someone who had broken the law. I've been driving for twenty-eight years now. Never had a ticket. Not even for over-parking. Linda said that you were doing a favor for a friend, but I still have to wonder about a boy who has friends who intentionally break the law. None of my friends would ever break a law. It all seems the same to me. I don't want my Linda to associate with the wrong kinds of people. What would you do in my place, Kelly?"

"I'd stick that foul-smelling pipe up your ass and puff until my lungs collapsed. Jerk! I'm scared as hell! Back off!" I thought. I was worried about more important problems than role playing. There was Dan Phillips's car, traffic court, my breath, and how I would work up my nerve to kiss her. Who the hell needed a lecture from an insensitive son-of-a-bitch? It was Eddie Haskell time.

"Well, sir, I don't believe the violation is a major crime. After all, it was just a noisy muffler and it wasn't even my car. I was just helping a friend, who had to stop by the hospital on the way home to see his mother; I'm not sure what she has, but I think it involved surgery." "Helping a friend so that he could get laid by Gloria Steiner," I wanted to add.

His beady eyes stared at me, trying to pierce the façade. After a close scrutiny he returned to his paper, resolved that Linda and I were going out together, no matter what he thought. One parting shot from behind his paper. "Just be sure to have Linda home by 11:00. At 11:01 I call the police and put an APB out on you."

I deduced that we were dismissed, as Linda grasped my arm and started to pull me toward the door. All that time the old lady had just smiled, knitted, and peered through us. As we reached the door, I heard, "Damn it! I dropped a goddamn stitch!" I immediately liked the old lady more than the pompous ass that she had married.

Being Joe Cool, I opened Linda's car door and sauntered to my side. Crisis #1 was over – meeting the parents. I had the uneasy feeling that the old man really would call the cops at 11:01. Linda slid across the seat to be next to me, and I smiled because I had wanted her to and I hadn't said a word.

"Sorry about my father, Kelly, but he's very strict. He really didn't want me to go out with you, but I talked him into it. I really wanted to. I should be taking you out for doing all those complicated chemistry experiments for me."

I really started to appreciate Linda. It was as though she knew the anxieties I was feeling and was doing everything humanly possible to help alleviate some of those worries. I wondered if she had the same fears. I enjoyed her company and was thankful that I hadn't been resigned to doing something gross with Jerry Hogan. It seemed to be my time to step over my friends and reach the other side.

On the way to the district municipal court, we made small talk about chemistry, Bates' English term paper that was due the following Friday, and what evil guidance counselors we had. The only lie I told her was that the car was mine, a gift from my aunt Amy, and that I didn't drive it to school because it was easier to take the bus. It was a lie for which I would pay dearly, of course.

Parking near the court house was impossible, and we had to walk three blocks. We bumped hands a few times, and I was tempted to grasp hers and hold hands for the short walk, but I chickened out. After presenting my ticket at the check-in table, I was told to go in and wait until my name was called. It was nothing like I had expected, and I was grateful that Linda was there to help me through the ordeal. It was terrifying!

Instead of a dark, oak-paneled vault, the courtroom was more like a gymnasium. There were at least a hundred people present, all casually boasting about their offenses and how they were going to beat them. The atmosphere was so boisterous that it gave the appearance of a high school assembly. Despite all the joviality, the idea of standing up in front of all those people and talking to a judge scared the hell out of me, and it showed.

"Are you all right, Kelly? You look pale."

I was shaky. "Sure, Linda. I'm fine. To be honest, I just didn't expect all these people. I thought it would be just me and a judge."

"I know what you mean. This is more like a zoo than a courtroom." Then she took my hand in hers, squeezed, and smiled at me.

We sat on a bench toward the rear and awaited my fate. All shyness gone, I held onto Linda's hand, not for the usual pleasure – I was really getting scared. It was worse than facing Swedarsky in the gymnasium, being chased in the museum, bluffing my way into a strip show, and seeing those flashing red lights behind Muff's car. For the first time I had a true sense of what it might be like to be locked up with the mummies overnight. I sweated as I watched the clock inch its way toward 8:00. Finally, a voice filled the room.

"Hear ye! Hear ye! Night traffic court of the twelfth district of the city of Chicago, Cook County, state of Illinois is now is session. The honorable Clarence Lewis presiding. All rise."

Everyone stood and I craned my head to see over the

multitude of faceless heads. A pudgy man, about sixty years old with a rim of gray hair and dressed in a black robe, floated in like Christ walking across water.

"Be seated," he bellowed with a rap of the gavel.

He put on a pair of wire-rimmed glasses and began scanning the list of cases before him. The gymnasium atmosphere had become funereal. I wanted to go to the bathroom so bad that I had to cross my legs. Again, I just hadn't planned. I gave up all hope of making it through the ordeal.

"First case is the city of Chicago vs. Thomas Appleton. Approach the bench."

Judge Lewis never looked up from his papers as poor Tom Appleton pleaded his drunk-driving case. All ears were receptive to the first case, trying to ascertain whether the judge was a human or a hangman. After Appleton finished his story and Judge Lewis, still not looking into the face of the man who groveled before him, sentenced him to one-year probation, mandatory driving school, and a $200.00 fine, everyone gasped. We had drawn Judge Roy Bean – the only law west of the Pecos.

There was no doubt I'd end up in jail. Life as I had known it would cease to exist. I would learn to appreciate the gentleness of Joseph Swedarsky. Even Linda had winced at the sentence and given my sweaty hand a strong, reactionary squeeze.

Time progressed as though I was attending a three-day seminar on Chaucer given by Mr. Bates, for no credit! It was absolutely endless, and I chanced a trip to the men's room, risking extra prison time if I wasn't back when my name was called. No case lasted more than three minutes, but the volume was staggering. Once in a while a defendant would have a lawyer speak for him, but the pleading usually fell on deaf ears with Judge Roy Bean on the bench. During the following 1 ½ hours he never looked at the defendants. No pity was shown – he hung everyone without discrimination or remorse.

My memory took me back to the time I had been caught shoplifting. I was six years old and had slipped a small bottle of dime store perfume into my pockets – it was for my mother's birthday. Unfortunately, an old crone hiding behind a pegboard display had seen me and marched me into the manager's office.

He was an old man with a stern temperament, not unlike Judge Clarence Lewis, probably well-accustomed to the proper procedure for dealing with thugs. In his most vicious tone he berated me, threatening a boys' home, until I broke down and cried. His goal obtained, he softened and asked me if I was sorry. I was so sorry that I couldn't even get out the words. He let me go with a warning, and I never thought about shoplifting again. I had been humiliated, but I had learned. Sitting in that courtroom I prayed that Judge Clarence Lewis would not employ the same tactics, but this was adulthood, a foreign playing field. There was no need to humiliate me – I had already learned that I never wanted to return to any courtroom. I hoped that Judge Lewis was aware of my disposition, too.

At 9:35 I was called, the courtroom nearly empty. Half of the victims were serving time or awaiting transfer to Devil's Island. The other half was on its way to various death rows throughout the country. My time had come. I don't know how he knew I was there, because his eyes never looked up.

His voice was ominous but tiring. "You have been charged with a traffic pattern violation and a noise violation, Mr. Elliott. How do you plead?"

I could not speak. My eyes started to tear; it was the worse experience I had had, and Linda was there to witness it. "I, I guess I'm guilty, sir. I was being attentive while driving, but I really didn't see . . ." My voice cracked and I thought the windows would shatter.

Shocked by the piercing sound from a human being, the judge finally raised his head. Through my misty eyes I saw that he squinted, as though stepping from a cave into the noon sun. Then I realized why he never looked at the other defendants – he had had his eyes closed the entire evening. Judge Clarence Lewis was sending people to their deaths in his sleep! He was one tough son-of-a-bitch! As he focused on my cringing figure, he seemed to grow more alert.

"How old are you, Mr. Elliott?" His voice became more human than automaton.

"Seventeen, sir."

His faced seemed to show some sympathy. "Don't be scared, son. I haven't sent anyone to Devil's Island in years. Is this your first offense?"

"Y,Y,Yes, sir."

There was a long silence while I fought to regain some composure. I had never considered myself as tough, but I had never realized how sensitive I was. The courtroom was not some game with mummies – it was real and I had become old enough to be part of it. I didn't want Linda to see my misty eyes and made sure my back was completely toward her, grateful that she was all the way in the back.

"Well, Mr. Elliott. Kelly. I can excuse the missed street sign, but I cannot overlook a noisy muffler. I'll go easy on you as it's your first offense and you're still a minor. Are your parents here with you?"

I was regaining control. "No, sir."

"Very well, I fine you ten dollars plus five dollars court costs, with the explicit promise that you'll get that muffler fixed. Do you promise?"

My worst fears dissolved. I wasn't going to jail. I wouldn't be gang-raped and become a homo. I would finish school and go to college. Just when I was prepared to be kicked in the groin, the kicker held back. I beamed.

"Yes, sir. I'll tell the owner of the car on Monday. I promise."

Judge Lewis looked like he might smile but merely waved to the side table. "Pay your fine to the clerk," and I was dismissed.

"Thank you, sir," I said softly, but he had heard it and smiled down at his papers.

I eagerly paid my fine and dabbed my eyes in a futile attempt to cover any trace of tears. Still, the redness and glossiness clung, but I didn't really care. I had spent three fourths of my life hacking on adults and finally felt that not everyone in authority was a complete bully. I felt foolishly happy, knowing that I had the rest of the now short evening with Linda.

I walked down the aisle with my head high. Linda stood at the end of the rear bench. I confidently grabbed her hand and strode out of the courtroom with my girl.

When we got back to the car, there was a $15.00 parking ticket on the windshield for over-parking in a one-hour time zone. The irony of getting a parking ticket while in traffic court seemed ludicrous and upset me for all of ten seconds. It wasn't my car; it was Dan Phillips's. Once Linda was inside I tore up the ticket in secret celebration and with a sadistic joy in my heart. Linda felt sorry for me, but I assured her that it was worth it.

I hadn't felt so good since I had married Laura LeDuc on my living room sofa. I could not comprehend how my body was able to cope with the opposing emotions that streaked through my soul from moment to moment. Everything had turned out perfectly; it was just getting there that took its toll on my spirit.

Since there was only an hour before I had to have Linda home, we decided to go to a place near her house – the Tally-Ho Fountain. I hoped someone we knew would be there; my ego just wanted to be seen on a date. With my luck Swedarsky would be the only one at the Tally-Ho, and he'd probably throw a rubber on my cheeseburger and wish me luck. I really hated the son-of-a-bitch!

The Tally-Ho proved to be a good choice. There was a good crowd with a lot of Talbot High letter jackets jammed into the booths. It was a good hang-out, the kind that served greasy hamburgers with lettuce and tomato garnish that was rarely touched, and probably reused fifty times before the lettuce wilted. People on dates ordered the cheeseburger "platter," which meant that they served the burger on an oval plate with some ageless and tasteless fries, a tiny paper cup of "creamy coleslaw," and a pickle spear. Those delicious additions allowed the management to charge an additional dollar, and they could always reuse the coleslaw and pickle. A dollar for an order of fries always killed me, but nobody wanted to be labeled as "cheap" when on a date. I had done research.

We were able to get a booth by the window overlooking the parking lot, wedged up against a middle-aged couple arguing about something – probably sex or money. It seemed that all arguments were about sex or money. I had spent my first date in court so that Muffler Mulhouse could have sex with Gloria Steiner, and because I had to see a strange redhead who might be attractive. I had to sleep weekends in a crummy all-night theatre so my mother and some over-sexed pilot could play house. Practically any argument between two people could be directly or indirectly related to sex and/or money. So I thought at seventeen.

The waitress became comatose when we started to order two cheeseburger platters and two chocolate malts. She was used to six kids crammed into a booth, ordering four small cokes with six straws. Linda surprised me by saying that she wasn't really that hungry, and would it be okay if we just ordered some cherry cokes and fries. I really started to like this girl.

Linda didn't feel that she should have any chocolate because it made her face break out in pimples. When she saw me blush, she realized that she should not have said that to someone with a pockmarked face, so she tried to cover her social gaffe by saying that it was only a stupid article by some Minneapolis quack that she had read in *Seventeen* magazine.

We sat in silence, the first real gap in our conversation. Still, it was nice not to have to say anything. I was never sure why non-stop conversation was a measurement of a "good" date.

"Hey, Elliott, getting any?"

It was Ralph Jacobsen, the only kid in school that I felt confident about being able to pulverize. I felt sure that he had been born six months prematurely and had never caught up, physically or socially. His diminutive size was equaled only by his intelligence. Undoubtedly, he would be one of those who went through high school without even a hint of a date. Inbred obnoxiousness dictated it. Ralph Jacobsen had less social poise than Swedarsky, because Swedarsky could at least back up his offensiveness. Ralph was a zero.

Ralph was in the next booth, craning his head over Linda's side with a mischievous smirk. He would never have been able to attract anyone with half of Linda's looks or style. I decided to play it cool, determined not to let Talbot's lower life ruin my evening.

"Hey, Ralph. How's it going? You know Linda Martinsen?"

Linda turned her head and smiled. She was really nice, even if retard Ralph was trying to stare down the front of her dress.

"Sure. Hi, Linda. Nothing else to do tonight, huh?"

I could feel myself turn red and start to rise from the booth, deciding it was time to tear out Ralph the Runt's heart and make him eat it. Linda grabbed my hand, a sign to remain collected and to ignore him.

Failing to get the desired embarrassing result, Ralph tried another approach, still staring down Linda's dress. He had no scruples. None!

"Hey, Elliott. I never got a chance to congratulate you on that great fart on Laura at the basketball game. I was two rows behind you and thought the loud speaker would blow out. And that smell! Whew! I was afraid someone would light a match and blow out the walls of the gym. Great fart, Elliott!"

I was willing to go to jail and get gang-raped by horny homos just to kill that slimy bastard. I stood, outraged and blind, shaking off Linda's hands.

"Outside, Jacobsen. Now!" It was a command, perhaps the

first that I had meant in my entire life. Linda looked scared, but not as much as Ralph the Runt.

"Please, Kelly. It's all right. Forget it. Look – here comes our food."

The waitress approached with our orders and placed them on the table. I glared at Ralph Jacobsen, wondering if the cliché that "if looks could kill" might be true. He had stopped peering down Linda's dress and stared at me with wide, frightened eyes, as though I was an animal about to maul a treed victim. He was right.

Acquiescing to Linda's "please" but looking for a graceful way out of the dilemma, I sternly dictated, "I'll see you Monday, runt. Be in the gym after school or I'll come and get you."

It was my second undeniable command and it forced him to shakily turn and slump back to his place. On Monday I really would kill him.

Linda and I sat in silence and drank our cherry cokes and shared our fries. The meal was unappealing, and I was glad we hadn't ordered cheeseburgers. I was determined not to let that little mental case know how much he had rattled me. I grabbed the salt shaker and began to season our fries. Plop! The top of the shaker had been loosened, a favorite trick of Talbot High School students, and I just held the shaker until the entire contents formed a mound on my plate.

Linda stared at the calamity, broke into a stifled smile, started to giggle, then broke into a hearty laugh. At first I thought she was laughing at me; then I realized it was just the absurdity of the entire evening. I broke into a mild laugh, which grew. I couldn't recall the last time I had had a good laugh, and it felt good. She understood and it was good, also.

We finished our meal and left before Ralph Jacobsen. I shot a parting, "Monday!" at him, feeling the victor as he cowered.

The ride home was like the ride going – we sat next to each other and we talked mostly about school. I foolishly boasted that I had outfoxed Judge Roy Bean into letting me off with a light fine, which made me stupid, because Linda had seen the whole episode and knew that the judge had been kind to me. I hadn't done anything to brag about.

As we approached Linda's house, a deathly silence crept over us. The moment of decision drew near – would we kiss? I kept licking my lips like a cocker spaniel, so that I wouldn't be too dry and have Linda feel like she was kissing her grandfather. I wanted a peppermint but couldn't think of a graceful way of getting it. I'd have had to offer Linda one, and then she would know what I was planning, not that she wasn't necessarily expecting it. I really wanted to kiss her, but I hadn't ever kissed a girl. Linda was not the same as my aunt Amy. I didn't know how I'd be able to face Jerry Hogan if I couldn't honestly say that we had at least kissed. He had great expectations of me.

I stopped in front of Linda's house. It was 10:55 on my Timex. I had little time to work up to anything.

"Well, here we are." It was the most profound thing to say that I could think of at the time.

"Yes, here we are." Linda was also in a profound state.

I turned in my seat to face her. This also afforded me the opportunity to put my arm around her. I really wasn't touching her; I had just put my arm around the area in which she was sitting. God, it was awful! What the hell was I supposed to do? There were only four minutes left.

Linda would not look me in the eyes. She just stared at the steering wheel. Why she did that, I would never know. I had heard that it was easy to tell if a girl was willing to be kissed by reading her eyes. All I was able to see was the top of her eyelashes. Who the hell could tell anything by reading eyelashes?

I thought about reaching over and getting something from the glove compartment. The move would have put me in closer contact, and I might accidentally brush her boobs with my forearm. That was what was called "copping a feel," I think. But what the hell would I need from the glove compartment? A map? A screwdriver? Then I remembered

Dan Phillips' advice to get the flashlight for safety. I could pretend to need it to light the way up the already well-lit sidewalk. I didn't know if she'd buy it. Would I have bought it? Three minutes!

The porch light flicked on and off twice. She finally looked up at me, as though pleading to get the kiss over.

"I have to go in, Kelly. My parents will be mad."

It was my last chance. "Sure, Linda. Just let me get the flashlight and I'll take you in."

"Flashlight? What do you need a flashlight for?"

She didn't buy it. I could hardly blame her, but it was too late to change tactics in the middle of an assault.

"To light the walk. I don't want you to trip or anything," I said in my most authoritative voice, as though what I was saying was accepted common knowledge.

"Don't be silly, Kelly. The porch light is on. I've walked up there a million times. I don't need a flashlight."

"But I'll need one to get back. Besides, my mother always told me to use one. It's proper manners." Christ, I sounded like a fool, but I had cornered myself. The sensitive Linda grew leery of my puzzling behavior.

"I'll get it." And she turned away, reaching toward the glove box. I got the uneasy feeling that she didn't want to kiss me. She probably felt as uncomfortable as I did. Her mind had probably been racing a mile a minute, too. I cursed the complexities of the simplest things.

Linda lifted the latch and opened the compartment. An inner glove box light came on, revealing an avalanche of foil packages. Rubbers! Son-of-a-bitch! Phillips' glove box was packed with a gross of Trojans, and they had spilled all over the floor and onto Linda's dress.

"What . . .," but she had stopped short. When I finally got a look at her eyes, they were glassy and enraged at the apparent deception. She still thought it was my car, and that I had planned one hell of an evening. Damn him, anyway! He had set up this whole trap.

"Linda! Linda! It's 11:01. You're late. Now get in this

house immediately." It was her old man dressed in a plaid bathrobe. God dressed for bed.

She was hurt and her words were paced in a tense, definitive voice. "Don't . . . you . . . ever . . . speak . . . to. . . me . . .again. Ever!" Before I was able to mutter a single syllable in my defense, Linda was out of the car, racing up the well-lit sidewalk and safely inside. The light went out.

CHAPTER 8

Mary Harker and the Sleazy Hotel

Hours seemed to drag as I sat in a deathlike trance. My emotions had pushed one another aside, bouncing them around inside my brain like wild atoms. I was embarrassed for us. I didn't even know what had tumbled out of the glove box at first, and I certainly hadn't expected Linda to recognize them. Where had she seen rubbers before? I had seen one at Jerry's house – his brother Paul had given it to him, and Jerry carried it in his wallet, even though time had dried it beyond use. But where had Linda seen one?

It appeared that I had lost the only girl I might have had a chance with. At least I had had one date while in high school. Despite the unusual circumstances of my first date, I thought that most of the evening had gone well despite the nightmarish finale. That night could have led to more enjoyable times, but showing a gross of rubbers to a first date is bound to make her never want to speak to me again. Circumstances like those made dating very difficult.

I wanted to kill Dan Phillips and realized for the second time in one evening that I had enough malice in my heart to actually carry out a threat made by every child – "I'll kill him!" Maybe Dan Phillips and Ralph Jacobsen could have a fatal accident together.

Besides embarrassment and hatred, I sensed and hoped that in later years I might see some humor in the situation. In ten years I suspected that I would be able to laugh at the disaster. Nobody would ever believe such an absurd story, yet it had happened. I decided that my first date night was important enough to give the evening a title – "The Night of the Gross Rubbers." Friday, March 26, 1965, was a night of historical significance for me, but I doubted if it would ever be recorded in history texts. Important events of a person's life never are – just important events of other people's lives.

Slowly I picked up all the foil packets, each clearly labeled "condoms for comfort and security." What had seemed like a gross of rubbers turned out to be fourteen; the package was marked "24 pleasure sleeves." Phillips had used ten of the original two dozen or carried them with him now. I opted for the former, remembering where my mother was at that moment. At least I had the satisfaction of thinking that I possessed his weekend supply. (Was it possible to use ten in one weekend?) Of course, I didn't want my mother pregnant, so I secretly prayed that she wouldn't let the horny bastard near her, and that he would die of a heart attack while choking the chicken in the bathroom. It would serve him right. He was to blame for my evening fiasco.

Trying to be quiet as I started the car, I pulled away from Linda's house, hoping to see her staring out the window. She didn't, but I thought I saw her father with a shotgun. Not wanting to spend another night in the Brighton Theatre, I drove south on Cicero, trying to think of a good alternative. The street was lined with motels because of its proximity to Midway Airport, and I thought about the forty dollars still in my wallet.

In my entire life I had never spent a night in a motel or hotel. I had plenty of money according to the neon signs blasting "Rates starting at $19.99." Those animated lights blinding me from both sides of the street excited and relaxed me at the same time, if that's logical. Many "No Vacancy" signs were flashing. I thought it odd that so many motels would be filled when I remembered the locker room gossip about the motels on Cicero Avenue. According to high level sources, the rooms were rented for two hours, four hours, or all night, depending on the intended use. Also, according to the same experts, most of the motels were owned by the Mafia, and sometimes they shunned certain clientele. I didn't know if I was in that undesirable category, but I decided not to embarrass myself any further. It had already been one hell of a night, without bringing mobsters into the mix.

I carefully merged onto the Congress Expressway and headed for downtown. Despite it being Friday night, traffic was light going into the city, so I could concentrate on finding a place to stay. As I passed under the post office, which straddled the freeway, a brilliant idea struck me -- the Palmer House. I had always been curious about where those elevators led. Why not? Because it would probably have taken most, if not all, of my forty dollars. Nobody would have believed me anyway, and if they had, they would have pretended that staying there alone was no big deal. With half the night already gone anyway, I didn't see any sense in blowing my wad in one place for such a short time.

Then I remembered the hotel I'd seen the night that Jerry and I went to the strip show. It had once been an established hotel, and I had vowed to go there when I had worked up enough nerve. After living through my first court appearance, having a row in a public restaurant, and surviving an avalanche of rubbers, I decided that I was ready.

There was a parking spot on Wabash, under the el tracks a block from the Swan. Like the motels on Cicero Avenue, the flickering blue, swan-shaped neon light beckoned. I gawked at the double doorway. I figured the cost would be minimal for the excitement of a different world. My peers would believe that I had stayed there. I would be able to create all kind of stories about hookers coming to my door, and the horny bastards would be on the edge of their seats begging for more details. My mind began to clear itself of the calamity with Linda Martinsen, and I felt the adrenalin revive the old Kelly Elliott – the one who survived best alone. The Kelly Elliott I knew and loved.

When the Swan was first built, the LaSalle Street Station was a major depot for commuters and a short walk to the hotel and downtown. Time and freeways made the depot almost obsolete, but the hotel kept its established name. The entrance was wedged between a shoe repair shop and a fast-food hamburger stand, which had assumed the space once occupied by the old lobby entrance after the hotel had aged past its prime. I climbed the twenty steps. As I neared the top I found that I had either tired or was losing heart. My brief bravado had been left somewhere around step fifteen.

The lobby, a narrow rectangle which disappeared into blackness, was dimly lit by a single gooseneck lamp behind the desk. Through the dark to the left I could see a coke machine with a shattered glass front panel. The black and white tiled floor looked like a chess board that had last been cleaned in 1952. I was grateful that the darkness concealed the walls. From a far corner echoed a resounding snore. The total atmosphere was eerie, making me feel as though I was a child intruding into forbidden territory.

"Whatcha want, kid?" I heard a gruff voice but saw no one. It was either Big Brother or I had climbed the steps to heaven and God was pissed off at me.

I was hoping for a "Welcome to the Swan Hotel, sir."

"Ya' want sometin' or ya' here to look?"

I craned my neck over the desk and saw a man with a ten o'clock shadow on the bloated face of a prize fighter. He was in a wheelchair. Dark, beady eyes, like those of the alley rats below, stared up at me.

I thought, "Guts, Elliott! Guts! He's in a wheelchair, just like your pal Little Joey, and he can't chase you downstairs. I wonder how he ever gets out of this place. Is it possible that perhaps he . . ."

"Come on, kid. I ain't got all night."

Why? You have a hot date on the Gold Coast? Of course you have all night.

"I, I'd like a room, please."

He threw the registration card on the desk. "How long ya' want it, kid?"

As I started to fill out the card, I hesitated, remembering the stories about the Cicero motels. "What do you mean by

'How long'?"

"Christ, kid. Ya' deaf or just stupid? Ya' want the room for an hour, two hours, a day, a week, a month? We get all kinds here. Ya' wanna' live here? How long do ya' want the goddamn room? I gotta' charge ya', ya' know. This ain't no mission. That's on State Street."

I wondered how long he had checked in for.

"Just for the night. I just want the room for one night."

"Six bucks. Ya' got some I.D.? If you're under eighteen I have to charge ya' an extra five as a minor without any parents present. If ya' got someone coming up, I get three bucks extra for that. Change of sheets and all."

Again I was faced with the real world. No games – just all kinds of people.

"No, there's no one else. Just me." I paid the six buck plus five bucks being-a-minor fee, and he grabbed a skeleton key off the rack.

"Room 18. The one is off the door, so go to seventeen, then one more. Next floor up. The elevator stopped working in '58. Be outa here by noon or it's another six bucks plus five more. Have a pleasant stay."

He turned his wheelchair and sat staring at the television set three feet in front of him. I was dismissed and left the clerk and the hidden snorer to their own privacies.

The next flight of stairs was sixteen steps, divided into two by a landing. I counted steps in order to measure the extent I was taking myself from the secure world I knew. One dusty, pink shade hanging from the ceiling above the landing cast a subdued light over the grimy pink walls of the hallway. I began my search for room seventeen. The doors could not have been spaced more than twenty feet apart, center to center. I wondered if the locks actually worked, or if there were even locks on all the doors. From the flimsiness of the walls, I had the feeling that locks would be superfluous. The hall was dead quiet, but I could smell no urine, an expected part of the stereotype I had created.

Once I had found room seventeen, I went to the next door

and could barely discern an "8" and the added space once occupied by a number "1." The dime store skeleton key fit easily but turned stiffly. I pushed open the stubborn door and stabbed blindly for a switch inside the door. The duplicate fixture from the hallway lit my first hotel room until I found the floor lamp next to the bed.

At that moment I felt like the dregs of humanity. If there existed a living organism lower than the amoeba, I was part of its class. I did not feel that way because the room was of such a low caliber, which it was, but because I actually liked it. I had never had my own room, and to me room eighteen was the bull's balls. However, at that same instant I also realized that anyone with an ounce of self-respect would have been repulsed. I doubted if the lowest caste and prisoner in India would have chosen it over the Black Hole of Calcutta, but I still liked it, and it was mine. I had become an "untouchable."

Despite my expectations, the wallpaper was not peeling off the walls. It was a very faded green and white vertical stripe pattern, saturated with smoke. It seemed that my aunt Flora, from my father's side, had had wallpaper in her bathroom like it at one time, but Aunt Flora had not been known for her elegant taste in décor; she thought that matching hand towels added superior class to her bathroom.

To the left was the double bed, with a splitting laminated headboard and a sagging mattress covered with a bedspread that looked like it might have been a carpet roll end from the old hotel lobby. The bedspread was disheveled, and I chose not to think about how recently it had been used and by whom. Very chic!

To the right was a dresser to match the headboard, with the bottom drawer missing. It had probably been chopped up for firewood. The floor was covered with gray and red tiles in a checkerboard design, with a moth-eaten rag rug by the bed. In the far corner was a sink which might have been clean when new, but now bore the signs of overuse and neglect. Still, it didn't drip and the mirror above it was not even cracked. I assumed that the toilet was down the hall. The place was not the Palmer House, but it had a certain class – lower class. I shoved the door closed, locked it, and with a smile I could not stifle, crossed the room to the bent venetian blinds hiding the window above the hot water radiator. The blinds went up without a struggle, and I gazed at my first "room with a view."

Directly outside my window was the blue neon eye of the swan, as though keeping watch. I remembered reading *The Great Gatsby* in Bates' class, and the "Eyes of Dr. J. T. Eckleburg," and I couldn't help feeling a chill up my spine at the similarities. At least Gatsby's symbolic eye wasn't flickering as though winking at me. I probably would have requested a different room, which I'm sure would have been answered with a "Get the hell out of here, kid!"

My distorted reverie was shattered by the thunder of an el train passing a half block up Van Buren. They ran every fifteen minutes all night long past midnight. I felt sure that the glass would shatter and/or that I'd go deaf. I remember hearing that if you slept next to a train, after a while you would get used to it. I don't think so!

I cupped my hands over my ears in a futile gesture. The brakes screeched and the earthquake temporarily ceased. I could see the people exit the well-lit interiors of the cars, suspicious of everyone else, yet alone in their individual worlds. I could understand why the hotel had not made good for very long. I gazed at the neon eye and thought about murdering that son-of-a-bitch in a wheelchair who had put me so close to the el tracks; I'm sure the Swan Hotel had many vacancies in a more quiet location. It would have been more restful at the Brighton Theatre, where there was an even din, perverts, and the mysterious lady in back, but I had paid my eleven bucks and was determined to stay the night. I thought of Mrs. Erickson's sophomore lit class and her concept of "growth."

"Growth," she had said, "comes only by allowing yourself to become vulnerable, then surviving the consequences.

People who always take the easy and safe way through life grow very little."

That lesson had stayed with me because I was always finding myself in awkward situations, though I felt they were not all of my own creation. I had always liked Mrs. Erickson for allowing me to rationalize my social ineptness, thus allowing me to feel better about myself. She was one of few teachers to whom I had never given a derogatory nickname. She was, and always would be, Mrs. Erickson.

With nothing to do, I decided to try the bed. It squeaked as though I had sat on a nest of rats, and I felt more positive that the bedspread had indeed been the carpet from the former hotel lobby. I liked being there, or, at least, liked the adventure of it. I lay back and stared at the ceiling, which was brown from smoke stains, but not peeling. For once I felt like having a cigarette. At that moment I think it might have even tasted good.

Other than the intermittent trains, the hotel was graveyard quiet. I heard another train roar by but didn't flinch as much. By night's end I figured on being used to being blown out of bed every fifteen minutes. The silence returned and I continued my vigil, trying not to think about the evening's events but instead about how people would react when I related my adventures. Then the squeaking started.

It was rhythmic, so I ruled out the stories I had heard about rats in the walls of seedy hotels. I recognized the sound, and then it dawned on me that it was the sound that my own hotel bed had emitted when I had first plopped on it. The squeaking came from behind my head from the next room. It sounded like somebody was using the bed for a trampoline, but quick thinking suggested otherwise. I tried not to reach the only possible conclusion -- someone in the next room was getting laid, and I was eavesdropping. There was nothing to be done about the activites of a couple two hour renters, and I remained very still, wondering how long the cadence would continue. My listening was a true act of voyeurism, but strictly unintentional.

Straining in an attempt to hear the voices and sounds of heavy sex, I hoped that they might start talking dirty and tell each other what to do next. I had never seen a stag film, but I considered my voyeuristic plight as being the closest to a stag film's dialogue as I would likely approach for a while. Trying to envision the action on the other side of the wall, I intensified my listening, wishing there was a drinking glass in the room to help my hearing. The Palmer House would have had one – and clean, too. Still, there were no sounds other than the consistent, rhythmic squeak of the bed springs.

Then the possibility hit me like a gunshot – there were no voices because there was only one person! Someone in the next room was "going solo"! I felt betrayed and cheated about the eavesdropping, so I sprang as quietly as possible from my bed, not wanting whoever it was to know that I had had my ear to the wall. I stared at the stained wall, feeling bad about my indiscretion. I could not understand how I could have justified listening to two people screwing their brains out, but not accept listening to someone spanking the monkey. It was a real hypocritical mystery.

Ironically, I stood still so that I might not be heard. I wasn't sure exactly how long I remained transfixed, but by the time the second el train had passed, so had the squeaking of the bed springs. Afraid of being too conspicuous so soon after the incident, I went to the window and remained there until two more el trains had passed. No other sounds were present, so I cautiously returned to my bed and continued my reverie, gingerly lying down.

Feeling awkward about what had happened, I decided to slightly alter the story that I would tell the guys at school. The participants on the other side of the wall would become a guy and a twenty-five buck hooker. That story would open a floodgate of questions, and I would be able to fabricate anything. I could make it two girls and a guy. Or maybe just two girls; guys really liked hearing about that action.

No matter what I told them I felt that they'd be anxious to hear Kelly Elliott speak. Even fat-ass Swedarsky would listen with half an ear, though he would probably pretend not to. He would probably accuse me of not even being here, so I decided to steal something from the hotel, maybe a book of matches, just to prove myself. He was able to pound the stuffing out of me, but for once I would be one up on him.

The excitement of the night sank into me and made me realize that I hadn't gone to the john all night. In the courtroom I had thought my bladder would burst, but I risked a prison term to go, anyway. I could not recall even seeing a bathroom in the hotel. It must have been somewhere down the hall or maybe in the lobby. The more I thought about it, the more I realized that I had no desire to see the bathroom of the Swan Hotel. The image of a drunk lying in piss on the floor in front of Ginny Dare at the Follies Theatre tended to make me cautious of bathrooms in sleazy places.

I got up and went to the sink, turning on the water to cover any displaced sounds. A sputtering of brown water flowed out. When it cleared, I unzipped and peed into the flow. The whirling of water, scum, and pee became hypnotic, like creating an abstract painting, and it was almost orgasmic just to relieve the pressure on my bladder.

As I stood peeing myself into a near-orgasm, angry shouts came from the hallway. I turned my head and kept my eyes on the door, afraid someone would crash in and catch me in a relatively perverse act. I wished my bladder would hurry. It felt terribly embarrassing and awkward to go into a sink with screaming people outside my door. I also felt that by turning my head toward the door I would be able to hear better. It was irrational, like shouting at a blind person.

An enraged man's voice screamed, "You old slut!"

The shaky answer came from a terrified woman. "I'm sorry, Ron. It was a goddamn accident. I just had lousy timing. Give me a chance, will ya'?"

The male voice grew more intense. "I doubt if it's even

mine, with all the tramping around you do. It's probably some pervert or that cripple down at the desk. That's more your speed. Ya' probably been doin' him for the rent, ya' lousy whore!" The stinging sound of a slap made me wince.

My sink peeing had stopped, but I stood spellbound, holding myself and listening to the war outside my door. It was absurd.

There was sobbing from the wilting woman. "No, Ron. I haven't been with anyone but you. You're not being fair. I never . . ."

A resounding thud at my door stopped her words. I jumped back, waiting for a body to come crashing through the thin barrier. He had hit her and she had reeled into my door. The cry of pain was instantaneous.

"You dirty bitch!"

Footsteps stomped down the hallway. I scurried to the door and listened. She was directly outside, crying but still conscious. Gently I turned the key and opened the door, fearful that her body would collapse into my room.

In the center of the floor huddled a weeping woman with raven hair, holding the right side of her face with both hands. She sobbed controllably, but the side that I could see was red and streaked with tears. She was the epitome of sorrow. Dressed in a floor length blue terry cloth bathrobe, she looked more like a stressed-out suburban housewife with three kids and a station wagon than someone who should be crying in the hallway of the Swan Hotel. Hesitantly, I ventured forth, fearful that I might upset her even more.

Softly and sincerely I asked, "Are you okay? Can I help?"

The sobbing ceased and she slowly lifted her head. Her right eye was already beginning to swell and darken; she looked like the loser of a prize fight. As she looked into my eyes, I got a weird sensation that I knew her. Her glassy brown eyes begged for sympathy. Then she let out a gasp and recovered her face.

I panicked, not knowing what I had done. "What's wrong? I only want to help. Really."

The words came between sobs. "Christ, kid. Do you always walk around like that?"

In my haste and surprise I had forgotten to reposition myself and to rezip. It was just hanging out, like I suspected any unrespectable pervert would have had it. I blushed and rearranged myself quickly.

"God, lady, I'm sorry. I was just getting ready for bed when I heard the noise. I'm not a pervert or anything. Honest! I was just getting ready for bed."

I thought I detected a slight ease of the tension. "Help me up, will ya', kid?"

"Sure," I said, relieved that she wasn't going to cause a scene by my inadvertent flashing. She grabbed my arm and was soon up on her feet, shakily.

"Help me back to my room, would you, please? Down there."

I held her arm while she kept her face covered with her free hand. She was a mess and I hoped she knew how to care for herself. This was not my area of expertise.

Her door was open, revealing a room at least twice the size of mine, with a small refrigerator and hot plate in the far corner. There was room for a worn red-velvet couch, a rocking chair in need of caning, a cocktail table, and a small, chipped, Formica dinette set for two. I surmised that she was a full-time resident. She stumbled to the couch and pointed to the refrigerator. Her crying had stopped.

"Would you get me some ice? Wrap it in the washcloth on the sink and run some water over it."

I shuffled to the refrigerator and did as she had asked. I sat next to her on the couch and watched her wince as she applied the cold compress. I stared, trying to place her bruised but vaguely familiar face. She was probably at least forty years old, judging from the wrinkles and weathered appearance of her face and gauging everything from my own mother. I had seen her before; I knew her.

"What's your name?" she asked. Her voice even sounded slightly familiar.

"Kelly. Kelly Elliott," I replied nervously, forgetting that I was an intruder on the mysterious woman's most private affairs. She still had half her face covered with the compress.

She weakly extended a hand. "Please to meet you, Kelly Elliott. I'm Mary Harker."

I shook her cold and shaking hand. The name meant nothing to me.

"How's it look, Kelly?"

She removed the compress and for the first time looked directly at me. I was dumbfounded.

"My God! You're Ginny Dare!" Tact had been waylaid by sincere shock. She involuntarily smiled and winced from the pain, quickly replacing the cold washcloth.

"Oh, you've seen me on stage, then. You're a bit young for that kind of show, aren't you?"

She showed no embarrassment at my having seen her almost totally naked, but I supposed that I had only been one of thousands. Still, I knew that I would not have been able to be so casual with a stranger who had seen me naked. Moron, I forgot! She had just seen my most important naked parts! But she had the class not to mention it. I spoke quickly, trying to cover my awkwardness.

"I was at your show a few weeks ago. My friend Jerry and I got in. We're both seventeen. You talked to me in the lobby. Don't you remember?"

I was almost pleading for recognition, but I did not know why.

"Sure, Kelly, but talking is part of my job. I talk to all the customers. I don't even see faces. Everyone is the same."

Not to be denied a closer relation with the first "older" woman I had fallen in love with, I continued my hopes that something would trigger a memory. I played my trump card, in spite of the embarrassment that it might cause me.

"I came out of the bathroom and a bunch of guys were giving me a hard time. There was a drunk lying on the floor. You must remember that."

Either she really did remember or she was just trying to

be kind without being condescending. I could not interpret her half-hidden face.

"Yeah, I guess I do recall something like that, but to be honest, that happens a lot. So, how's it look?" she asked, lowering the compress again.

Her eye had almost swollen shut and turned livid.

"I'm afraid it doesn't look too good, Miss Dare. It's pretty purple and spreading."

She replaced the compress angrily. "Shit! There goes a good two weeks' salary down the toilet. Russ won't let me dance looking like this. That son-of-a-bitch!"

I figured that son-of-a-bitch was Ron, the guy who had hit her, but I remembered Russ, the manager at the Follies, and how he had ridiculed me. I thought "son-of-a-bitch" a suitable epithet for either man. I felt sorry for her but had no idea of what use I could be to her. Besides, it had not been the best of nights for me, either.

Meekly I asked, "Is there anything I can do, Miss Dare?"

She tried a slight smile again but flinched in pain. "Call me Mary. Ginny Dare is just my stage name. If you'd like, you can call me Ginny, but I prefer my real name. Maybe you could turn on the tea kettle for me, Kelly."

I turned on the hot plate and checked to be sure there was water in the tea kettle. When I returned to the sofa she was crying, and I thought that she would prefer to be alone. I mumbled, "If you're okay, I'll leave now."

"Hmmm?" A broken reverie.

"If you're all right now, I guess I'll be going."

I really didn't want to go, but I didn't want to stay either. I wasn't ready for the situation; Again I felt awkward, a child intruder in an adult world.

Ginny Dare looked up at me as though seeing me for the first time, as a stranger who had just entered her open doorway. I thought she had been reading my mind.

"Kelly, why are you here?"

Defensively, like I had been caught peeking through a bathroom keyhole, I blurted, "But you asked me to come in. I heard all the fighting and opened . . ."

She grasped my hand to shut me off, shaking her head. "No, no. I don't mean here in this room. In this fleabag hotel. What are you doing in this hotel? You obviously don't live here. You seem too nice to be here with a hooker. Why are you here?"

I was a little embarrassed at my emotional outburst and honestly did not know how to answer.

"Well, it's a long story and not a very good one."

She squeezed my hand firmly, relating a genuine interest. "Please. Tell me. I'd like to talk or just listen. I need someone just now. Would you stay for just a little while? It would help me temporarily take my mind off my own problems."

Trying to conceal the lump in my throat, I looked down at the floor; her eyes were so pitiful. I felt that she really wanted me to stay, but I just did not know what was happening. It was a new land. I had endured a strangeness with Linda, but at least I had had an idea of what my expected behavior should have been. With Ginny Dare I had no idea of what to do, or say, or what was expected of me. She was practically begging me to trust her. A strange woman who made a living by taking off her clothes in front of a bunch of horny men and perverts. It muddled my mind.

"Sure, Ginny. I mean, Mary. I can stay if you'd like."

She did not wince from her slight smile and grasped my other hand, pulling me onto the couch beside her.

"I'd like." The whistle of the kettle intruded on the moment. "But, first I'll get us some tea."

She rose from the couch, went to the kitchen, and grabbed two cups marked "Mom" and "Dad" from the cupboard. Handing me one hot cup, she commented, "The cups came as a set," as though explaining their labels.

We sat on that couch, she holding my hand, and I talked, while she listened for real. She asked me to tell her everything about myself, and I hoped that my monologue might divert her concentration from her current catastrophe.

I told this strange woman how my mother and I had lived

a comfortable existence the past seventeen years without my father. That story led to Dan Phillips and the reason that I was at the Swan Hotel that particular evening. Mary listened with intense and apparently sincere interest, occasionally interjecting an understanding comment about my various dilemmas, something nobody had ever really done for me before, not that I had ever sought such counseling.

As the night passed, I found it easier to talk to her than to anyone. Perhaps she saw herself in parts of me, because she seemed to relate to some of what I said, and she was a good and sympathetic companion. I asked her about herself, more about why she lived at the Swan Hotel, but she did not want to talk about her problems and asked me to continue talking about my own tribulations.

I related anecdotes about Swedarsky and how he had intimidated me throughout high school, and I got the feeling that she had gone through some of the same bullying experiences on the female side, because she would nod her head in agreement with events most people would have considered absurd and inane.

Mary Harker was the easiest person to talk to in the whole world. Her honesty encouraged me to ramble as though I were a patient talking to his psychiatrist. Ma always heard what I said but rarely really listened. I could always tell that her mind was elsewhere, whether it was on her job or Dan Phillips. Jerry Hogan always waited for some comment he could jump on and twist to make some idiotic sexual innuendo. Baldy Smith, the guidance counselor, was an asshole who knew nothing about the people who came to see him, except for their California Achievement Test scores. Linda would have probably been all right, but she had vowed never to talk to me again, so I was left alone. But Mary Harker listened and understood.

Daylight was crawling through the slats of the venetian blinds by the time I completed my story about my first date, including the glove compartment full of condoms. She laughed at the story, though I could sense by a single flinch that it caused her some pain. Her laughter was contagious, and I soon found myself laughing with her, and it felt good. The absurdity of the situation demanded laughter, and I began to believe that I should not take everything that happened to me personally. I had thought it would take me ten years before I would be able to laugh about the "Night of the Gross Rubbers," but with Mary's presence, it had taken only a few hours.

Finally, I was exhausted and the silence was welcome. We both felt better, our individual tragedies alleviated for a time. Sometimes simple talk and sincere concern were all I needed, but they were so often elusive. I felt that I had been useful to her, as she had been to me, and I prepared to leave.

Shyly, I said, "I'll go now, if you'd like."

She looked genuinely taken aback. "Do you have to?" she asked for the second time that night.

I still did not have the experience to enable me to read people's minds, though I had advanced leap years that night.

"No, I don't have to go. I just thought you'd like to finally be alone. It's four a.m."

"No, not yet, Kelly."

It looked for a moment as if the tears might reform, and I realized that pain does not dissipate after listening to someone else's problems for hours; it is merely suspended. She stood and tenderly took my hand.

"Come with me, Kelly. We're both exhausted."

Panic seized me as she led me to the bed. I definitely was not ready for what appeared to be inevitable. Talking and daydreaming came easy – reality was too difficult without more preparation. I wasn't ready yet, and she did not seem to understand like I thought she would.

"Lie down, Kelly. Relax, nothing's going to happen."

I did as she asked, trying not to be stiff like a corpse, and she lay next to me. She put my left arm around her neck and nestled into my shoulder. She took my hand, squeezed it firmly, and spoke gently, "Thanks for being here, Kelly. Now go to sleep."

Relief, mixed with disappointment, flooded my brain. It was as close as I had been to a woman in my life, and I was relieved and grateful just to lie there with Mary next to me. Somehow, she had known that I was not ready, but that some day I would be; she understood me better than I understood myself.

I wanted nothing more than the warmth and satisfaction that settled between us. I appreciated her tenderness and lightly kissed the top of her raven hair, a gesture that seemed so natural that I later wondered about all the anxiety that had built up in me over kissing Linda.

In a half-sleep, she whispered, "Thanks again, Kelly. Good night," and she was sleeping at the last syllable.

I looked down at the strange woman I held. Her face was badly bruised, and I empathized with all that she had suffered. Despite her trauma, she took time for someone like me, and I hoped I could help her in return. It was an emotion I felt that I would probably never experience again.

Her robe had slipped open and I could see the tops of her breasts. I delicately pulled the robe closed, turned my head, and went to sleep. It seemed like the proper thing to do.

CHAPTER 9

The Zoo, the Scandal, and the Cheater

Mary Harker and I slept until one o'clock the next afternoon. When I awoke she was sitting at the kitchen table, still dressed in her robe, sipping coffee and staring emptily at the table. I said, "Good morning," but she only replied with a weak smile.

"Would you like something to eat, Kelly?" she asked. "I could scramble some eggs." I found it difficult to believe that this quiet, troubled woman was a raucous stripper when we met.

"No, thank you. I'll be going now."

The time had come when she really needed to be alone. I felt sorry for her and ambivalent about myself. Did I feel bad for her or good for myself because I had helped her through the night? I had a difficult time feeling both at once.

"What will you do now, Mary?" I asked. The name "Mary" came more naturally to me now. The night we had spent together had killed the character of Ginny Dare and substituted the real Mary Harker.

She spoke firmly, a woman with a definite stop-gap measure in mind. "I may go home to my parents in St. Louis. After a month, we'll see."

I felt possessive, not wanting her to leave. It was important for me to be the one to help her, though I could not determine the cause for my need, unless it was selfishness. Of course, I had to resign myself to her decision.

"Will I see you again?" I whispered.

She looked up from her trance, again understanding my confused state. "Sure, Kelly. I may be back in a month, at least to pick up my things if I decide to leave Chicago. I'll probably see you then."

And I'll probably be playing quarterback for the Chicago Bears, I thought. I knew that I would probably never see her again, and it hurt me deeply. All I had left was a souvenir picture, which I kept hidden in volume "D" of an old *World Book Encyclopedia* set at home.

"Okay, Mary. I'll see you then. Bye."

I reluctantly started for the door, feeling sad, my eyes downcast.

"Wait!" Mary commanded.

I stopped and she came to me. Her arms flew around me and she hugged me tightly. I hugged back and didn't care if the day ever ended, never wanting to relinquish her to the world that had hurt her. A tear began to roll down my cheek, but, of course, I didn't want her to notice. An important person was about to leave me forever. It seemed that people could spend an eternity doing very little of importance, but unexpected occurrences of a few hours could alter lives forever. I understood that, and I was saddened that our meeting had to end quickly and with tears.

Mary Harker slowly released her grip. I turned and left in silence, not looking back, not wanting her to see my profusion of tears.

I decided to spend Saturday night at the Swan Hotel, since I'd missed the noon check-out requirement. I had given my mother the complete weekend for her own "joy." A good portion of the day I spent silently weeping, trying to purge my system of the aching emotions. I went to the Chicago Theatre on State Street to enjoy a movie, not to sleep. *Cat Ballou* with Lee Marvin and Jane Fonda was playing and I stayed for two showings. The first was for brooding, the second show for enjoyment.

Several times during the night I walked past Mary's room but saw no light under the door. I forced myself not to knock, which was one of the most disciplined decisions I had ever made. Asking Linda for a date had been nothing compared to passing Mary's door in silence.

I was half-tempted to go to the Follies Theatre to see if she might be there, but I really did not want to see her other persona, not today. Also, she said that she would not be performing for at least a couple of weeks because of that blackened eye, so I spent the night in my luxurious hotel room, accompanied only by the squeaking sounds of the unknown self-satisfying neighbor, hoping for a knock on my door from Mary.

Life wasted little time in returning me to its proper form. Dan Phillips was gone by the time I returned on Sunday evening, and Ma seemed to be more miserable than Mary Harker or myself. Sorrow seemed contagious. She did not even ask me about my first date (it seemed ages past!), which hurt me somewhat, but I had become professional at sympathizing, so I did not press the minor issues.

Monday brought school and the usual drudgeries of being a seventeen-year-old in a sea of 2,000 other trapped teenagers. Jerry Hogan pressed me for details about my "hot date" with Linda, and I drove him insane by not revealing a single detail. He tried to prod me into saying that I had at least "copped a feel," but I would not budge. I always felt that the ones who did the most talking probably did the least, so my sustained silence emitted all kinds of inferences. I enjoyed his helplessness.

Linda kept her word – she would not say a word to me, even when I tried to talk to her in the halls. She would do an about-face and go out of her way to avoid me. Chemistry class also passed in silence. Jerry noticed her attitude and assumed that I must have scored. He figured I had tried something really kinky to earn that kind of treatment. I was a god in the mind of Jerry Hogan.

Ralph Jacobsen also tried to avoid me, but I finally caught him hiding in the gym, of all places. I grabbed the twerp by his shirt collar and hauled him to Shipstead's office, explaining that we had differences to settle after school. Shipstead leered at the thought of the two school weaklings slugging it out; he loved blood in any form.

The after-school fight lasted as long as my first fight with Swedarsky. I had a new confidence that the little weasel would not be able to hurt me, even if he landed every punch. Ralph Jacobsen never got the opportunity. As soon as he was within my reach, I faked a left cross, a move that I had learned from Swedarsky. Ralph threw up both hands to cover, like I would have expected a girl to do, leaving his entire left side open. Using my waist as a pivot, I swung a round-house right, punching him below his left eye and continuing through, past the headgear and to his nose. A slight crunch indicated I had broken it, but I felt no remorse. I wanted him to stay on his feet, so I could pulverize his body. I was an uncaged beast. Blood spurted out of the bridge of his nose, and Ralph Jacobsen dropped to the mat unconscious. Shipstead watched me with his mouth open, never imagining such anger getting into me.

Not saying a word or offering any assistance, I sauntered out of the wrestling room, as if what I had just done was routine. I was Swedarsky, Jr. I left Shipstead to take care of his little kingdom and his messes. It would be interesting to hear how Ralph Jacobsen's parents would handle it.

The one-punch knock-out had brought me more respect; nobody liked Ralph Jacobsen and his smart-ass mouth. Along with my mythical triumph over Linda Martinsen, I began to enjoy some new status, which helped me suppress unhappy thoughts of Mary Harker. People who had rarely spoken to me before said "Hi" in the hallways, and I cockily nodded my head in acknowledgment. Even Laura LeDuc, who I had mentally abandoned for a few days, nodded and smiled at me. Perhaps the ultimate triumph was Swedarsky. He ceased his "pizza face" taunts and once even said, "Elliott" as he passed me in the hallway. My star was on the rise.

My final victory for that week occurred with Muffler Mulhouse. After my new-found popularity, he started talking to me, trying to grab the coattails of someone on his way up the social ladder. He asked me how I did with that "court thing." I smiled, looked him in the eye, and politely said, "Eat it, Mulhouse."

Ordinarily he would have gotten pissed and pushed me in his defense, but he played statue while I strolled away, never informing him about the noise violation warning concerning his car that I had received from the judge. I knew that some day that bastard would get caught.

By Wednesday Ma was talking again and finally asked me how my date had gone. I fabricated a simple story about a movie and a hamburger, the way things should have been, which she seemed to accept. It just seemed easier to leave out the parts about the traffic court, the glove box rubbers, the sleazy hotel, and sharing a bed with a middle-aged stripper. I asked her if Dan Phillips would be coming back the following weekend, meaning, "Should I leave the house?" She whispered, "No," and returned to her pensive mood. I realized that I had touched a nerve and wondered if the loser pilot had finally crash-landed with my mother. My recent surge in ego had made me ready to punch out the son-of-a-bitch.

When one's social life is in order, so follows everything else. My attitude toward school work changed, and I actually found myself willing and eager to attack my assignments. I took books home with me and even checked out a few from the library to use for Bates' term paper. Such activity was unheard of, especially by a senior, who was practically guaranteed graduation. I worked on the term paper until one in the morning on Wednesday and had even completely typed it by supper time on Thursday; most seniors would be starting theirs when I had already finished.

The paper was an analysis of the guilt of the character Billy Budd, from Melville's novel of the same name. Being victimized was a subject with which I could clearly relate, and I took the side that Billy should have been acquitted, not hanged from the yardarm. He was a likable person; even his shipmates had said so, and I didn't see any sense in hanging the youth for something he could not have avoided. Bates actually gave me an "A," the first I had ever earned from him. It made me curious how well I could have done my first three years of high school with the same effort, but the system accepted mediocrity as above average, so I had never really exerted myself.

By Friday I didn't even mind getting out of bed and going to school. As I looked in the mirror, I felt sure that my face was clearing. Nobody else had noticed it, but I rejoiced when I counted only fifteen zits, including two on my chin that were almost closed. The previous week I had counted twenty. There was no doubt that my acne was on the decline. Besides the clearing complexion, my voice had not cracked under any stress for an entire week!

The first weekend after the "Night of the Gross Rubbers" was quiet. Jerry had taken a bus to Oak Lawn for the beginning of the state basketball playoffs, but I decided not to go. I hadn't attended a game since farting in front of Laura LeDuc, and despite the mellowness of my social situation, I felt that appearing again too soon would revive some unpleasant memories, for all of us.

Since Dan Phillips was out of town, Ma and I were left alone together. It was the first time in months that I could recall being home with my mother on a Friday night. I didn't really mind, though I could still detect her sensitivity about something. I asked her if she wanted to talk, but she just said "No," and added that I couldn't possibly understand. My assurance did nothing to change her mind.

In an attempt to cheer her up, I asked if she would like to go to the zoo on Saturday. She had always taken me there when I was a kid, and we'd spend hours tossing marshmallows to the bears. She half-laughed at the idea and said "No," but I could tell that she was taken off guard by the question and might leave that door open. It had been one of our favorite places, and there hadn't been an "us" for a long time. I knew I'd be able to talk her into it, and I did.

Saturday was the second weekend of spring, the day when the sidewalks finally melted completely clean and the rivulets started to trickle down the gutters. It was the day that everyone prematurely shed the winter coat for a windbreaker or sweater, refusing to use the heavy coat until next season, no matter how cold it became. It was the day that people escaped their fortresses, came out from every crack in the city, and flocked to Grant Park to walk and feed the pigeons. It was the unofficial first day of spring.

While Ma dressed for the zoo, I washed the breakfast dishes, "like a good little boy." She wore her gray skirt and pink and gray striped top, an outfit that she had spent an entire year knitting. It wasn't flattering to her, and it was easy to see her mistakes, but she took great pride in her handiwork, and I thought it looked just fine for a trip to the zoo.

The buses were crowded for a Saturday, as people flooded the Loop for window shopping and desensitization to the harsh Chicago winter. Ma found an aisle seat and I stood beside her. Looking down at her blue-scarfed head, I could clearly see her age advancing. The gray roots protruded from her dyed hair, and her cheeks had begun to sag like her chin. There were visible crows' feet. I studied the face of aging carefully, wondering why I had never noticed it before.

I appreciated the fact that she had raised me on her own, and that her nagging was probably therapeutic for her as well as for my own good. It felt good that I had won the scholarship and had decided to go to college. I really wasn't sure what I wanted to do with my life anyway and was relieved that the decision had somewhat been made for me. She deserved something; she hadn't had much her entire life. Even the worn, pink coat with the artificial fur collar was ten years old, one of her countless sacrifices to "make ends meet." For the first time in a long while I felt like a son and not an antagonist. I just wished that I had started sooner, but I was learning that everything came with time – nothing could be forced.

Lincoln Park Zoo was jammed with every teenage couple in Chicago, along with countless parents pushing rented orange strollers. It hadn't been that long ago that one of those children had been me, but I was content knowing that I didn't have to relive what all of them had yet to confront.

Ma and I walked in a relative silence, mentally pondering our more simple, joyful past. The tigers paced their cages like the trapped animals they were, while the monkeys picked and ate the lice from their brethren. All of the animals could also sense the change of season.

When we approached the polar bears, Ma's reflective mood seemed to lighten. I could see a nostalgic memory enter her eyes -- the satisfaction that some things never changed. We threw a few marshmallows as the bears sat on their haunches, applauding with their huge paws and snapping the flying treats out of the air like Willie Mays.

There was an unoccupied bench opposite the area, so we sat while we watched the polar bear show. When most of the people had drifted away from our vicinity, Ma spoke softly, taking her eyes away from the bears for the first time.

"Kelly, why did you want to come here today?"

I didn't want to tell my mother that I felt sorry for her; she was too hardened to merit sympathy and sons weren't supposed to pity their mothers, I thought.

"We haven't been here in a long time, and we always liked it. In fact, we haven't really done anything together for a long time."

She wanted to accept that answer but could see through me, as she always had. When I was ten, Jerry Hogan had loaned me a nudist magazine that his brother Paul had bought. Ma had gone to the store, and I had been lying on my side on her bed with my head propped up on one elbow, getting my first look at a fully naked woman. The door was shut but suddenly I heard Ma approach and stop, probably puzzled by the closed door. I quickly shoved the magazine under a pillow and lay there like the proverbial cat that had eaten the canary. She knocked once and entered. Ma asked what I was doing, and I gave the standard reply, "Nothing." She cocked her head to one side and said, "You look like you've been looking at girlie magazines and your mother walked in on you." Then she left with no other comment. I could feel my jaw drop; somehow she had known. It didn't seem possible, but she had known. She always knew, just like she sensed that I had asked her to the zoo because I felt sorry for her.

She resumed the subtle interrogation. "There's no other reason, is there, Kelly?"

I could not hide my hidden motive from her. "Well, you have seemed a bit down lately, Ma. I thought maybe you'd feel better if you got out a little. And it's true – we haven't been here for years."

Ma resumed her vigil of the polar bears and spoke with a strength in her voice. When she was troubled, she had to vent her frustrations. "You're right, Kelly. I have been down the last couple weeks. Do you know why?"

Guilt gripped my throat. "It wasn't anything I did, was it?"

She smiled. "No, it's nothing you did."

Relieved, I knew there was only one alternative. "Does it have to do with Dan Phillips?"

I waited for half a year or more for her answer. My bluntness and accuracy had cut deep. She hesitated at first, then mustered the courage to speak concisely.

"Last night I said that you were too young to understand. I feel I may have been wrong in that judgment." There was a substantial pause, enough to make me shiver. "I found out last week that Dan Phillips is married. He has a wife and two kids in New York. "

That rotten, selfish bastard! I hoped his Phillips head screwdriver would get gangrene and fall off in the midst of the Christmas mob at Marshall Fields. I hoped his head imploded. I hoped he'd rot in some stinking prison and be viciously gang-raped by fifty disease-infested inmates. I hoped . . .

My train of thought was cut sharply by Ma's stare, and the pain on my face must have been clearly visible.

"His wife called me Tuesday night." I recalled being

startled by a late call one night, but Ma had picked it up on her bedroom extension. I assumed it had been a wrong number and had forgotten about it, until now. "Sarah is her name. It seems that she found my name and phone number in the classic little black book of women's phone numbers. Apparently he has known many women in many cities. It seems almost corny, except it happened to me. She found the book in his underwear drawer, under some Valentine's Day shorts he only wore once a year. I suppose he thought it would be safe there until the next Valentine's Day. Seems rather appropriate, finding his women in his shorts, don't you think?"

A rough attempt at humor, but I was still too numb to speak rationally. Ever since my promise as a kid to watch my language even as I got older, I tried to watch my words, especially when I was angry. Ma could detect my discomfort and continued.

"Dan had called me at Amy's a few Sundays ago from his apartment in New York. I thought I could hear a woman and kids in the background, and he had to hang up abruptly. I suspected something then, but just let it go. After all, he has a sister there, too, but his need to hang up disturbed me. I read in *Redbook* magazine that men who cheat for long actually want to get caught – too much tension, poor guys. Anyway, Sarah must have come in unexpectedly.

"I suppose he figured that his wife would never see the phone bill, but she saw it and matched it to one in his black book. So Sarah called me. It seems that she and Dan had met and married under the same circumstances – an affair with a married Dan Phillips. She just thought that I should know. She was actually quite nice about it and said that I was welcome to him if I wanted the bastard. Much nicer than I could have been."

Tears were forming in Ma's eyes, but by now she was too hardened to let them escape. I was sure that it was the first time she had vocalized her dilemma and I felt useful, like I had with Mary Harker, merely by being present and listening. A new pride swelled inside me, knowing that she had decided to confide in her son. Her Sunday moodiness and the late night telephone call took on new and clearer meanings, and I realized that my traumas were minute compared to other people's. Everything was relative. I wanted to hug her like I had Mary Harker, but Ma was not the type who catered to displays of sentiment, especially in public.

I said weakly, "I'm sorry, Ma. What are you going to do now?"

She grasped for more courage. "He called me at work yesterday, and I told him that I never wanted to see him again. Hopefully, he'll respect my wishes and leave me alone. Like so many women my age, I'll continue until I stop. What else can I do?"

God, she was tough, and I wondered where my inherent weak character had come from. I would never have her fortitude.

"I'm sorry, Ma. I'm sorry it didn't work out for you."

She gave a slight smile and grasped my hand. I felt a wave of déjà vu. "Thank you, Kelly. Now let's go see Sinbad, the 500-pound gorilla. He reminds me of what I'm losing."

My mother seemed once more relaxed after her confession, and she was willing to make a full effort to enjoy our Saturday. I felt that she simply did not want to go home in case of an unwelcome visitor or telephone call, but I was enjoying myself more than I had with Linda Martinsen and readily agreed to all she suggested.

We had a deep dish pizza at Gino's on Rush Street, then decided to catch a movie. I wanted to go to one of the ornate downtown movie palaces, but she wanted to start the trek home, so we ended up at the Brighton Theatre. They were playing a Vincent Price triple horror shock show, and Ma loved horror films. It seemed ironic, taking my mother to the theatre where I'd made my home while she had been with Dan Phillips. Jorge greeted us with a, "Hello, Kelly," which totally shocked my mother. I did not explain.

The seven o'clock crowd at the Brighton was nothing like the late crowd with which I usually attended. I didn't see anyone sleeping, and the mysterious lady of sexual tension release (a term from one of Jerry's magazines) was not her usual visual self. In fact, the place was packed with shrieking couples, and I could scarcely believe it was the same theatre. We only stayed for one and a half movies and were safely home by 10:00. Ma went to bed and I watched another late horror movie starring Vincent Price on channel 2.

Sunday passed quietly. Ma, in slightly raised spirits, went to her sister's, and I lounged around the apartment, watching the Blackhawks beat the Bruins 4-3. The phone once sounded twenty rings, but I didn't answer. There was something ominous in the ring.

Monday brought the scandal of the century to Talbot High School. There was enough energy in the halls to light Michigan Avenue at Christmas. Students became frantic as they quickly exchanged the latest details during the four-minute passing periods. Since I had lost all contact with my classmates over the weekend, I was one of the last to find out the news – Old Man Shipstead got caught pumping Old Lady Winegarden in the school library!

After school on Friday Becky Burns had gone into the library with Mr. Schwarz, the principal. She had lost her math folder and thought that she might have left it in the library. The door was locked, but Mr. Schwarz, who was passing by the library at the time, agreed to let her in. Making sure that she took nothing more than her folder, he followed her in and waited.

From the blind corner of the stacks, between philosophy and theology, came the sounds of grunts and groans, as though two sophomores were in combat, both afraid to throw a punch. Mr. Schwarz and Becky rushed to the scene, and there was old Shipstead, bare-ass up, pants around his ankles, sticking it to Old Lady Winegarden on a study table. Her dress had been pulled up and her white nurse's panties dangled from one ankle, which rested on the wisdom of

Confucius, while her other leg stretched up to the third shelf and *The Power of Positive Thinking*. What a sight it must have been!

Becky Burns screamed, more horrified than Janet Leigh in *Psycho*, while Schwarz stood spellbound. He could hardly throw a bucket of cold water on two consenting adults. At the exact moment of Becky's scream, Old Lady Winegarden gasped and brought her legs tightly around Shipstead's back, like a Koala bear hanging onto a eucalyptus tree, pumped with everything she had left, and climaxed. Becky screamed a second time, again in harmony with Winegarden – an orgasm and a shriek of terror. Stereo screams to shatter the finest Waterford crystal!

Shipstead realized that there was one scream out of synch and craned his head, his eyes exploding at the sight of two audience members in the gallery. He instinctively jumped back, unable to say anything, his pants still around his ankles. He dripped from the banquet of Winegarden's flower basket (a metaphor that became a Talbot High standard), and Becky, a naïve spectacled freshman, pointed, screamed again, and bolted from the library as though Shipstead had put her next on his list of sexual conquests.

Rumors had it that Becky ran the entire mile to her house in record time; it was not posted in the gym as the official school record, but everyone knew. Terrified, she locked herself in her bedroom, refusing to respond to her parents' pleas to tell them what had happened. She only answered with further shrieks. When her parents finally jimmied the lock, she was lying flat on her back staring at the ceiling, both hands covering her crotch, and mumbling, "Not me! Not me!"

No questions asked, the following week Becky was officially withdrawn from the roles of Talbot High and transferred to St. Bernadette's of Lourdes in Evanston, where she would have no contact with evil men, but was still intimidated by the priests. Nobody actually learned what happened to Becky, but rumors flew that she had become a nun in a convent somewhere in the French Alps.

All of these details were brought to the students courtesy of Ray Windsor, a senior, who had heard the screams and raced to the library to investigate. Everyone interrogated Ray to learn how long Shipstead's Johnson was, but he never told, fearful that some day Shipstead would catch him alone. Most of the students hated Shipstead and insisted that Ray had told them that he hadn't really seen anything, which students twisted to mean that it was so small that an eyewitness could not even see it. Ray denied such an assumption and kept his vow of silence, much like the oath Becky Burns allegedly took.

Because of the strength of the teachers' union and the due-process clause, Shipstead and Winegarden could not be fired immediately. They were "temporarily suspended without pay," until a hearing could be held. I know that I would never be able to respect a teacher who had been caught screwing Winegarden, especially in the library. Teachers weren't supposed to have sex, least of all in the school library with the librarian. It would have been difficult to even pass Shipstead in the hall without picturing him naked and grunting. The mere idea was gross and nauseating.

Excitement of the scandal made the week pass quickly. Conversation knew no other topic, and it seemed that even the rest of the teachers were embarrassed, though sometimes I'd see a couple of them talking out of the sides of their mouths, then breaking into subdued laughter. It was always a puzzle to kids – what did teachers talk about to each other? Did they talk about sex and booze like normal people, or did they talk about school and the most effective way to instruct Jimmy so-and-so? It has always been one of life's most puzzling mysteries.

The aisle where Shipstead had pumped Winegarden received more than its normal flow of traffic, as everyone wanted to inspect and walk over the scene of the scandal. It was like a pilgrimage to Canterbury. People tried to estimate where Winegarden's ass had been, and find the exact books on which her feet had rested, according to Ray Windsor's account. Mr. Schwarz probably should have roped off the area but that would have elevated the aisle to the level of "holy shrine," drawing more attention and pilgrims to it.

During his free time Swedarsky conducted free guided tours through the stacks. "And here is where Miss Winegarden, our former librarian, rested her right foot, while her left foot rested here. If you look closely at the area that I have outlined in chalk, you can actually see trace drops of their passion, leaving an indelible impression in our archives." It was probably the most literate Swedarsky had ever sounded.

The substitute librarian had a difficult time coping with the large, gruff senior, and finally called in Mr. Schwarz, who banned Swedarsky from the library for the rest of his natural life. The tours had ended by Thursday. Swedarsky's punishment did not affect his education or class ranking.

A late spring break followed the scandalous week, which gave time for the excitement to diminish. I passed the break doing my usual inane activities – watching TV, going to the movies, hanging out with Jerry, all the while trying to collect my paradoxical emotions and putting them into perspective with the rest of my life. After a week of contemplation I had partially accepted the fact that Mary Harker was gone forever, that it was not my fault, and that I would simply have to continue life to the best of my abilities, but I clung to her picture.

On the Monday of the first week after vacation, (the second week since Mary Harker had gone), another event occurred which threw me back into the quagmire of fanciful dreams from which I had finally begun to emerge. Just as I started to live in the real world instead of my imagination, Laura LeDuc was transferred into my world lit class, and she occupied the seat in front of me.

After all I had recently experienced, from Mary Harker to Ma's trials and my confrontation with puny Ralph Jacobsen,

I was beginning to handle life's conflicts and feel good about my changes. And then Laura reentered my life and crashed open the gates to my former Fantasyland. Every day during the eighth period I was forced to stare at her luscious gold hair, perfect legs displayed from her short skirts, and an occasional profile of that angelic face. Again, I was drawn back to the daydreams of our orgasmic nights of love-making, complete with heavy necking, heavy petting, and an enviable marriage. I knew the fantasy cycle would start again, because we still had eight weeks before the end of the year. There was nothing to do in Bates' English class except to daydream, and those thoughts could only encompass one subject – Laura LeDuc sitting directly in front of me. I felt like a mental patient whose psychiatrist had informed him that after two years of intensive therapy, he was worse off than when he had started. He was certifiably nuts.

Laura did offer some entertainment to the class. Bates finally emerged from behind his desk in order to get a better look up her skirt and down her blouse. Everyone in that class of seniors knew what he was doing, except for Laura, who seemed oblivious or silently enjoyed it. There were times when I could actually feel my face flush and my temperature rise. I damned Laura at the same time I loved her, and thought of how stupid I had been to temporarily give her up for Linda Martinsen in my future plans. Laura had recaptured my mind and she went everywhere with me. To compound difficulties, she would even talk to me before class, usually about the assignment she had forgotten to read, in the event of a pop quiz. It probably didn't matter – she could have turned in a blank exam and aced it. Good old Bates!

With all my loving devotion, it took only a week before my infinite passion had turned to animosity, a previously not remotely considered possibility. It began at lunch on Tuesday, a week after she had transferred into eighth hour. As usual, Jerry and I were voicing our fantasies about various girls – what we'd do to Sally Jameson if . . . . I had never told Jerry about my night with Mary Harker, which made our game seem like so much drivel, but I still played along so I wouldn't totally alienate my best friend.

Jerry kept bringing some gross magazine from his brother Paul. During lunch, we'd sit across the table from each other so that he could quietly read his latest craving. He'd read absurd stories (also available on 8mm films) about Dick the Plumber and his cast-iron wrench, and all the perverted things he'd do on his daily house calls. Since Dick usually worked in the kitchen, there was a multitude of stories involving whipped cream, pickles, mayonnaise, cucumbers, and even olives. Then we'd add our own details with local girls. I had to secretly confess an interest, though I tried to play it semi-cool.

We had just talked Diane Kyrk into dancing on our kitchen table top when I felt a tap on my shoulder. It was Laura. I was too shocked to blush, but still conscious enough to feel Jerry's kick under the table.

"Kelly, could I speak to you alone for a minute?" she asked meekly, as though troubled by something only I could cure. It was a major step toward our first destined night of passion.

"Sure, Laura," and I got up, leaving a mesmerized Jerry Hogan.

We walked the length of the cafeteria, and my eyes pushed their peripheral vision to see who noticed us together. Unfortunately, we seemed to generate no interest. Laura faced me and gently placed her hand on my arm. Like Pavlov's dogs, I immediately began to salivate.

She spoke beseechingly. "Kelly, did you get Mr. Bates' library assignment done?"

I was still too enraptured to infer the intent of her question.

"Sure, Laura. I finished it last night."

She continued, using her best cheerleader captain smile. "Kelly, I had some problems at home. My mother got sick and I had to stay home to look after her. I couldn't get to the library, and I'm still missing three answers."

Her implication became clear, and I didn't like it. Bates

had given us twenty obscure questions that required us to use twenty different reference books. I had worked my tail off, skipping some lunches and spending two late nights in the city library. I had successfully completed it without help, and I was proud of my accomplishment. It had taken a solid eight hours of hard work, and Laura wanted to take five minutes to copy my answers. I loved the girl deeply, wanted to marry her and eventually father her children, but I wasn't sure if I was ready or willing to let her copy my homework!

"Why don't you tell Mr. Bates? I'm sure he'll give you some more time," I said with emphasis on the "you."

She had prepared for my answer. "I'm not sure when I'd be able to get it done. My mother's really sick, and I'm so upset that I don't know if I could even concentrate. Please, Kelly. I'll pay you back some time." Seduction had finally crept into her voice.

I thought I could see her eyes turn glassy, the way Mary Harker's and Ma's had, and I began to understand something of the weapons in a woman's arsenal. Women didn't fight fair with me – at the first appearance of tears, they usually won.

"Sure, Laura. It's in my notebook. Bring your paper over and you can copy them."

I started to turn but she grabbed me, panicky. "It's in my locker upstairs. Why not just give me your paper and I'll return it to you before class."

I didn't like her implication – she didn't have any of the answers. She was using me because she felt I was the most vulnerable. She felt that I would welcome the opportunity to assist the lady in distress. I saw through her façade but not through my own gullibility.

I returned to the table like a prisoner walking his last mile. It deeply hurt. Reluctantly I gave her the results of my hard labor. She thanked me and hurried out the door. Jerry was perched like a rattlesnake about to uncoil.

"What she want, Elliott? She going out with ya'?"

Jerry's face was so tense it looked like it would shatter in a breeze. It would have been easy to lead him astray, but I was too disheartened for games.

"She just wanted my homework. No big deal."

Jerry's face did shatter. "You mean she wanted to copy it? And you let her?"

"Yes, Jerry. I let her. Her mother was sick and she didn't get three of the answers."

He practically shouted, "Her mother was sick? You don't believe that, do ya'?"

I began to really dislike Jerry Hogan. He was the kind who would request a polka at a funeral.

"Yeah, Jerry, I believe her. And you would have, too. Besides, she said she'd pay me back."

The comment was meant to pacify his primeval cravings, but I did not wait for any reaction. His honesty was hurting as much as Laura's dishonesty.

Eighth hour finally arrived; I was pacing nervously in front of Bates' classroom door as I waited for Laura. She got to English just before the bell rang and after I had taken my seat. She smiled and winked at me as she sat, which helped alleviate some of the pain. I still wasn't content – her smile was the kind seen on a girl who had just cheated on her boyfriend with his best friend.

The bell rang and Laura took out her assignment. I waited for her to return mine, but she made no such motion. Bates had almost completed taking roll, which meant he would soon make his sweep around the room to collect assignments. I tapped her on the shoulder and whispered, "Laura. Do you have my paper?"

She furled her brow like she didn't know who I was or what I wanted. Then a panic spread across her face. She opened her folder and started ravaging through her mess of papers. After the initial check she still hadn't found it. Another quick search gave the same result. That once beautiful face turned with a look of shock. Her words came quickly and sharply enough to cause pangs in my heart.

"My God, Kelly. I loaned it to Brad Eveland for seventh

period. I forgot to get it back!"

I couldn't decide whether to suicide or to murder. Our marriage plans definitely ended at that point. I might have laid her to recompense for my missing paper, but I would never have been able to marry someone so irresponsible. If it had been her intent to screw me, she had done one hell of a job.

"Did you have something to tell the class, Miss LeDuc?"

It was the voice of doom. He hated to lose his absolute authority, even to Laura LeDuc.

"No, Mr. Bates. I'm sorry."

Anyone else, except Diane Kyrk, would have received an hour's detention. He let Laura off with a nod and a smile. The irresponsible slut!

Bates started at the other end of the room and began collecting the homework from the upper right hand corner of each desk. I sat like a frontal lobotomy experiment. He finally arrived at my desk, the only one without a paper.

"Where's your homework, Mr. Elliott?"

I waited for an eternity for Laura LeDuc to say something in my defense, but all I could see was the back of her head. Ironically, she was willing to sacrifice me so that people would not think of her as a cheater. I refused to believe that she would let me die.

"Well, Mr. Elliott, again, you are holding up the class."

I waited until my forehead began to sweat, but Laura was not going to help someone below her station at her expense. She was not the girl of any man's dreams.

"I left it at home, Mr. Bates."

A sneer crossed his face as he shook his head.

"You didn't do it, you mean. Very well, Mr. Elliott. That's one less for me to check. You may take the zero."

Laura had to speak up for me. She was the only one who could have helped. It wouldn't have been right for me to tell the truth. Why is it that if I had told the truth, I would have become the outcast? Still, the stone maiden did not move. Bates picked up her paper with my answers and proceeded with the class. Laura remained perfectly still, posture perfect, the entire period, never offering me even a profile. My fantasies had turned into nightmares, via Jack the Ripper.

When the final bell of the day sounded, Laura raced from the room. I sat, having expected her to offer some explanation and apology. She had descended from my queen list to my bitch list. Even Swedarsky had more ethics than to let someone take a bum rap. I realized how I had misjudged the proverbial book by its cover and extinguished Laura LeDuc from my life.

News did not take long to travel in our high school, the Shipstead-Winegarden affair being a prime example. At the end of the day I stood at my locker like a zombie. My mind was absolutely numb – I felt no malice; I felt nothing. I wasn't sure if I had been more stunned by seeing all of my homework go to waste or by watching my goddess disintegrate before my eyes. I asked myself what I really knew about Laura LeDuc, and if I should have been so shocked by her action. I guess I was appalled by the thought that even Swedarsky, who was the crudest slime ever created on God's Earth, would not have done what Laura LeDuc had done to me.

"Hey, Elliott, I heard Laura really put the thumb screws to ya'; I told ya' she was screwin' ya', didn't I?"

It was Jerry, of course, eager to humiliate a defeated cripple rather than to offer sympathy. I was surprised that he knew. School had only been over for twenty minutes.

"How'd you know, Jerry?"

"I went down to the locker room to get my gym stuff for tonight's intramural game. Brad Eveland was telling everyone about it." I felt relief that the news was out and hoped it reflected the truth. I couldn't stand the idea of returning to the status of senior class whipping boy.

"Was he bragging?" I asked, afraid of the answer.

"Nah, he felt kinda shitty about it. He said he didn't even know ya', but he's thinking about telling Bates the whole thing. Everyone is on Laura's case."

Brad Eveland was a track jock who seemed to be a decent human being, but I doubted that he'd take the rap and pull Laura down with him. Not for Kelly Elliott, anyway. I had little confidence in human nature, especially when it affected me. But I felt that my side was becoming stronger than Laura's, and upstaging her was no small feat.

"I'll see ya' later, Kelly. Why don't we plan something for Friday night. Maybe we can catch a flick or something."

He was trying to be kind, for once. "Yeah, sure, Jer. Thanks for telling me. See ya' later."

I turned back to my locker and mentally went over the books to take home, allowing for some study time in first period study hall. Realizing what all my hard work on Bates' research assignment earned for me, I threw in all my books. They would graduate me, no matter what. I was a senior without a police record.

"Hello, Kelly," said a feminine voice.

I anticipated Laura with an apology, but it wasn't Laura – it was Linda Martinsen. She hadn't said a word to me, even in chemistry class, since the "Night of the Gross Rubbers." Disappointment was quickly replaced with welcome relief. At least Linda was honest. She spoke meekly, her books clutched to her chest.

"I'm really sorry about what happened in English today, Kelly. Everyone pretty much knows what really happened. It's not fair."

It felt so good to hear her voice again and to just look at her. It really felt great.

"Thanks, Linda. Jerry said the word was spreading, but I assume you didn't hear about it in the boys' locker room. "

I had meant to get a smile from her, but she lowered her head, as though afraid of me. "No, I didn't."

"Where then?" I pushed, feeling that she was hiding something. I had had enough games for one day. She would not look me in the eyes, that ominous signal once again.

"Laura's locker is in the same hallway, just a few down

from mine. You know, she's an 'L' and I'm an 'M.' I eavesdropped."

Praying that Laura was feeling some remorse, I had to choke on my next question. "Did she say she was sorry for what happened or have any guilt?"

There was still no direct eye contact from Linda. I feared the worst, almost becoming weak in the knees.

"Well, not exactly."

The sickening tightness I had felt in Bates' class was returning. "What did she say?"

Linda looked like a scolded child, and I could see how difficult it was for her to tell me the truth, but I knew she wouldn't lie.

"She was sort of bragging. You know."

"Bragging?" I shouted, drawing stares from the few malingering students. "What do you mean she was bragging? What did she say?"

Linda could not look at me, feeling as much pain as I felt. She was the innocent victim of circumstances she had not created, but my ire was difficult to control and had unintentionally trapped her. She spoke quickly and I began to regret that I was venting my anger on Linda. That's what the Kelly Elliotts of the world were for.

"It was just her cheerleading friends. Nobody else listened. You know how that clique is."

"What did she say, Linda?" I pressed, sure that she regretted ever renewing our speaking relationship.

"She said that she had given you some story about her sick mother, and that she had actually spent the week with her college boyfriend at his frat house, drinking and stuff. You know."

Her last "you know" painted a devastating, unhappy picture in my mind, and my numbness returned. Seeing no visible reaction, Linda continued, like a doctor telling his patient that his time had almost run out.

"Honest, Kelly. No one but her cheerleading morons even listened. Everyone else thought she was a rat. Trust me,

Kelly. It's a side of her that nobody on the outside of her clique has seen before, and now people are starting to think she's a real creep. You never saw her before, Kelly. Not on the inside, anyway."

I had to know, like a masochist. "Did they laugh?"

The long pause was sufficient answer.

"Only her group, Kelly. They live in a different world from ours. We're not invited. You know that. They use anyone for what they need. Anyone who lets them. Anyone who wants some of their phony social status. We, you and me, aren't meant for people like Laura LeDuc. Every time we cross the line, we get hurt. They're on top because they're pretty or athletic or rich. We're in the middle and always will be, but our place is actually better. Just forget the whole incident, Kelly. About 80% of the school will know who the real Judas was. Be glad about that."

There was another sustained silence as she waited for me to respond. My mind was less concerned about my image to the upper crust than to Linda. I was concentrating on what she had said about crossing lines. I had been a fool to waste my time fantasizing about Laura LeDuc – the pert, blonde, and beautiful cheerleader with more outward class and finesse than anyone I had ever met. Fantasies were never meant to happen or they wouldn't be fantasies.

"I'll see you later, Kelly," and Linda started down the hall, her head bowed like the ancient Roman messengers. Linda was my kind.

"Linda, wait!"

She stopped and looked back at me. I slammed my locker shut after grabbing my chemistry book. An uncertainty in her face had appeared; the face of the punished child had returned. I strode determinedly to her.

"Can I buy you a coke?"

A slight smile appeared. "Sure."

We went to a nearby Walgreens and sat in a booth sipping two cherry cokes. The words came easily. Eventually, the conversation led to our first tragic date and I explained about the car I had borrowed and forever sealed the subject of the "Night of the Gross Rubbers." Linda actually laughed and confessed her fear, anger, and disappointment at the time. She even understood my lying about the car, but made me promise not to lie to her again. She didn't lie to me about Laura's comments, even knowing how hurt I would be, and she didn't tell me in order to maliciously hurt my feelings either. It was easy to make a promise, but I wasn't sure how that would play out in reality.

I walked Linda to a nearby bus stop and waited with her for the southbound bus. We had talked for more than an hour, and the hypocrisy of Laura LeDuc was soon behind me. Linda was right – it was being accepted by my own kind that was important. Some day I would be able to look down at those others with the same contempt that I felt now and be able to break that invincible aura that protected the elite. Laura LeDuc had actually done me a favor · a real wake-up call to reality. Thanks, Laura!

We made a date for Friday night just as Linda's bus arrived. She waited at the back of the long rush hour line, willing to surrender a seat in order to talk longer with me. Our eyes spoke a new and comfortable language.

I edged up the line with her, and before she stepped into the bus, she reached up and we kissed. It seemed perfectly natural, and on the way home I relived all those awkward moments of our first date – of how absurdly I had acted when reaching across her in a vain attempt to put my arm around her. I relived the very real terrors and anxieties of those moments and felt foolish. Our first kiss was over in a second, but it gave me an elation I had never felt before. Unlike my night with Mary Harker, there was no trepidation accompanying my joy. I wasn't in love again like I thought I had been with Laura LeDuc or Mary. I just felt good. Laura LeDuc had been pretty much purged from my mind, and I didn't even care.

CHAPTER 10

Sex, Baseball, and the Return of "The Thing"

When I got home that evening, Ma was sitting at the kitchen table, smoking a rarely seen cigarette, and blankly staring at the radiator. Nothing was said about my lateness. Nothing was said at all. I knew immediately what the problem was. We ate our pizza supper in relative silence. I mentioned having a date with Linda on Friday night, but she only acknowledged with a "That's nice." I was sure that she hadn't heard a word I said, and I was ready to confess posing nude for a gay porno magazine, but I didn't want to antagonize an already delicate situation.

After supper I retired to my desk in the bedroom and started my chemistry homework, but that night I could not balance an equation under any circumstances. I felt an ominous giant pounding at the door of our lives; it was a premonition stronger than my usual paranoid instincts. This time there was something important – something dangerous. On the radio WLS played "Martian Melodies," but I had a difficult time laughing at Dickie Goodman that night. Ma sat in a hypnotized state, a constant highball at her side, staring at the television screen.

At 9:45 the telephone rang, and I let Ma pick up the receiver in the kitchen. Anxiety twisted my insides as I waited for her to pick it up after the seventh ring. I tiptoed to the bedroom door to try to hear the conversation. Ma's voice was as tense as the atmosphere of the evening.

"No, Dan. No. It's over. Just stay the hell away from me!"

A long silence followed. "No, Dan! Don't bother!"

She was almost screaming and I could hear that her voice

was about to crack from the strain.

"Well, I won't be here!"

She slammed down the receiver and stomped back to the couch. Not able to bear the suspense any longer, I went to her. She was sitting on the couch, her legs folded under her, an empty glass in her hand, and tears leaking from the corners of her eyes. At that moment she reminded me of the pathetic figure of Ginny Dare huddled on the hallway floor of the Swan Hotel, but it still didn't seem quite right to compare my own mother to a stripper. Still, I had a certain kind of love for both of these women, and I wanted to help. I knelt beside her on the couch.

"What's wrong, Ma?" I asked softly.

There was a silence, but I could tell that her mind was planning a scheme to overcome the dilemma. She was a woman never to be outdone. Besides me, she and Mary Harker shared a common bond. Surprisingly, her voice was strong and determined.

"Kelly, I'm going to Aunt Amy's Friday night to spend the weekend. I'd like you to come with me."

The son-of-a-bitch was actually going to pay a weekend visit, even after knowing that his wife had called. My previous wishes became stronger as I hoped his plane really would crash, but then again I began to feel guilty for all the innocent people who would be killed. Could a plane crash and just the pilot die? My mind was working strangely then, and I wasn't positive that I liked the change.

I spoke angrily. "He's coming here, isn't he? That bastard is coming here to see you."

The word "bastard" hardened her face. She glowered at me as she back-handed me with a sharp slap. I was too stunned to feel the pain. It had been so long since she had actually struck me, but it hurt.

I sat staring at the back of the sofa, unsure of how to react. Then I heard her weeping. My mother rarely openly cried, but something had obviously stabbed her deeply. Instinctively, I threw my arms around her. We sat for a few moments while my mother wept her pain. The slap was forgotten and I felt sorry for her.

"It'll be all right, Ma. Don't worry about anything. I'm here. It'll be all right."

I had never thought of me taking care of my mother; it had always been the other way. I wasn't sure if the feeling stemmed from the malice I felt for Dan Phillips or the recent occurrences in my own life. The series of life's dominoes were continuing their cascade. Ma looked at me, her face red and streaked with tears, but her composure returning.

"I'm sorry I slapped you, Kelly. I didn't think. You're right, of course – he is a bastard. We can take the 4:40 train to Wheaton on Friday and come back on the 2:30 on Sunday. I'll call Amy now."

Her edict meant that I'd have to cancel my date with Linda, but I knew Linda would understand, as long as I was truthful.

One desperate ploy. "Okay, Ma. Let me call Linda first and tell her that something came up. She won't mind." I started for the phone but was stopped short.

"Linda? Who's Linda?"

I knew she hadn't heard a word all night, and I wished that I had told her that I had posed nude for a gay porno magazine. How often did a guy get to tell his mother something like that without severe reprisal?

"Linda Martinsen. The girl I took out a few weeks ago. I mentioned her at supper. We made a date for Friday, but we can go out next weekend. N.P." (N.P. was our standard abbreviation for "no problem.")

Suddenly she was very interested. Knowing my mother, she was probably waiting for me to bring Linda home. She grabbed my hand so I couldn't escape her interrogation.

"Tell me about her, Kelly. Is it serious?"

I was surprised at the idea of our relationship being "serious," but I got comfortable and related the lengthy story. At least it took her mind off her problems. Mary Harker had taught me to "keep talking," and I found that the tactic worked equally well with my mother. Besides, I enjoyed talking about Linda. As with Mary, I began hesitantly, unsure of how much I dared to relate. Within an hour I had told her the entire truth, from my initial ticket on Muffler Mulhouse's car to the "Night of the Gross Rubbers." Of course, I didn't think she was ready for the detailed Mary Harker saga. I thought she might be offended, but at the rest of the story she laughed like a psychotic drunk, and I found myself again laughing at the absurdity of the evening.

By the time I finished, Ma was beaming. Despite the terrible threat of Dan Phillips hanging over her head, she was almost radiant. It was as though she had found something to be proud of in me, but I could not detect what it might be.

"Kelly, I didn't realize I had such a resourceful son. I'm sorry I missed so much of your adventuresome life. Please forgive me for that. Listen, I can go to Amy's by myself. Why don't you go out with Linda, who you'll have to bring home some day. I'll be fine."

I didn't want to leave her alone; not then.

"No, Ma. I'll go. Linda and I can go out next weekend. There's nothing that . . . "

"Kelly, I want you to go out with Linda Friday night. I'd feel bad if you were bored at Amy's when you could be enjoying yourself with what I'm sure is a delightful young woman."

Wow! "Young woman" no less. Her voice was determined and excited, as though she were digressing to her own high school days.

"It's important that you have your date. It's important to you. It's important to me. You'll be out of school in a couple of months, and you may not have the chance to see her for a while."

It felt impossible to desert Ma during the time when I could be of the most use. I was adamant.

"No, Ma. I want to be . . ."

"Kelly, don't argue. Amy will be there and there's nothing

for you to do. That bastard has already screwed up my life; I'm not going to let him mess up my son's life, too. Just don't let him in the apartment if he does try. Now go out with Linda on Friday night."

I could tell that she would derive more pleasure from my dating Linda than by my accompanying her to Wheaton. Besides, I very much wanted to be with Linda as soon as possible.

"Okay," I agreed, and the subject was closed.

On Thursday Linda verified our date, although she mentioned that her father wasn't too pleased. He had vivid recollections about the boy who had broken the law and sent his daughter home in tears. She felt that it might be better if we met someplace, and I was more than happy not to have to face the scrutiny of Ward Cleaver again.

When I got home from school on Friday, there was a note and a twenty dollar bill on the kitchen table. Beside them was a sealed envelope. The note gave instructions to not open the door but to slip the envelope under the door to Dan Phillips, "if that bastard should have the nerve to show up." Since I opened that can of worms, Ma had become rather liberal with her use of the word "bastard." I knew Ma would be all right, so I began to plan my evening. Just the idea of having the apartment to myself for the entire weekend was exciting, and my wheels began to turn. I quickly washed the dishes, vacuumed the rug, and cleaned everything in sight. Subconsciously, I suppose I was attempting to create the proper atmosphere. For what, I wasn't sure. I had seen too many romantic movies.

Digging through the record cabinet, I took out a few of Ma's Frank Sinatra L .P.'s, throwing in her only Mantovani instrumental album for good measure. It seemed corny as hell, but that level of the game called for specific rules. Linda seemed to be an old-fashioned girl. I usually listened to the radio and took little interest in building my own record collection. Ma's would be just fine.

Too nervous to eat, I checked the refrigerator out of habit.

There sat a half bottle of Mogen David concord grape wine and two cans of Schlitz. Wheels kept turning and I was surprised at my growing confidence. If events went perfectly, and I actually was able to get her to my place, maybe . . . I had learned not to get too carried away with plans, but still.

Linda was waiting in front of the Rockne Theatre as I got off the bus. We were going to a double feature horror show. One of them was the movie I had seen with Ma the week before, but I had let Linda select the movie. I was glad she had chosen horror films – it would afford me an excuse for putting my arm around her, not that I needed one anymore. Girls were supposed to go crazy at horror films and grab their dates for security. I was all for that. I had gotten my feet wet, but I hadn't yet dived in. Any help was welcome, even if it came from Vincent Price.

The other movie was titled *Mr. Sardonicus*. It was a William Castle film about some guy who was so frightened at the sight of an opened grave that his facial muscles permanently froze and he always had a huge, terrifying grin. Every tooth and most of his gums protruded, and he scared the hell out of anyone in the movie who saw him without his mask. Mummies would have feared Mr. Sardodnicus. Seeing that eternal smile I couldn't help but think what a perfect husband he would have made Laura LeDuc. They could have gone through life together, always smiling, and spreading misery wherever they went. The perfect couple. Rah! Rah!

Before the movie started, I bought Linda a box of jujubes, small, fruit-flavored, soft candies that everyone loved. I started to laugh as we took our seats and she opened the box. I had to relate the story of my former best friend.

When I was eight years old, my best friend, Jeff Frey, was known as "Melonhead," because the back of his head stuck out like a cantaloupe. He claimed the deformity was brains and that he was actually quite intelligent. Everyone else knew better.

Melonhead and I always went to the Saturday matinees together and had a great time. Once he bought a box of jujubes. During the movie, *Abbott and Costello Meet the Mummy*, for some inexplicable reason, he stuck the trapezoid shaped candy up his nose. Soon he began to nudge me and there was real panic engraved on his face.

"Kelly, I got a jujube stuck in my nose, and I can't get it out!" Melonhead was scared.

I had absolutely no choice but to roar out loud. I got a side ache from laughing so hard. It was a good thing that it was a Saturday matinee, because only kids were there. Adults would have had us thrown out. When I somewhat regained my composure, I looked at Melonhead, who was still pinching his left nostril in a vain attempt to extract the candy.

"It's not funny, Kelly. I can't get it out. Should I tell the manager?"

It was too much and I resumed my hysterical convulsions. The picture of an eight-year-old kid going up to the crotchety old manager and saying, "Excuse me, sir, but I have a jujube stuck in my nose" was too much to bear in silence. I grabbed my side to alleviate the pain.

Melonhead stormed up the aisle and returned five minutes later. I never asked him how he got it out, but our friendship was never quite as close after the incident. I did ask him if he ate it, and he moved to a different seat. So much for the brain power of Melonhead, and so much for eight-year-old best friends.

Linda went insane over the story, and we shared a comfortable feeling with each other for the rest of the evening. During the movie I had my arm around Linda while she occasionally popped a jujube into my mouth, whispering afterwards that she had marinated it in her nose, which caused both of us to burst into muted laughter. After an hour, my hand draping over her shoulder went totally numb. I could have driven spikes through my hand without pain. Still, I was not about to move it, just as I had suffered when my foot had rested under Laura LeDuc's luscious derriere.

Once my hand even dropped down to Linda's right boob and my fingers lightly grazed the surface of her cotton dress.

I cursed my luck at having no feeling in my fingertips at such a key moment, as Linda did not seem to mind my graceless intrusion. Occasionally, she grasped my left hand when a scary part came on, and I derived some satisfaction from the small intimacy. Still, a hand squeeze was not as good as a breast fondle. It was an unwritten law of mankind.

As the second movie started to get toward the end, my mind left the screen and focused on the apartment. My anxiety over whether she would go there caused my heart to quicken and my forehead to sweat, but I would not relinquish Linda's hand to wipe my brow. It was the longest conclusion to a movie I had ever sat through, especially considering the fact that I had already seen it.

The movie ended by ten and Linda had a midnight curfew. We had two hours, and social custom dictated a pizza and a slow ride home. It was my time of resolution. We stood outside the theatre on a warm spring evening. Everyone was in a good mood now that the last vestiges of snow had vanished. I prayed that the atmosphere would permeate Linda's being. I tried to act nonchalant, concentrating on preventing my voice from cracking.

"Linda, would you like to go to my place for a nightcap?"

Joe Cool – I had seen it done in the movies hundreds of times, but at seventeen some of the suaveness was absent.

"What do you mean by a 'nightcap'?" she asked, warily.

She was hedging and I was unsure of the proper response. Our previous mutual easiness had digressed to our first pre-date jitters. I could hardly tell her that I had wine in the refrigerator, and that I hoped to get her tipsy and on the couch. I didn't want to bang her or anything – I wasn't really sure what I wanted, but my natural masculine instincts told me that I should get her alone on a couch as the next stage of our relationship. The term "making-out" dominated my mind

"Oh, you know. I have some coke, or my mom has some Mogen David in the fridge."

I thought to impress her by label-dropping. At school the drinkers always boasted about getting wasted on

Thunderbird, but I thought I'd bring in a little class.

"Does your mother allow you to drink wine?" She was perplexed.

I hadn't planned on her mentioning my mother, and it temporarily threw me off guard. I also remembered my promise not to lie to her again.

"Sometimes. We drink Mogen David with dinner on Sunday." It was time to disclose the make-or-break point. "Besides, my mother's gone for the weekend."

I watched her reaction but could detect none. Her mind must have been moving faster than mine. She appeared to be looking for an answer on the sidewalk that she kept staring at.

"Your mother is gone for the whole weekend?"

I nodded affirmatively. "All weekend, but I'll be a perfect gentleman."

Another quick search of the street. "Okay, let's go."

I could hardly withhold my elation and I felt like Mr. Sardonicus; I just hoped that I didn't look like him. "Don't worry, Linda. We'll get you home by curfew." I felt like I was working on a jigsaw puzzle and had just finished the frame; now I had to fill ln all the pieces.

Grabbing a bus, we were at the apartment by 10:30. I unlocked the door and stumbled through the darkness in order to turn on a muted table lamp, blocking-out the glaring ceiling light. Mood was crucial, and a glaring hundred watt bulb was not conducive. I had thought about candles but figured that was overstepping the bounds of suave seduction.

"Let me take your coat. Have a seat."

She sat on the couch and I draped her coat over the armchair. It was a move to make that chair inaccessible. This was the minor league for me, a place to start.

Having previously placed five "easy listening" LP's on the stereo, I casually turned it on. The increased tension as I approached the "moment of truth" made me want to hit the bathroom before things became too involved. I turned up the volume so that she wouldn't hear me splash. Noise like that could definitely curtail a romantic mood. I was learning the logical rules of the game quickly; my only concern was how much of the game Linda knew. It's possible she had dated hundreds of guys, or I might have been her first.

When I returned from the delight afforded by the bathroom, Linda had removed her shoes and was sitting on the couch, her legs folded under her, like my mother sat. Good sign or bad sign? She looked ready for anything – offensively or defensively. It would have been nice if she had been naked and straddling the coffee table – even I would have been reasonably confident of my interpretation of her body language.

"Would you like a glass of Mogen David, Linda?" What girl could say "No" to Mogen David?

"Just a little, Kelly. My dad will kill me if I have liquor on my breath."

Everything was going too easy. I turned down the volume on the stereo to a more acceptable decibel level for seduction, and went to the kitchen for the wine. Cursing my misfortune at not having two stemmed wine glasses, I had to use two jelly glasses decorated with purple grape clusters. It was as tacky as humanly possible, but I hoped that she'd assume that the grape clusters indicated that they were real wine glasses. I poured each of us a half glass and returned to the living room, where Linda sat like a victim awaiting an assault.

"Here's how," I said as we clinked glasses. It was an ungraceful toast for the setting, but I really had not planned on getting so far. We sipped from our glasses and I was surprised that it actually tasted pretty good.

"It's good," she said, but what else could she say?

What had been relatively easy to that point was about to become increasingly difficult. I only had about forty-five minutes to conclude my stratagems, and I just wished that I had planned more thoroughly. My mind raced through all the Bogart films I had seen at the Brighton Theatre festivals, and I decided that the only reason he was able to score so easily was that the script called for it, and the director told him what to do next. Chicago was not Casablanca, and Linda was not Lauren Bacall. We were two seventeen-year-old kids sitting on a couch, and I wished like hell that I had a director, even Hitchcock, to tell me what to do next.

We sat in silence, ironically listening to "As Time Goes By" and sipping wine, as the clock hurled me toward another gutless failure. The opportunity would not present itself like this again for an eternity – of that much I was sure.

The awkward silence was broken when Linda said, "Kelly, I have to use your bathroom." I debated telling her to turn the volume back up on the stereo.

"Sure, Linda. It's right there," as I pointed to the door just down the short hallway. She got up gracefully, pulling her skirt down like a lady.

The time had arrived! How was I to get her closer to me? How would I be able to get my arms around her without throwing myself across her body? What signs would she give that would allow me to proceed to the next stage? My speculations were interrupted by the coarse sound of Linda's going to the bathroom. I snickered at the irony of it and realized that I had control of the elements. It was a home game; I just had to use the advantage correctly.

I had to get her to lie down on the couch. If I was lying down when she returned, what would she do? It was not intimidating enough to frighten her to hysterics. She wouldn't want to seem frigid and sit in the arm chair. With a half hour to go on "Beat the Clock," I had to move, not think.

I grabbed our wine glasses and rushed to the kitchen. Neither of us had had more than a sip. Instinctively, I poured mine down the sink and refilled it, adding just a drop to her glass. Like a waiter at his finest hour, I waited until I heard my customer returning to her table. Walking out at the same time, I put our glasses on the table and sat in the middle of the couch.

"I really shouldn't have any more, Kelly."

"Mine was empty, so as long as I was filling it, I thought

I'd just top off your glass, too." I hadn't lied and she bought the story and sat next to me without comment on my sudden shift of position. We clicked glasses again, sipped, and sat in silence for another minute. Finally I put my left arm around her shoulders as I had during the movies. This time she grabbed my draped hand and held it.

After another thirty seconds of mental turmoil, Linda spoke. "So, are you going to kiss me, Kelly, or are we just going to sit here?"

My God! Did I hear that right? It hadn't dawned on me that maybe she wanted to "make-out" too. Girls weren't supposed to think in those terms, were they? I had assumed it was the man's role to seduce the woman with overwhelming temptation. She had been as uncomfortable as me, sipping that wine in silence. I had been a real fool again, but then Linda saved me from complete humiliation.

I moved a bit too fast toward her waiting lips and we lightly bumped teeth. We puckered and kissed with an increasing passion, not like the bus stop kiss. After a short while, I swore I could feel her take the lead and we gradually leaned into the couch and onto our sides.

"Mind if I take the inside, Kelly?"

You have to be kidding me! This girl's been around, I thought as I gratefully followed her lead. In the background, Frankie was crooning "Fly me to the Moon." It was just like in the movies only we didn't smoke. It felt comfortable to lie there with Linda, smashing our faces together. It became time to consider my next move. I was content but I speculated on my disappointment in the morning if I hadn't tried something more.

Swedarsky and Curtis had been talking in the locker room about their alleged sexual conquests, comparing them to a baseball game, the object being to hit a homerun every time at bat. Curtis, who was a greaser but had the reputation of a stud, said that he concentrated on baseball when the excitement of sexual entanglement began to propel him to an early finish. He boasted of the powerful feeling it gave him to be "grinding pelvises" while visions of Ernie Banks at the plate dashed through his mind. Probably something to do with the bat as a phallic symbol. One time he claimed to have emulated Cubs' game announcer Jack Brickhouse and yelled, "Hey! Hey!! It's outta' here!" at the moment of climax. The whole conversation seemed a bit ridiculous at the time, but it was my only reference point at that moment.

I looked down at Linda, who had worked her way completely underneath me.

We kept kissing and were soon "grinding pelvises," as Curtis had so elegantly phrased it. Linda put her hands to the back of my head, her fingers in my hair, pulling me tighter. Then something seemed to intrude on our privacy – something other than Linda's lips was between our mouths. I wanted to open my eyes to see what the hell was happening, but assuming that I was in control, I was supposed to be omniscient.

It seemed an eternity before I realized that the interloper was Linda's tongue pushing on my teeth. It was step two of the kissing procedure – Frenching. Everyone at school called it "swapping spit," and I wasn't sure of its purpose. I only knew that I was supposed to yield my incisors and allow the slimy, alien object into my mouth. I saw no sexiness in Frenching, but it seemed to be the next required step, so I parted my teeth slightly. I was grateful not to have a large overbite, or I would have felt ridiculous.

Linda stuck her tongue deeply into my mouth and ran it across the back of my upper teeth. I prayed that there were no popcorn hulls stuck. What the hell was I supposed to do with Linda's tongue in my mouth? Was I supposed to suck on it? That seemed a little odd, but I knew I could not just lie there without reacting. The woman seemed to have experience and expected some in return. My animal instincts gave no clue – my logical mind would not allow them.

Slowly I moved my tongue around hers, and I felt her tongue retreat into her mouth. Had I offended her or was I supposed to chase it? She didn't even seem upset and emitted a slight moan. Charge! I stuck my tongue deep into her mouth and mimicked her dental cleaning drill. Finding those movements more stimulating as I realized the parallel implication to the actual sex act, I became impassioned and let my glands control my mind. As appreciative as I was of her response, my tongue and its routine grew exhausting.

One thing that was not getting tired was the erection pushing at the crotch of my pants. I cursed the fact that I wore jockey shorts, which kept me imprisoned and in pain. On Monday I would change to boxer shorts so that any future activity would allow my good friend some breathing room to roam. I also wondered if Linda could feel some discomfort with all this pelvis grinding we were doing.

Having rounded second base (Frenching and preliminary petting), third base became clear to me. After "swapping spit" and grinding pelvises came heavy petting. Although she was lying on my contorted left arm, my right was free to explore, if I dared. Events were moving too rapidly, and I hesitated ruining a perfect evening. But when would I ever get Linda in that position again? I had to "go for it." My hormones commanded me.

Slowly my hand slid up the side of her body until it was even with her breast. No signs of protest were apparent. I could even feel the gyrations quicken against me, and the discomfort in my pants became almost unbearable. Then it happened! Twang! Like a diver going off the high board, it had found its way through the passage of my jockeys. It was lying flat between us, like sandwich meat, and the cessation of pain turned to pure ecstasy as I started rotating my hips. She moaned and I lost my mind.

Without weighing the consequences any further, my mind slid to her breast, and I squeezed it like an orange. My first! It was soft and I squeezed it like Swedarsky trying to crush a golf ball. Linda pulled her head away, and I could see beads of perspiration on her forehead.

"Careful, Kelly. Not so rough. That hurts," she

commanded, then closed her eyes and pulled my head back to her anxious mouth.

I was so happy that she hadn't called me "filthy pervert" that I hardly noticed what she had said. We returned to our "love-making" and I continued to caress her breast, feeling hotter as we moved into a mutual rhythm.

My next goal was to touch her bare breast – to see her naked and to kiss them, but I didn't know how I could possibly get her dress off. Swedarsky and Curtis had skipped that rather important step. I would have to settle for cotton.

Linda's pelvis was grinding with more fervor, and I had a new feeling, like I had to relieve myself, only more urgent and better. I had masturbated rarely, from fear of being caught, but I knew what was happening to me. Ernie Banks had stepped into the batter's box to face Don Drysdale, and the Cubs needed a grand slam homerun.

With brief relief, I wanted to fondle both breasts. I freed my numb left hand and grabbed her, like someone playing a pinball machine. It was just as soft, and my desire to touch her skin drove me crazy.

She spread her legs and I settled between them. She moaned and I was lost. The more I rubbed on her, the better I felt. Sweat was dripping from my forehead and trickling down my cheek, which itched and forced me to relinquish a breast to wipe it. But I never missed a cadence in our motion. I was approaching climax, so I had Banks foul off a 3-2 pitch.

Then it happened! Linda's moans grew louder, and soon my sounds joined the harmony, just like Shipstead and Winegarden must have done in the library. I started to grind harder and faster. Our crescendo grew with our fervor, and Linda pulled back her head in an excited, yet muted scream. The dam broke, and I could feel my elation as I saw the ball leave Wrigley and bounce onto Waveland Avenue.

I buried my head so Linda couldn't see my contorted face, and let my system conclude its needs. I was exhausted and lay on Linda like a dead man. My first successful sexual experience, and I hadn't quite known the proper way to finish it. But God, it felt great!

Frankie had stopped singing some time during our passionate exchange, but bars of "That Old Black Magic" kept running through my head. I had no desire to move and did not care if anyone found us there. There was a buzzing in my head, and I assumed it was the post-coital bells of all lovers. What a night it had been! I had hit a homerun, though it had been inside the park.

"Kelly!" It was Linda's voice – not the tender and moaning of moments before, but one of alarm.

"Kelly, there's someone at the door. Your bell's ringing. Maybe it's your mom!"

She was scared and panicked, but I was somewhere between death and euphoria and could not have cared less. But she was right – the door buzzer was sounding like a madman was standing on our threshold. I tried to calm her.

"It's okay, Linda. My mom has her own key. She'd just let herself in."

Then I heard the key enter the lock and the bolt slide back. Like two teenagers caught in the act, we sat up and quickly straightened our rumpled clothing. My beige levis were stained in front, and I felt an uncomfortable stickiness clinging to my stomach. Linda pulled her dress down, and I averted my head. The real Kelly had returned. I did not care who was there – I was intoxicated. We sat watching the door, awaiting our intruder. It was Dan Phillips, looking cock-eyed drunk as he trespassed into our Eden.

"Hey, kid. How ya' doin'?" He was drunk as evident by his slurred words and sadistic smile. "I'm not breaking up anything, am I?"

My hands went to my crotch in an instinctive effort to cover the dark spot. I doubted that he saw the stain, but he did not miss the gesture.

"Getting a little, are ya', kid? What would your old lady think?"

He stared at Linda, who was more fearful of his drunken presence than his verbal implications.

"Nice lookin' girl, kid. Aren't ya' goin' to introduce us?"

He leered like the sick son-of-a-bitch he was and if I hadn't the wisdom to know that he could have hurt and embarrassed me even more, I would have knocked the bastard on his ass. For Linda's sake, as well, I tried to act cool but firm.

"We were just leaving. What do you want?"

Dan Phillips did not like my tone of voice and changed his leer into a sneer as he peered at me with malevolence.

"You know damn well what I want, you little prick. Where's your old lady?"

The menace in his voice made me angry, but fear and practicality dominated. I had to get Linda out of there as soon as possible. It had already been an embarrassing encounter. Physical harm would not make matters any easier.

"She's not here. You knew she wouldn't be. She told you she'd be gone for the weekend."

He knew that I was telling the truth, but his drunken obstinacy would not allow him to simply leave.

"Okay, kid. I'll wait."

He staggered into the kitchen and opened the refrigerator. I put my arm around Linda and squeezed her hand, but she was too terrified to react and remained frozen, watching the imposing threat of Dan Phillips. We heard the can opener bite through the lid of the beer can, and a moment later he was standing in the kitchen doorway, leaning against the frame, chugging his Schlitz. He still glared at us, trying to decide what to do with the extra baggage; then he belched loudly. Linda turned her head in disgust.

"There's only one more beer, kid. Get some more on the way home. It could be a long wait."

Anger was gradually surmounting my fear. I resented his intrusion and coarseness. Sanity pushed us toward the exit. "I'm too young to buy beer. You know that."

He smiled pompously, then chugged down the rest of the can. His eyes would not move from Linda's legs.

192

"That's right. You're still a child, aren't ya'? Didn't look like a couple of kids when I came in. Looks like you had your dipper in the honey pot. I mean, two kids . . ."

"Shut up, Phillips! Shut the fuck up or I'll call the cops and have them haul you out of here for trespassing. Just shut your goddamn mouth or I'll . . ."

He stomped at me and towered like the bear in Faulkner's story. I could smell his stink and sense his ire, but I didn't care any more. I was ready to fight.

"Don't you talk to me like that, you little punk, or I'll bust your goddamn face!" he roared as he poked his finger at me; I wanted to bite the damn thing off.

"Kelly," Linda broke in, "I don't feel good. Please take me home now."

Tears had formed in her eyes. For a moment I almost wished that she hadn't been there to intervene. I was ready for Phillips, no matter the consequences. He had so enraged me by that time that I honestly felt I could have taken the drunken bastard and was sure that some day I would kill him.

Regaining partial control, I said, "Sure, Linda. I'm sorry. Come on. I'll take you home."

Phillips's fire had waned somewhat and he backed away to allow us through. I steered Linda away from him, avoiding any further eye contact with my nemesis.

"Come with me, Linda. I have to get my wallet before we go."

I did not want to leave her alone with Phillips, and I led her to the bedroom, locking the door behind us.

We spoke in whispers, "Are you okay, Linda?"

The tears in her eyes were about to burst forth. I held her chin, forcing her to look at me. Like my mother, she was strong and would not concede to her true despair.

"Yeah, I'm okay. Just scared. You know."

I could see that she would be all right and kissed her gently on the mouth. She threw her arms around me for strength, and I found myself stronger. At that moment I needed nothing else.

"I'm embarrassed, Linda, but I don't have any time to think of something clever to say. I need to change my pants. Then we have to get you home. It's 11:30." Her eyes opened wide.

"Eleven-thirty! God, my dad will kill me! It'll take us at least a half hour to get home."

I was in control. "It'll be okay. We'll call and say the movie got out late. We'll be a half hour late. He won't mind. After what you've been through tonight, a mad father will seem like a cake walk. Sit on the bed while I get some clean clothes."

Luckily I had not picked her up at her house. No doubt her eagle-eyed father would have noticed the change of pants, and that would have made the road impassable. I had to change, in case he decided to have one of his Ward Cleaver talks with me. The stain was evident. I began to unzip when I realized that Linda was sitting there like a member of an audience.

"Ah, Linda, would you mind turning your head for a second?"

It seemed like a ridiculous request after we had just finished dry humping on the couch, but I was somewhat embarrassed at removing my pants in front of her. She seemed to understand and graciously turned her head while I backed into an opposite corner. I changed as fast as I could, not wanting to be naked in the same room for any longer than necessary. I quickly cleaned myself with the already soiled shorts. I would have to remember to throw them out before Ma found them. In spite of my newly found strength, I also felt very vulnerable.

Cleaned and dressed, I took a firm hand and led Linda out of our sanctuary. She returned the reassuring pressure for support, but I was no longer afraid. The worst was over.

Dan Phillips sat in front of the television, staring blankly at an old Cagney movie. It seemed a sacrilege.

"We're leaving. Ma won't be home until late Sunday. You

may as well go."

He craned his head, a drunken stupor overtaking his viciousness. "I got no place to go, kid. I'll just wait here for her."

Knowing that it was impossible to rationalize with the drunken bastard, we began to leave, after we shared a quick wash in the bathroom; that, too, was weird.

"Kid."

I had no desire to turn back, but the tension was absent from his voice. Leaving Linda at the doorway, I went to him. He fumbled in his pocket and withdrew some keys.

"Here. You can take my rental. It's a blue Plymouth parked down by the Beer Depot."

I waited for some smart-ass comment about the rubbers being in the glove compartment, but he remained silent. It almost seemed like an apologetic gesture, and I wondered if all animals had a compassionate side. Perhaps for the first time I was witnessing the element in him that had attracted my mother. I took the keys and we left.

There was a light spring rain in the air, and it felt cleansing after the night we had spent together. We walked briskly to the corner store, feeling rushed not by the rain but by the fear of her father's wrath. We were almost to the car when I had one of my rare flashes of brilliance – the kind I usually got when I was alone. We entered the Beer Depot.

Little Joey sat in his corner, counting his receipts, preparing to close for the night. He seemed pleased to see me with a nice girl, and I introduced him to Linda, whose hand he shook. Explaining most of our situation, I asked him for a slight favor. He obliged as he dialed Linda's phone number. He spoke ln an articulate voice that I did not know he possessed, but which had probably been part of him before his tragedy.

"Hello, Mr. Martinsen? This is Mr. Moscotti, manager of the Rockne Theatre. We had some projector problems here tonight, and the show ran a little later than scheduled. I have two young people here who were caught up in the misfortune and feared that you would be angry with them concerning the young lady's curfew. They asked me to call and explain the situation. He seems like a nice young man, and I wouldn't want them to get into any trouble for our error."

There was a long silence as we waited for the reply. "Very well, Mr. Martinsen. It was no problem at all. Thank you and good night."

Linda sighed with relief. I was impressed with my ingenuity and assumed that she must have been, too. Little Joey got a charge from his impersonation and thanked us for affording him the opportunity to demonstrate some prowess.

As we left the store, Joe said, "Careful going home, kid. Kelly," and he smiled for the first time in a long time that I could remember.

Dan Phillips was probably bouncing off the walls, needing to buy some more beer and make good on his promise to wait as long as necessary. I made a mental note to call Ma and warn her. I had the uneasy feeling that he would not leave until he had seen her.

On the way home Linda snuggled on my shoulder and we rode in silence. I could feel her head jerk as she tried to conceal her tears. The night's tensions had reached her heart, and I wondered if she was crying about the crudeness of Dan Phillips or about the guilt she may have felt from our semi-sexual activity on the couch.

"Linda, are you okay about what happened at my place tonight?" I almost whispered.

"Yeah, I'm fine, Kelly. He just scared me a little, that's all. I'll be okay."

"I actually wasn't referring to Dan Phillips, Linda. I meant about what we did on the couch."

I could feel Linda's head turn up so that she was looking into my face. "Yeah, that was fine, Kelly. It's not like we went all the way or anything. I was a little surprised at first. You seemed to have been around the block a few times."

Was she kidding me? Me, around the block a few times?

"Why do you say that?"

She was getting less sad and more assertive. "Really, Kelly. Dim light, wine, mother gone, and Frank Sinatra albums stacked up and ready to play."

"I was that obvious, huh?" Maybe it was time for some more of that honesty I had promised. "Can I tell you something that you need to keep secret?"

"Of course, Kelly. We just shared an intimate moment followed by a violent interlude."

I hesitated, uncertain if this was the right track to take. "Actually, that was my first trip around the block."

I looked down at her and she broke into a huge smile. "Really, Kelly? Huh! Well, as long as we're sharing truths, that was my first trip around the block, too." Then she reached up and kissed me.

Fifteen minutes later we pulled up in front of her house, and I jumped out without any preliminaries. We kissed at the door and she embraced me. I felt that despite the evening's tribulations, everything was going to be all right.

On the way home I thought of how lucky I was to have her in my life. Could anyone have had two worse dates? Yet, she seemed to like our times together, and I felt sure that she would want to go out again with me. How many girls would respond so gently and willingly to some jerk who had put her through what I had? I wondered if we were an unofficial couple now. We had reached the maturation stage it took some couples months to achieve. I started to have stronger feelings for Linda. It wasn't the love I had once felt for Laura LeDuc – it cut deeper, and it made me feel good, not frustrated. The more I thought about it, the better I felt.

Subconsciously I had driven downtown and by the Swan Hotel. Mary Harker was due back soon, and I thought about stopping in to check on her. Maybe she would be able to verbalize my emotion. I wanted to tell someone I could trust. I was elated, but there were too many paradoxes – I shouldn't feel as good as I did. My first sexual encounter would have been labeled a failure by most guys, but I considered it a personal triumph. I didn't know if Mary held the answers, but I had no one to turn to for clarification. I drove past the hotel, not wanting to be too intrusive too soon.

When I got back to the apartment, Dan Phillips was snoring on the couch, answered by a static-filled television screen. Ma's letter lay torn and scattered like confetti on the floor beside him. I turned off the TV and went into the bedroom to retrieve my stained shorts. After stuffing them into my coat pocket, a base gesture, I quickly removed the wine glasses and, surprisingly, six empty beer cans from the coffee table. Phillips never moved. "Let sleeping dog lie," I thought.

Feeling unable to spend the rest of the night under the same roof with the bastard, I left. The rain was increasing and I lifted my face to absorb as much of the cleansing water as possible. It washed away the alleged sins and troubles of the night. Life was good. There was an important girl in my life. School was almost over. My mother would be fine. If life is a cycle, I was at my high points.

The Brighton Theatre had its usual late night crowd. Several winos could be heard snoring in the back rows. The theatre's in-house hooker also sat in the back, waiting for her usual customers. A young man with long hair, one of the current crop of "hippies," smoked a strange cigarette called a "reefer," shielding the glowing tip behind his cupped hands. For a change, I sat in the middle and watched the antics of Bob Hope, Bing Crosby, and Dorothy Lamour as they joked their way through the "Road to . . ." film festival. Two months before, I had cried during the Marx Brothers film. I was soaking wet and cold, but this time I only looked at the bigger-than-life silver screen and laughed. I was the only one in the theatre who did laugh and I just did not seem to care about anyone else, or what they might think.

CHAPTER 11

Giant Killing Again and Return to the Swan

From the moment I had told Swedarsky "up yours," events in my life had seemed to snowball, propelling me up and down hills with little regard for personal control. In a single day I could be on top of the universe, looking at my past with ecstasy, only to find myself in the deepest chasm of hell a moment later. Had I been wiser and able to vaguely analyze and prepare for my fate, I would have sought professional counseling, but at seventeen everything that happened was so unique that my curiosity kept me from insanity. I realized that I could not control the muses of life, but I still had to deal with the consequences. Ecstasy and despair were as common to me in a single day as morning and night · witness the week after Linda and I had semi-consummated our relationship.

We continued our congenial companionship at school, with me falling into the "I'll walk you to class" syndrome, then racing back through the halls to make it to my own classes on time. Our sexual liaison was never mentioned, though at times there was an uneasy silence during which we each seemed to be reliving that night. Some embarrassment and guilt forced us to continuously contemplate what we had done but stifled free expression between us. Both of us wanted to talk about it, but neither of us wanted to be the first to mention the subject. Although we hadn't gone "all the way," in the back of our minds it had seemed somewhat sordid, like something Dan Phillips would have done, and our sustained silent moments served as a mild penance.

Perhaps I owed Dan Phillips a small debt of gratitude for diverting the focus from our sexual encounter to his violent behavior. I thought Linda felt as I did · the opportunity probably wouldn't come again for a long time, so it was useless to feel guilt over a "maybe, if . . ."scenario. My emotions were confusing – I was elated that we had done it, and I wished that we hadn't. We had progressed another step, no matter how simple it may have seemed to most people, which had altered our lives forever. Did it count as being each other's "first"?

Life in school seemed to continue normally despite our secret, and I somehow felt cheated of a manhood debt owed me. Surely something in the routine school life should have been different to let us acknowledge or celebrate what we had done, but nothing unusual happened. The excitement of the Shipstead-Winegarden affair had ebbed to the point of nonexistence. There were no more pilgrimages to the library stacks, and that historic aisle began to collect dust again. References to the incident donned a literary quality. Guys would ogle girls and say, "How'd you like to Shipstead-Winegarden her?" It was an interesting metaphor which spread like influenza, and soon everyone was Shipstead-Winegardening all over the place. But the namesakes themselves became ghosts.

Laura LeDuc still posed in front of me, but she didn't have the nerve to look directly at me. Her golden hair was still hypnotic, but I would shatter my brief relapses by envisioning blood seeping between the strands; I really hated the bitch. Apparently word of Laura's indiscretion had spread through the faculty too, because Bates gave me the opportunity to write a substitute paper about anything for the missing grade. I wrote an essay to prove that Ernie Banks' influence extended beyond baseball. Of course, I left out the most important effect. I thought it had been pretty decent of him – I never thought that English teachers had any common sense or heart.

Jerry Hogan remained the eternal inquisitor. Under

pressure I mistakenly told him that Linda had gone to my place that complex Friday night, after my mother had left for the weekend. I believe it was a Freudian slip. His eyes lit up like Comiskey Park for a night game, and he began a non-stop interrogation for details. I knew that if I told Jerry anything, word would rapidly spread throughout the school, Linda would be labeled a "good date," and she would never speak to me again. I should have known Jerry better, and five minutes after my initial "slip" I regretted having hinted at anything. Still, I refused to give any of the intimate details, until Thursday, when I viciously snapped Swedarsky in the balls with a wet towel.

The gym class was in the locker room, drying after our mandatory showers, when Jerry pursued his inquisition.

"Come on, Elliott. How far'd ya' get? First base? Second? Third? You didn't hit a homerun your first time at bat, did ya'?"

I ignored him with a smile, from which he inferred a round-tripper.

"God, Elliott! How was it? Was she any good? Do you think she'd go out with me?"

I would have resented the vulgar comment from anyone else, but I knew that Jerry was incapable of intruding on anyone's relationship. He could only fantasize and drool, like I had always done.

"Jerry, I didn't score! We just went up to my place and made out a little, that's all!"

I did not dare tell him about even getting to second base, let alone my inside the park homerun. Still, he foamed like a rabid dog, standing naked, frozen like a Greek statue.

"How much is making out? Did you get in her blouse at least?" He had kept it up since Monday, and the pressure was about to crack me, when the voice of doom echoed from behind me.

"What's this, Elliott? You nail some broad this weekend? Wasn't that girl I saw you walk to class one day, was it? She could do much better. Who helped ya'?"

Of course, it was Swedarsky, grinning like Mr. Sardonicus. Silence deadened the normally reverberating locker room. The guys had witnessed the identical situation a thousand times, but the conflict was always spellbinding. Again, Swedarsky had forced me to try to save face, with Linda's reputation as an added incentive. If I denied him satisfaction, within an hour everyone in school would have heard that I had screwed Linda Martinsen on the couch, even though I hadn't. His leer told me all I needed to know.

"I didn't screw anybody, Swedarsky. Nothing happened! Hogan's just making up stuff, that's all."

Swedarsky was not going to let the opportunity for public castration evade him so easily. He had resented my recent rise in popularity, and it was his chance to drag me back to the whipping boy status that he had always enjoyed.

"Sure, Elliott," he sneered with a stinging slap on my bare back that almost sent me reeling. "Nothing happened because you probably finished as soon as you held her hand. You did get that far, didn't you, Elliott?"

I wasn't sure if I was stunned from his slap, his cruel taunts, or because he had touched the nerve connected to the secret truth. I felt totally vulnerable inside as well as outside. If someone as shallow as Swedarsky had deduced the truth, everyone else in the school could have easily reached the same conclusion. I could not allow the comments to go unanswered, or I would have been called "Quick-shot Elliott" the rest of my life. It had happened to Chuck Peterson, who was still known as "Chuck Petersout."

"Up yours, Swedarsky!" I shouted again. It had worked once. He turned with murder in his eyes and froze, allowing me time to absorb his malicious ugliness. Nobody moved, waiting for one of us to convert our verbal combat to physical warfare. Swedarsky just stood there, leering and waiting. He was totally naked with everything just hanging, and I had a wet towel in my hands. He had just recovered from his accident on the pommel horse, and I knew his most sensitive and vulnerable Achille's heel.

With all the nonchalance I could muster, I locked his stare into mine as I twisted my wet towel into a long, single whip. The stillness was stifling, and I could feel thousands of Roman eyes poised on the Christians facing the lions. I had only one shot; his response would be fatal if I missed. I let it go with a sharp jerk of my wrist.

Thwack! The towel snapped across the three feet separating us and came up under his balls, almost driving them up through the top of his head. The combined screams of all the Marquis de Sade's victims could not have equaled Swedarsky's anguished shriek. He fell like a bull elephant, his hands grasping his crotch, and I knew that he would not recover for a long time. I had gone too far, but I had had too much to lose. I stood over him, David over Goliath again, and glared at the writhing behemoth. He could only kill me once, so the advantage was mine.

"Hey, Swedarsky, don't play with yourself in the locker room. The guys will talk."

Everyone, including those terrified of Swedarsky, roared with laughter as he continued to grimace and grasp his throbbing groin. The potential name "Quick-shot Elliott" died at that moment, and "Sure-shot Elliott" took its place. I could have taken another shot to the head with the boxing gloves, but with Shipstead gone for good, the "gentlemen's satisfaction" was defunct. Swedarsky would extract his pound of flesh in another way, and I knew that my triumph and glory would be fleeting, but I was going to enjoy every second until then.

I marched naked to the coach's office, admiring eyes on me with scattered applause, and told the substitute that Joseph had fallen and reinjured himself. He rushed to Swedarsky, who was still squirming in obvious pain, and helped him up and into his clothes. Swedarsky spent the rest of the day behind a screen in the fetal position on a cot in the nurse's office. Visitors were not allowed.

Despite my desire to let Swedarsky honorably even the score, he was not to be found after school. The anxiety of awaiting my tormentor would not be as bad as that of my first date, and I began to appreciate the triviality of so many events of my life. Swedarsky did nothing for the entire next week, until the following Thursday when he stopped me in the hallway and intensely whispered, "I'm going to cut your balls off and shove them down your throat."

I hoped he hadn't meant it literally, but it was hard to tell with Swedarsky. As time passed and nothing happened, my fears increased. I had even fantasized that he would forget the entire incident, but I was realistic enough to know that he was a supreme torturer. His delay increased my fears, and every moment at school had the potential to shatter my life.

Word of my triumph and impending doom spread throughout the school. Because people hated the crude arrogance of Swedarsky, they were gratified by my act. However, they also realized that Swedarsky was a time bomb with a sensitive and unpredictable detonator, and soon the words of tribute became muted by sympathetic glances. With Swedarsky healthy, no one wanted to be associated with me any longer.

Although Linda probably knew all the details, she played naïve. She noted that I'd been acting moody and asked if there was anything wrong. I shrugged off my uneven humor as a minor argument with my mother, though I was certain that Linda knew everything. When it came to gossip, people rarely left out any of the juicy details, including those that never occurred. Linda probably felt that I had been protecting her reputation, and on some uncertain day I would have to pay the penalty. Sensitive to my anxiety, she never pushed me to talk about that night. Thank you, Linda.

When I went home each night, I would go to the bedroom and stare at the ceiling, building myself up, then tearing myself down. During dinner, of which I could eat very little and taste nothing, I sat in silence, answering Ma with only minimal answers. As always, her maternal instincts could tell that something was wrong – something I would not openly discuss with her, but would have to work out for myself. Castration by Swedarsky: It sounded like a new Illinois state penal code option.

The one person I most wanted to talk to was Mary Harker. I relived the entire night at the hotel, trying to recall how I had obtained enough composure to sleep with Mary Harker and not even look into her open bathrobe. We had talked for hours, about everything, and she had never hinted at disinterest. She had even said that if I ever needed anything, I should go to her. Mary already knew my whole story up to date night. She was a patient listener, and not the type to make fun of someone. We had slept together and protected each other. Despite our age difference, we sincerely seemed to be friends, even after only one night.

With a definite plan of action, my confidence rose slightly, and I no longer held my head so low. It seemed that people were whispering less. Swedarsky's ever-present threat took a back seat to a possible solution to my distress. It had been two weeks since our fight, and he had done nothing but threaten to cut off my balls. Linda had to babysit that Friday, clearing the way without deceit, if only I would be able to contact Mary.

Ma had decided to spend the evening watching the NBC Friday night killer line-up—Bob Hope's Chrysler Theater, Jack Benny, and Jack Paar. I prayed that Dan Phillips was not planning any unexpected or unwelcome visits. She had not heard from him for two weeks, so I hoped that the affair was at an end. Just to be cautious, she hooked the chain lock after I left; I was to knock three times as a signal when I returned home. It placed an automatic twelve o'clock curfew on me, but I didn't mind – my business would be concluded by then, and I wanted to be with Ma in case she needed protection from the drunken pilot.

Looking out the el windows on the way downtown, I could feel the approach of summer zest in Chicago's people. Everyone reacted differently to each of the seasons. The city seemed to come more to life on an almost summer Friday night. Couples strolled from restaurants to theatres, rejuvenated with the presence of a mild spring and rapidly approaching summer. I enjoyed none of it.

Van Buren Street was empty, and I found it difficult to catch my breath as I stood before the Swan Hotel. Then it hit me—Friday night! She was probably dancing at the Follies around the corner. I couldn't wait until after the show. Maybe she hadn't started yet. I had no choice but to hope she might still be home. If she wasn't, I didn't know what I would do.

Nothing had changed in the hotel lobby – there was still the darkness, the broken coke machine, and the phantom snorer. Behind the desk sat the crippled clerk with the broken face, his half-smoked, unlit cigar plugged into his mouth. I wondered if it was the same stub from last month.

"Watcha want, kid?" he growled. I thought he might say that he didn't have all night, but I wasn't afraid of him anymore and spoke firmly.

"I'm here to see Mary Harker."

His single eyebrow rose in surprise. "Why? You a friend or a customer?"

The comment stabbed, but I would not allow the bastard to deter me from my purpose. "I'm a friend of hers. What room is she in?"

"If you're a friend of hers, you should know what room she's in." There was always an asshole around when I needed it the least. I found myself deteriorating to his level of language.

"I ain't been here in a month. I forget."

He looked long and hard, then decided I could not be intimidated as easily as he had hoped.

"Room 13. Next floor up," and he returned to his *Stag* magazine.

My heart throbbed from the anxiety as I took the steps two at a time. The hotel seemed more seedy than it had during my first adventurous visit, and I began to wonder what the hell I was doing in such a dive.

I stood before her door and listened for signs of life. All was silent, and I feared the worst. I knocked lightly at first, using the coded three knocks I had worked out with Ma, feeling that it was bound to bring an open door. I tried again, harder. The silence grew maddening, and I pounded the door, calling her name. She was not there, and I felt disappointed and confused. Too much depended on her. Reluctantly, I left. As I shuffled through the lobby, the voice of Big Brother stopped me.

"She ain't home, kid."

The son-of-a-bitch had known and was playing games. Anger made me slam the counter as though I was trying to shatter it in order to reach the monkey behind it. I was in no mood for games.

"Then why didn't you tell me?"

He had a smirk I would have liked to erase with a bulldozer. "Ya' didn't ask."

It was the oldest line in the book, and I was getting pissed as hell. Little Joey had been crippled and spent his life in a degrading corner store, but he wasn't a complete, bitter jerk. I could not comprehend the differences between people, but I assumed that everyone was crippled in some way.

"Did she say when she'd be back?" I barked.

"Yeah. She said." He returned to his magazine, indicating my dismissal. I felt like pushing that chair down the steps. If the fall didn't kill him the traffic on Van Buren would. Who would know and care that I did it?

I snarled, "Well, when?"

He casually finished his paragraph, then looked up at me as though he had lost his train of thought. He probably had.

"When what?"

The game had gone too far, and I wondered if the phantom snorer would notice me push the bastard, but the answer was too important.

"When will she be back?"

The sadistic glaze was in his eyes. "Who?"

He had won; I had lost. I simply didn't give a damn.

My best Swedarsky came out. "Up yours, Crip!" I shouted and stormed into the night, the sound of his sadistic laughter following me down the stairs.

Mary Harker had apparently returned from St. Louis and had gone out. Perhaps she had just run to the store, or perhaps she would be gone all night. I needed her and waited by the hotel door.

Nobody noticed me as a few displaced persons walked by, and I felt alone again. Van Buren was the survivor end of the Loop, where people rarely noticed each other. Old men carrying heavy plastic trash bags trudged down the sidewalk, their bodies permanently stooped, their eyes ever fixed on the ground.

A half hour passed and I was beginning to get a damp, bone-deep chill as the lake wind started to penetrate my skin, forgetting that it was almost summer. The same police car drove by twice, its occupants eyeing me like I was a pervert. Since the Palmer House was only four blocks away, I decided to wait there and make periodic checks. Besides, all that pressure had made me need to use the can. It seemed that whenever anything important had to be accomplished, all I could do was try to find a bathroom.

At that time of the night, around 9:30, the hotel lobby was relatively quiet – everyone had either gone out or retired. No matter, I was in no mood for more play. I used the bathroom and even tipped the valet a quarter for the towel he had thrust into my hands as I stepped back from the sink. At least I had some dignity left.

As I sat in the vacant lobby, I rehearsed how I would present my situation to Mary Harker. I had done so a thousand times, but rarely twice the same way. My best strategy was to sense Mary's mood and play it by instinct, as long as I told her everything and did not turn coward.

Every hour I ran back to the Swan to see if she had returned, but I had no luck. At 11:30 I decided it was time to go home, but I could not force myself to quit in the midst of all that had happened and all I hoped would happen. I called

Ma to tell her that I had decided to spend the night at Jerry's. She sounded like I had just awoken her, so I assumed that everything was all right and that I had bought myself a night.

Around 2:00 the streets were almost empty, and I found myself becoming sleepy; all the recent tension had mentally drained me. I even began to question the entire venture, but I knew that I had to follow through or continue my unabated confusion.

"Who is it?" came the perturbed voice weakly from the other side of the door. With the surprise of finding her at home, I nearly forgot my purpose.

"It's me. Kelly. Kelly Elliott."

"Who?" She had forgotten my name and I prayed that she hadn't forgotten me.

"Kelly Elliott. I was the kid who was here last month when . . . when you had your accident." I spoke carefully, sensing ears at every door. Her voice sounded impatient and irritated.

"Just a second." There was the sound of a dead-bolt lock. She recognized me through squinting eyes. Her irritability was replaced by tired surprise but not unkindness.

"Oh, it's you. I just got home. Did you want something?"

I had hoped she would be ecstatic at the sight of my face, throw open the door, hug me, and invite me in. Like the last time I had seen her, she probably had more serious problems than a seventeen-year-old kid. I spoke haltingly, not wanting to intrude or to be turned away, but trying to convey the sense of urgency that I felt.

"I know it's late, but I needed to talk to someone. Could I please come in? I'll try to make it quick." She peered a moment longer, unsure, then acquiesced to the pitiful face outside her door.

"Sure, I guess I owe you one; I remember the last time now. Come on in."

I did not see the same Mary Harker I had met last month. She had cut her hair short, as though she was about to join a convent. The swelling caused by her bruises had been replaced with dark circles and bags. Her face gave the appearance of an eternal weeper, and I felt even more pity for her than I had the last time. By the end of our last meeting, she had become almost pretty, but she had changed to one of the haggard people. Despite her exhausted and gaunt appearance, she was congenial – I had probably been the last person to show her much kindness.

"What are you doing here at two in the morning, Kelly? Couldn't it keep until tomorrow?"

"I'm really sorry, but I had to talk to someone, and you seem to be the only one I've been able to honestly talk to. I've tried to see you every hour since eight o'clock, but you weren't home. It's that important to me."

She went to the stove and began to pour two cups of coffee. Her hair was wet, and she wore the same ratty, blue terrycloth bathrobe. A soft scent of bath powder helped counterbalance her appearance.

She avoided my face as she sat on the couch and spoke defensively. "I was out on a date. I just got back. Would you like a cup of coffee? It's already poured."

I had not moved from the doorway, trying to read between the lines as I looked around the room for a visitor.

"Sure, thank you." I sat next to her on the sofa, a repeat of last month's tableau. By just looking at her I could sense that my problems were miniscule compared to hers, and I felt guilty for troubling her with the problems of a teenage kid.

"What happened in St. Louis?" I asked hesitantly, hoping to ease the tension in the room. I wanted everything to be like it had been the last visit.

"My parents disowned me. Said they had warned me not to go to Chicago, and that I hadn't listened to them. I was back within a week."

Again I found myself in the role of the one to help, not the one to be helped. With slight prodding she related her entire story, and I could feel an ease begin to replace the tension as she talked. Besides losing her family, she had lost her job.

The man who had beaten her had been a booking agent (Yes, even strippers had to have an agent) and since then had made enough phone calls to make acquiring work nearly impossible. Any money she had saved was quickly spent to keep her alive, and she had taken some temporary employment, working some nights. As she talked I realized how everything only had meaning in relation to something else, and suddenly my problems seemed trifling. Mary Harker had found her place at the Swan Hotel.

I listened for almost an hour as she related her depressing story. She described the nasty "I-told-you-so" lecture by her father and the disappointment from her mother. In addition, Mary's only brother, John, had been drafted last year and was close to leaving for Vietnam. Nothing had gone right for the family, and the parents had hardened their attitude toward Mary and were not about to change. At her age and after all they had done for her already – schools, support groups, money ·· they had exhausted their good will, even for their own daughter. "Good luck and here's fifty more dollars to get you back to Chicago." She clasped her hands at the end of her narrative and I think she felt better. Her voice became lighter.

"I'm sorry, Kelly. You came here at two in the morning with problems and I've done all the talking."

Her miserable life had so completely captivated me that I had temporarily dismissed my problems. At that moment I felt stronger, but on Monday I would have to again confront the arena of my tribulations.

"I guess it's nothing much, Mary. Not after all that you've been through. Now I feel kind of weird about coming here."

She clenched my hands firmly and commanded me. "Nobody hangs around a sleazy street corner for six hours and not have major problems. You can't judge your life against mine. Obviously it's important or you wouldn't have made the effort. Now tell me everything. There's no rush."

I swallowed and it was difficult, but I could feel from the pressure in her hands that I was her prisoner, not to be released until a full confession. Slowly I began talking, telling her how much I had grown to care about Linda She tried to appear attentive, but I could tell that she was fighting to keep her eyes open. Even Bates, Laura, and Swedarsky entered my oration. I waited for her to interrupt and tell me to get to the point, but she politely clasped my hand while fighting exhaustion.

Too embarrassed to give much detail but feeling that I had to tell her about Linda's and my couch make-out episode, I simply said that we got "hot and heavy" one Friday night, and that the matter ended rather abruptly. Mary never once smirked or snickered, seeming to understand my meaning. With her troubled life, I'm sure she had experienced plenty of this kind of demoralizing behavior.

I moved on to the confrontation with Swedarsky, toning down the rhetoric to a "towel snap where he lives." Changing the subject from sex to violence made it easier to look her in the eyes again. It was almost 3:30 by the time I concluded telling her about my fear of Swedarsky "neutering" me.

Despite the late hour, Mary sat glassy-eyed and stared at me. I could envision the cogs in her brain analyzing everything I had said, computing a viable solution to a myriad of teen-boy problems. She may not have had much formal education, but she was street-wise, and I had street problems. She let go of my hands and sat back, almost smugly.

"Have you thought about confronting Swedarsky?"

"You have it backwards, Mary. It's Swedarsky who wants to . . . "

"I know, Kelly. It's Swedarsky who threatened to cut off your balls. I'm just suggesting that you take the offense rather than the defense for once. When someone plays cutesy with me, I go after him. It gets everything out in the open fast. Don't let him play the role of master torturer. He's winning by not doing anything. Go at him. Tell him that if he has a score to settle, do it or he'll get tired of hiding."

She was serious! "He'll kill me!"

"He won't kill you, Kelly. I doubt if he'll even hurt you that much. Let him gain back some face. You can't keep running and spending your nights staring at a ceiling. Stick it to him, Kelly. Confront him in front of a bunch of his gang, so he'll have to do something. He's playing dungeon master and you're letting him. Kick him in the balls, Kelly."

She made sense, no matter how suicidal her tactics seemed.

"Yeah, I could kick him in the balls," and I laughed the good laughter of friends.

"I don't mean to literally kick him in the balls, Kelly. I mean to push the issue. Of course, if the opportunity presents itself. . . Kelly, I have to compliment you on your restrained use of swear words. It's a nice contrast to most of the jerks that I talk to. Did your mother teach you that?"

"Actually, it was a promise I made to her when I was seven. I never thought I'd be able to keep it, especially when I got out of junior high school. I guess it became sort of a habit."

"Well, it's a nice way to be, especially with women."

My face felt beet red as I blushed. Did my mother and Mary Harker have too much in common?

"Feel better, Kelly?"

"Yeah, I do, except for Linda. What do I do about her?"

She shook her head. "You don't do anything about Linda. You don't need to. You're just fine. She'll let you know if anything has drastically changed. Trust me. I know quite a bit about women's feelings."

I nodded, feeling a rush of relief. The sincerity on her face confirmed what she said. Mary Harker knew a lot about everything, especially relationships between the sexes. I again started to feel the boyish love I had once felt for Ginny Dare.

"Kelly, it's almost four in the morning. I took a couple sleeping pills shortly before you came in, and I am dead tired. I think we've solved enough problems for one night. It's too late to send you home now. We can comfort each other again, the way we did the last time you were here, okay?" There was a different tone in her voice. She was right, practically speaking, of course. She stood, grasped both of my hands and led me to her bedroom.

When the morning light leaked through the blinds, I could see that the almost naked Mary Harker was not the illusion I'd held in my mind since that first night at the Follies Theatre. Then the make-up had hidden the three inch scar on the left side of her face, and the muted lights had concealed the imperfections of an abused, time-worn woman. On stage she had tried not to look exhausted and victimized; she had become a caustic, teasing vixen, and as I grew older, I learned to appreciate what she had lived through and shared with me. Like my first visit, we said very little that morning, as she took some more pills and submitted to a semi-comatose state in order to deal with the reality of another day.

I kissed her lightly at the door, like the last time. But this time I sensed that I would never see her again. She hugged me tightly for an extra moment, as though to confirm it, and I left. As I raced down the stairs of the Swan Hotel, I began to hurt inside from the thought of possibly never seeing her again, but I realized that I had to start looking towards the future that Mary Harker had pushed me toward. Who first— Linda Martinsen or Swedarsky?

When I returned home early Saturday afternoon, Ma was strangely quiet, and I could tell that there was again something amiss. It was nothing urgent, like the reappearance of Dan Phillips, but something inside that gnawed at her.

"Did you have a good time last night?" she asked as she took a bite from an egg salad sandwich. I found it difficult to lie to her, probably because of the importance of the previous night's happenings.

"Yeah, it was okay."

"What did you do?"

"Oh, you know. We just went to the movies and walked

around. The usual."

Her eyes held me as she took another bite of her sandwich.

"We, meaning you and Jerry?"

"Sure, me and Jerry. Who else?"

She knew the truth, but I could not fathom how. Her eyes held me firmly, and I felt myself flush. I turned around as she went to the sink with her empty plate. She knew!

"What do you have planned for tonight, Kelly?"

Fortunately, some motherly instincts told her not to pursue the issue, but she knew that something had happened.

"Nothing for tonight, Ma. Why? Would you like to do something?"

She smiled the ambiguous smile of the *Mona Lisa*.

"I thought we might go out for dinner. Maybe Crandall's. We haven't been there for a long time."

Thoughts of the old restaurant always triggered pleasant images in my mind. There had been serene Sunday afternoons when all was well, and I had fed French fries to the goldfish in the restaurant's wishing pond. We hadn't been there since I started high school, and it afforded me an opportunity to escape to a less stressful, nostalgic time.

"That would be nice, Ma." Unexpectedly, she hugged me, which took me completely unawares, and she casually walked into the living room. I let myself relax. The inquisition I had expected hadn't come. Maye she didn't know the truth after all.

The rest of the weekend seemed uneventful in comparison to that Friday night. I spent much of it staring into space, reliving Friday with Mary and wondering but no longer worrying about the future. Our dinner at Crandall's had been pleasant, and I even danced with Ma after our meal. As we awkwardly two-stepped, I felt very close to my mother, holding her as though I was about to lose her forever. Sunday night I called Linda just to talk, the way normal teenagers were supposed to. She said I sounded different, not as aloof as I had been, and she said that she was looking forward to seeing me at school. Mary Harker had been right – Linda was fine and would "let me know if there was a problem."

Monday brought the beginning of the third to the last week of school, and everyone was in a light-hearted mood. My conversation with Mary had made me feel better, and I was in a mellow frame of mind. There was no way to gauge how long the mood would take to dissipate, but I hoped that it never would.

My sense of peace was abruptly shattered after school, when I saw my opportunity to take the offense against Swedarsky. He was standing on the west campus with "friends." Linda had just left on her bus, but the school grounds were still crowded with people awaiting their rides and athletes waiting for the start of their respective sports. With a shaky assertiveness, I strode up to Swedarsky, who was in the middle of one of his raunchy stories, his puppets listening attentively. I rudely interrupted, my voice firm, no signs of cracking yet.

"Okay, Swedarsky. You want to settle our score now?"

All eyes turned to the skinny kid with the diminishing acne. They must have assumed that I had a strong death wish. Swedarsky snarled, "Bite me, Elliott!"

I stood undaunted, "You're the one who wants to get even. I'm here to give you the chance. Now!"

He poked me in the chest with a rapier finger. "Get lost, pimp. I'll settle with you when I get ready and on my terms."

I boldly swatted his hand away. "What's the matter with right now? You're not afraid, are you? You can't hide forever, you know." These were close to the words that Mary Harker had given me, and I had practiced enough to spit them out fluently.

His nostrils flared like a Komodo dragon. I didn't want to get him too angry – just mad enough to stop at maiming me. It was time. Swedarsky peeled off his letter jacket and tossed it to one of his lackeys.

"Okay, smart-ass. I'm gonnacrush your nuts." He

assumed a neutral wrestling position, his arms extended, awaiting mine. I interpreted his stance as a good sign. If he had put up his fists, there would have been inevitable pain. Nobody likes to chance pain. Even I was capable of landing a lucky, wild punch to his face, and I had the feeling that he feared bare knuckle encounters.

I had hurt him once and had shown that I didn't fear him, at least on the outside. By wrestling he could use his weight and do the necessary damage by throwing me to the ground and applying a painful half-nelson or an arm twist. I only hoped that his booted toe did not find my crotch.

Firmly I grasped his forearms, as taught in Shipstead's phy ed class, and we jockeyed for position. He started to throw me a few times, but I released my grip which threw off his balance, almost causing him to fall at one point. Finally, he lunged, toppling me onto my back with his full weight on my chest. The air expelled like a gust of wind off the lakefront.

He tried to pin my arms, but I kept them flailing in an attempt to stall for time to regain my breath. Despite the warm weather, the ground was cold and damp. I could see a crowd beginning to gather. I hoped that they wanted to see David slay Goliath again, but the conclusion would unquestionably be different this time.

Swedarsky was big, but slow. I was able to scramble from underneath him and gain an advantage by applying a full-nelson, a move I learned from watching the Crusher on WGN-TV's Saturday Night Wrestling. For once I was glad that Shipstead, along with the Crusher, had taught me something useful. Although I was on top, I did not know what to do next. It was kind of like sex. Finally, Swedarsky was able to toss me over his head, and I was stunned as my back slammed against the ground. Swedarsky was soon straddling my chest again, trying to capture my wildly swinging arms. He had me down, but he didn't know what to do with the advantage, either.

"All right, boys. Break it up! Get off him, Swedarsky.

Now!"

All eyes turned to Mr. Bates, who had the unpleasant task of trying to separate us; I was sure that teachers hated fights more than the combatants.

Swedarsky glared down at me. He clearly had the upper hand and would lose no face with his friends. I had been rescued. He had beaten the wimp and could have easily pulverized his face. Slowly he released me and stood, like a gladiator awaiting the emperor's signal. I got up hesitantly, over-dramatizing the injury by stumbling. Other than a shortness of breath, I was unhurt.

"Do you need the nurse, Kelly?" Bates asked, concerned but hoping that I didn't.

I shook my head "no" and waved my arms to show I was okay.

"You two report to Mr. Schwarz's office the first thing in the morning. You know the rules about fighting on school grounds. Now go home! Both of you!" I didn't know that Bates could raise his voice, but he was pissed.

Swedarsky grabbed his jacket with a sneer and strode off, the obvious victor of the brief brawl. I went the opposite way, feigning a limp, concentrating hard to keep the same leg stiff. It wasn't easy, nor was it easy to keep a Mr. Sardonicus grin from spreading across my face. It was over, and I was knocking down one windmill after another.

Swedarsky and I each got five hours of detention. We spent the time sitting next to each other in room 208, the detention hall, and once he even borrowed my chemistry book. I felt that everything would be all right and that maybe I had even earned some of his respect, two weeks before school was out. Linda was proud and kissed me in the hall, but nobody else saw it. She was still a little conservative about public displays of affection, or as Swedarsky unknowingly called it, with no hint of irony, "public displays of infection."

Sitting in the detention hall I thought of how important it was for me to tell Mary Harker about the success of her advice and how grateful I felt for her guidance. I decided to drop by, maybe bring her some flowers from one of those corner stands by the el train exit platforms. It had been enough time since my last visit so that I shouldn't seem too much of a pest. Especially if I brought her flowers; I bet no one else brought flowers to her.

On Thursday I was primed to see Mary the next day, overcoming that foreboding twinge I felt the last time. Feeling cocky and invincible, I sauntered into English class and prepared myself to take on Bates, now my savior, or anyone else. That was when Laura LeDuc walked in. In my eyes she had become a real slut; her hair seemed oily and snarled and her usually immaculate clothes had become spotted and unkempt. Even that treasured college letter sweater she wore had become nubby and soiled. Her college romance seemed to be taking its toll on her once perfect beauty and spirit.

If I hadn't hated her so much, I would have felt sorry for her, but it had been more than a month since our homework cheating confrontation, and she had not made any gesture of apology. I chose to think of her as Jekyll and Hyde (another of Bates' required novels) and in the month since she had committed her sin, her superficial attractiveness had been decaying inside and out. I was surprised when she spoke to me in her still angelic voice.

"I heard you challenged Joe Swedarsky, Kelly. That took a lot of guts. I already told you what I think of him."

Her words and tone were enough to melt the North Pole, but I would never be able to forgive her, not if she offered to ravage me all weekend. Well, maybe then. Bates wasn't in the room yet, and I was feeling brazen. I didn't need false compliments from the bitch. "Drop dead, Laura."

There was a round of "oooh's" from those within earshot, and Laura looked like she was about to cry. Her hurt made me feel small, and I could not understand my unnecessary cruelty to the girl I had once fantasized about marrying, etc. But thoughts of her boasting about how she had lied, manipulated me, and made me look like a fool pushed aside any impulses to apologize, and I soon returned to my recently cocky self.

Linda was somewhat disappointed that I had to break another Friday night date, but I had made up my mind to visit Mary that night. It was the three-day Memorial Day weekend, so there would be plenty of time to see Linda later. Since I had planned to see Mary for only a few minutes, there was no valid reason why Linda and I couldn't have gone out later. But something stopped me from making those plans. Subconsciously, I was worried about Mary and her uncertain future, probably more than I was worried about mine.

As I got off the el by the Swan Hotel, my adrenalin began pumping with anticipation and anxiety, enough to almost make me dizzy. I was there by 6:30 in case she had another "date." I brought a small bouquet of pink carnations and some yellow flowers wrapped in cellophane from one of the on-the-run vendors. Taking the steps two at a time, I tried to dart past the dragon in his lair, hoping to avoid a confrontation. I wasn't fast enough.

"Hey, kid. Where ya' goin'? Especially with flowers."

Against my better judgment, I stopped and glared at the sadistic, twisted demon behind the desk. I was not to be intimidated – not this time. I had defeated better than him.

"You know damn well where I'm going. To see Mary Harker."

His grin made me uncomfortable. He had me at his mercy again. Slowly he took the unlit cigar from his foul mouth and scrutinized the tip.

"You're too late." There was something ominous in his tone that I did not like.

"Why? Is she gone?"

A long pause. "Yeah, you might say that."

"Where'd she go? Did she say when she'd be back?"

He had me firmly by the balls and was twisting.

"Nope, she didn't say nothing. But I do have an address where you can find her."

I could not believe that she would leave without saying good-bye but who the hell was I? I waited for the cretin to give me the address.

He paused to make sure that I was looking him in the eyes. "She's at 2121 West Harrison."

"What is at 2121 West Harrison?"

He again made sure he could see my eyes. "Let me give you a hint. She's not coming back here and I think you might want to bring those flowers to the morgue, located at 2121 West Harrison."

I froze, sure that I would never be able to move again. Then my face began to twitch. I was too young for a heart attack. Maybe not. Satisfied with my reaction, he continued his sadistic taunting.

"Overdosed on some pills. Pretty sure it was suicide. Dead a few days before a smell started to bother her neighbor. They hauled her ass out of here on Wednesday. Still owes me last month's rent. If you're a real friend of hers and can afford to buy her flowers, maybe you got $100.00 for rent. Boy, lotta guys will miss that piece of ass, I bet."

My knees gave out and I grasped the counter for support. My body had been drained of every ounce of life. Still, I found enough hatred, and I started to whip the worm with the flowers. Over and over, until he started yelling to stop. I was too enraged to stop, so I kept hitting him harder, substituting my fists when the flowers had disintegrated. Visions of her body in the bedroom, probably the same bed that we had shared, flooded my mind, and I wretched inside. I wondered if she would have done it if I had been there earlier, but I would not allow myself to absorb all the sins of Mary Harker's world.

I stood for an interminable amount of time in the roaring silence before I was able to edge my way out of the Swan Hotel forever. I could hear the demon yell that he was calling the police, but I truly did not care. Grasping the rail with both hands, I sidled down the steps. Outside I could see the neon light flashing "Swan Hotel – Swan Hotel" in a never ending refrain. I was sick and wondered what everything that had happened between us was about.

My only comfortable refuge was the Brighton Theatre. Jorge asked if everything was all right as he took my ticket and gave me the return stub. I must have looked worse than usual. It wasn't just a normal, uncomfortable pain I felt. I had never dealt with the death of someone I was close to. It was a numbing, excruciating ache.

I shuffled from the left side aisle, making my usual check of the crowd, not even being aware of what was on the silver screen. I don't know how long I sat there. I know I cried, sometimes silently, sometimes muffling the sounds with my coat. I had been by myself before, many times, but I had never felt so alone.

CHAPTER 12

The Stag Party and the Pilot Crash

The obituary in the *Chicago Tribune* was a concise capsule of three lines. As I sat in the public library looking at Thursday's paper, I felt disappointment that the newspaper would take so little space to summarize Mary Harker's life. To the journalism staff she was only a name for a typist, a job to be completed without any deeper meaning. Probably not many people knew Mary or read her obituary. I wondered who even placed the notice. Her parents seemed logical, but how would they even know? The Follies girls were probably her only friends; one of them must have known her background and contacted her parents in St. Louis. Or maybe it was one of her rich "dates." I felt sad about the slighting of Mary Harker's life, but perhaps the terse obituary best encapsulated it – short with little impact on anyone of importance.

To my dismay the obituary listed her age at twenty-eight. Staring at the souvenir photo of Ginny Dare, I had assumed her to be closer to forty, but adversity has a way of aging people before they are prepared. Her only family were the parents who had disowned her, and I resented them for not taking her back, problems and all. Mary was their daughter. I wondered how her brother in Vietnam would react; he may have done more to honor his sister. Her body had been sent to Missouri for burial, and I knew that she had been taken from me forever. At least we had gotten to know each other and formed a bond, however short it was.

My mother knew that something was causing me pain and wanted to help, but I put her off by saying that someone at school had died. It took the rest of the school year and the following summer before the pain had ebbed.

And when Jerry asked me if something was wrong, I told him that there had been a death in the family. His usual crude self softened, subconsciously offering me a willing listener had I need of one. Jerry suggested I get out and away from the cause of my melancholy mood. Then visions of his excitement at the Follies careened inside my mind, and I felt that he would hardly believe the whole story without graphic details and would revert to the real Jerry Hogan.

Jerry's parents had flown to the Bahamas for the extended weekend, leaving Jerry and older brother Paul alone. This afforded Paul the opportunity to throw a Saturday night beer bash, and he invited me. I was in no mood to return to the world of boys playing men, but Jerry was persuasive, insisting that a good party and a few drinks would help raise my spirits.

Reluctantly, I attended Jerry's party, forgoing another date with Linda. I told her the same death-in-the-family story that I had told Jerry. My promise not to lie to her again had lasted about a month.

My tears were spent for that day, and I had to try to continue the life Mary Harker had advised. There was a total of only six at Paul's bash, including three from his fraternity. He had bought the beer for the evening and promised us all a "special surprise." I was briefly introduced to the three strangers, whose names I immediately forgot, and they treated me as an outsider for the rest of the night. But I knew that I had experienced things that they hadn't, and I felt superior to the college "jocks."

Strange as it may seem at the age of seventeen, I had never been drunk. The legal drinking age in Illinois was twenty-one, and liquor was not easily obtainable in high school. Getting drunk was reserved for a certain clique that needed to prove its social standing and coolness and that had access to booze. Drinking was used as a status symbol, and I also knew one of its purposes was to "drown one's sorrows." I had seen too many movies. It was for that reason that I found myself at Jerry Hogan's house that night. Mary Harker would have understood. It was important to do something other than mourn. I wanted to have either complete control of my thoughts or lose myself entirely.

"Hey, Kelly. How ya' doin'? Wanna square?" asked Jerry with two cans of beer in his hands.

"Sure." I took the offered cigarette and beer. I lit up and choked on my first inhalation; I had actually tried to inhale the stupid thing, but it was no use trying to fake anything else as a reason for my gagging. They all knew I didn't belong. There was no problem with puncturing the Hamm's can and I swallowed half of it immediately, trying to regain some of my "I'm cool" persona.

"Christ, Elliott! Take it easy! I didn't know you could drink like that." Jerry was impressed, which made me feel worse, not better.

The beer tasted good and went down easily. The impact was almost instantaneous, either from the alcohol or the loss of oxygen while I chugged the can.

"Boilermakers, everyone! Choose your weapon!"

It was Paul Hogan, who was wearing his grimy high school letter sweater but was playing the role of Joe College. He slammed a quart of Brennan's bourbon on the table beside six shot glasses. I was ready for the moron and was the first to grab a shot glass and fill it with the cheap whiskey. After everyone filled his glass, Paul proposed an elegant toast.

"Here's to sweet ass," and he downed the shot with one fluid motion.

I put the glass to my lips and slugged it down, figuring that I wouldn't be able to taste it if the liquid rapidly bypassed my taste buds. Wrong! My throat felt like it was burning from the inside out, and my eyes watered. I tried to extinguish the flame with the rest of the beer in my can, but I had already emptied it and craved more.

I remembered some movie with Ray Milland about an

alcoholic that I had seen at the Brighton Theatre at their "Here's to you" movie fest. It gave me pause, but I decided I wasn't heading down that road yet, not after a half hour. Apparently, the rest of the losers felt the same way, because everyone was sucking down a can like it held magical restoration powers.

"One more time!" announced Paul like a ringmaster. The absolute stupidity of the idea stunned me, and I was a little slower to pour, stalling for time to allow my system to return to a state of semi-normalcy. Still, boilermakers presented a shortcut to my evening's goal of obliteration.

The second shot went down easier, but I was definitely feeling the impact of the liquor. My vision was becoming blurred and my head was lighter. Thoughts of Mary Harker shifted from the tragedy of her death to the ecstasy of being with her.

"Chug-a-lug time!" proclaimed Paul with the crash of another six-pack on the table. "Then it's time for my special surprise."

I grabbed a can, opened it, and passed the church key to Jerry, who was beginning to look like a victim of the plague. He was sweating and his face was sickly white. Like me, Jerry hovered on the edge of catastrophe after only a half hour.

Everyone held his can to his lips, and at the cue from Paul, tipped them. I gagged and spit a few times, spilled several swallows on my sweatshirt and pants, and began to analyze the validity of such an exercise. I would never chug a twelve ounce glass of water, and doing it with beer was absurd. I could feel my head turn to mush, and soon I could feel its effect on my crotch.

Trying to look nonchalant, I staggered to the bathroom, leaving behind shouts of "We know where you're going!" I probably needed to sit and pee like a girl as my aim was less than perfection. Instead, I clung to the towel bar above the toilet to help steady my swaying. Still, I liberally coated the toilet and floor with my flow and drunken aim. The mess was too much to easily clean with tissue, but then I saw the dark brown hand towels. I wiped the floor, and returned the damp towel to its proper spot. Who would know?

When I had returned to the living room, grasping furniture to keep me from toppling, Paul Hogan was setting up a small reel on an eight-millimeter film projector. Jerry and an unknown body lay sprawled on the carpet, oblivious to everything. I fell into a corner of the couch and held the arm rest with both hands as the room whirled around me. I may have temporarily forgotten my troubles, but I hadn't yet decided if the effort was worth the consequences. It was only later that I realized that I had only substituted calamities.

"Okay, guys. What we have here are pictures of Simpson's mother," said Paul sarcastically, and everyone laughed like a bunch of drunks, except me, who didn't know who the hell Simpson was. I later found out that he was the other unconscious body on the floor.

I sat like a convict in an electric chair and stared at the white wall, waiting for the switch to be thrown. I could not move, had no desire to do so, and just wished the whole damn evening would end. The mere thought of drinking again brought a wave of nausea to my bile-laden throat, but I fought it back.

The lights went out and the projector clicked as someone who still had some strength left made shadow figures on the wall, intercepting the beam of the projector. There was always one child in the crowd who did shadow pictures, and I felt that they should all be neutered. Solutions were always easy when I didn't have to carry them out.

"The Babysitter" shone across the wall, and everyone who was still able clapped. I watched but really wanted to have my guts torn out. Stupefied, I stared at the wall as my first stag film rolled before me. I felt obligated to get more excited and show some enthusiasm, but I was too worried about throwing-up. I had to divert my mind to the movie and away from the queasiness.

The black and white film kept jumping and the quality

was poor, but no one seemed to mind. I could vaguely hear snide comments from various parts of the room, but my muddled brain was unable to discern a single word. The movie had managed to partially arrest my attention. A rather homely woman stood naked in a bathroom. A man came from behind her and gripped her tits while she acted surprised and giggled. That brought a wave of applause from the audience, but I remained comatose.

Something bothered me about the film, but I could not pinpoint the problem. The two went into the bedroom and began to devour each other, using positions that I thought were impossible for the human being. I found myself mesmerized but not stimulated by the action. Under different circumstances, I would have found the film erotic, but I was viewing it at the wrong time and in the wrong condition. Had I seen it a week before, I would have been one of them applauding the sexual acrobatics.

Pushing up from my throat was everything that I had drunk combined with some sort of moral sickness. Nobody noticed as I forced myself up from the couch and stumbled toward the bathroom again. As I reached for the light switch, I fell backwards into the bathtub, cracking my head on the porcelain. I would not feel the pain or the lump until the next day.

Using both hands, I clawed my way up from the tub. I barely got my head over the toilet before my insides gushed forth. I wretched as everything I had ever eaten or drunk in my entire life poured into the toilet with such force that it splashed back up onto my face, and I reclaimed the vomit. If I needed to die, I was willing to do so. Dying made sense at that moment.

When I felt that my body had purged itself of everything humanly possible, I weakly flushed away the remains of my shame. Dizziness held me to the floor as I listened to the relieving flush and swirl of the toilet disposing of my embarrassment.

Wicked dreams overcame my stupor as I lay in the fetal

position on the cold mosaic tile floor. Mary Harker came alive, and I dreamt that we were walking down Michigan Avenue to the Museum of Natural History. She was as excited as a five-year-old seeing it for the first time. I shared her enthusiasm and joy until she said that she wanted to see the mummies. I protested, but she pulled me with both hands, down the stairs leading to the Egyptian vault. She assured me that they were all dead and just preserved. I knew that, of course, but I was afraid of the dead. She told me that she was dead and started to pull my arm again, drawing me closer to the ancient cadavers. I began fighting her, twisting away from her grasp, and shouting. "No! No! I won't go," but she insisted and her strength had always been greater than mine.

"It's okay, Elliott. We're just taking you out of the john. Some people have to use it."

My eyes cracked open, and I could see a dim image of Paul Hogan and someone else, pulling me by the arms, out of the bathroom. I was unable to fight or help myself.

"Just drop him here," said Paul, and I was put to rest in the carpeted hallway. Fearful of more unwanted dreams but unable to stay awake, I curled into a ball and spent a long, restless night in the Hogan hallway.

When I awoke, the disgusting smell of greasy bacon and eggs whiffed my nose, and remembrance of the night's sickness returned. Grateful for being close to the toilet, I crawled back and again wretched over the bowl, but nothing came out. My head throbbed and I was too spent to even vomit.

Shakily pacing myself to the kitchen, I saw Paul Hogan at the table, eating a full breakfast. I hated that bastard's guts. Jerry sat propped up at the table, an untouched glass of orange juice before him, his head cradled in his hands. Body count: two dead, one survivor.

Paul had the audacity to be cheerful, and I secretly hoped that he'd choke on the sinewy bacon.

"Hey, Kelly, how ya' feelin'? Like some breakfast?" he

asked sadistically.

The mere idea of food forced me to gag again, and I weakly shook my head and dropped next to Jerry, who I could now see was actually sleeping sitting up. Paul poured me a tall glass of orange juice.

"Drink this. Vitamin C helps soak up the booze. You'll feel better in no time. Sorry about your sleeping in the hall last night, but you were blocking the major facility. I figured I'd leave you close to the john, in case you had to puke again."

Considerate but not worth a "thank you." Couldn't he tell what condition I was in? I didn't want to hear about puke! The orange juice went down easily, though I could scarcely taste anything pleasant. My tongue had been numbed, like a dentist had just given me a giant shot of Novocain. I even dribbled down my chin. Paul continued cheerfully and I felt the need to escape his obnoxious smugness. It was my first hangover – cut me some slack!

"Looks like my kid brother here is out for the day. You can stay until you feel okay, but the best medicine is a good romp in the fresh air. Make ya' close to normal. I gotta meet some guys for basketball."

If he was trying to impress me, he was totally failing. He rinsed off his plate and started to leave.

"Hey, Kelly, I almost forgot. There's a big end-of-the-year party next week in Evanston. Mostly frat guys, but we're always looking for new pledges. Jer said you might be going to Northern next year, so this could give you a little taste of college life. Lots of booze and stuff. Everyone loses their mind. Keep Saturday open. I think Jer's going if he's recovered by then. Be sure the place is locked up if little brother's not awake when you leave. Boy, you sure got blitzed last night. Nice going. Take it easy, kid."

Thank God, he was gone, the pompous asshole. I could vaguely recall the mention of a party, but I didn't care if I ever went to another party in my life. Swallowing another glass of orange juice, I slowly but eagerly made my way to the front door. Jerry never moved, and I wondered what his parents would say if they saw their youngest son in such a state. But it was every man for himself, and I was thankful to escape the Hogan Chamber of Horrors. I didn't bother to check the locks; it wasn't my house.

Paul had been right about one thing – the fresh air did feel invigorating, and normalcy slowly began to return as I walked. It was 12:30 by the time I left Jerry's, and I wanted to resemble the person who had left home on Saturday. I passed the next two hours riding the el downtown and walking through Grant Park.

At 2:30 I began to work my way toward home. I got off the el one stop sooner than normal, so I could walk and clear my head before my mother saw me hungover. Hunger was overcoming me and the hot dog carts were already out. I bought two Chicago dogs without peppers and a coke, then walked a couple blocks to McKinley Park, where I spent the next hour on a bench, engaging in one of my favorite pastimes -- people watching.

Lots of families with little kids playing on the jungle gyms. I fondly remembered Ma bringing me here when the weather was nice. I'd scale the monkey bars, and she'd watch from a bench while she smoked a cigarette. She'd wave and smile and I'd wave and smile back. It was nice to see that some things didn't change.

There were the young couples who stopped just short of making-out in public. I wished that Linda Martinsen was with me. I never had considered what an easy and enjoyable date a trip to the park would be. Maybe I'd ask Linda to come to the park with me for some Sunday.

The final six-block walk almost made me feel normal again. I hoped that my mother could not detect anything wrong. Inhaling deeply for air and courage, I sprightly walked up to our apartment.

Something was wrong. The door was partially open and the chain from the lock hung with a piece of the door molding attached to it. Someone had busted the jamb off the wall.

"Ma!" I shouted as I burst in. A strong but terrified voice

came from the kitchen.

"Kelly, I'm in here. Stay away!"

I raced toward the frightened shout and saw Ma crouching on the kitchen floor in the far corner, her hand clasping a butcher knife. Her dress had been torn and a welt was forming on the left side of her face. I had seen this picture before. The table had been pushed to the center, silverware scattered, and Dan Phillips leered like a drunken beast across from Ma. The hunter had its quarry trapped, waiting for the right moment to spring.

"Ma, are you okay?"

I was standing a couple of steps to the side of Phillips but did not know what to do. The vicious glare in my mother's eyes terrified me. I had never imagined that she could transform herself into the animal I saw clutching the knife. Phillip's determination scared me more; he had not recognized my presence as any indication of a threat. I was non-existent to him.

"I'm okay, Kelly. He just got here and he's leaving now before I call the police."

Her bravado was weakened by the tremor in her voice, and Phillips rose to the weakening challenge of his trembling victim. With one sharp yank, he parted the telephone cord from the wall. It was my move.

"Get out of here, Phillips! Get out of here now!" I commanded, but my threats had no impact. In his state of mind, Phillips was oblivious to danger. His mind was muddled but his ferocity was not. Just the look on his face froze me.

"Beat it, kid! This is between your old lady and me. Go and dry hump that little bitch of yours. I bet you didn't tell your mom about that, did ya'? Did you know that I caught your son pumping some slut on your couch one night? Did ya' know that they . . . "

I attacked with a scream and both fists flailing. The punches were wild and he easily grasped both my hands in mid-flight. Phillips quickly reversed my offense into an arm bar. Pain shot through my body as he brought my right arm high behind my shoulder blades, and the socket popped with a crack. He drove me into the wall, and my face slammed against the plasterboard, my nose crunching on impact. I slid down the wall in a heap, my right arm hanging lifelessly. My entire being was a mass of agony.

Mother's shriek distracted my mind from the pain as I saw her race around the table with the knife wildly slicing the air. Phillips was ready for her and grabbed the slashing arm like he had grabbed mine, but Ma was too enraged to be deterred. Hatred for Phillips and her maternal instinct gave her more strength than she realized she possessed.

Desperate, Phillips slapped her across the head. She loosened her grip and he seized the knife. Ma stood before him defenseless. He toyed with the blade, sneering as he began to back her into a corner. God only knew what would happen when she reached the corner of the room.

Using every ounce of energy I had left, I stood, bracing myself against the wall with my good arm. There was little I could do with only one arm; I had already proven myself useless with both arms, but I had to help my mother escape. Phillips was intent on the cowering woman and never noticed or cared about me. There was a fork on the floor and I picked it up. As I closed in behind him, I thought of how futile the situation was – a boy with a fork and one arm, but what else could I do? Ma saw me but locked eyes with the venomous Dan Phillips.

The only skin I could see was his neck, and I did not know what impact I could have. I could see the freckles on his dark skin, and a hair growing from the center of a mole. The fork would not cause much harm, but I had to aim for the exposed area. It was difficult to stick something, anything, into a living being.

Phillips began a sadistic laughter as he moved to within two feet of my mother, taunting her with the knife. Fighting the pain in my broken body, I raised the fork high over my head and clenched my teeth. At the last moment I closed my eyes and slammed the fork down. The stab was off to the side, and only two tines pierced Phillips' neck. The skin was strong, but I could feel his fibers tear as the fork entered his body.

Phillips shrieked like a stockyard pig and turned to look at me. The fork clanged to the floor as he grasped his neck. Enough damage had been done, and Ma darted around the table and ran to the front door, yelling for help.

Blood trickled onto Phillips' collar, and he was incensed by my audacity. He glared at me, not fully understanding what I had done, nor where my strength came from. The knife had fallen to the floor, and I hoped that he would not see it. His eyes became even more like those of a possessed demon, and I could sense that he would not continue his duel to the open doorway, where he might be seen. His prey had escaped and I was merely a remnant without value.

Without touching me, Dan Phillips lumbered through the kitchen, his hand still grasping his bleeding neck. I could hear his heavy retreat down the back stairs.

Defeated but victorious, I staggered back to the front room, grasping furniture for support, ironically, a talent I had learned while drunk. Ma was collapsed on the floor, slumped against the wall, crying, her pleas for help having been answered. The animal was gone; the worst was over, and she released her emotions. The scene was reminiscent of the night I had first comforted a stripper named Ginny Dare, who had been another victim of a man's vicious assault. The pain in my arm began to return with the departure of the peril.

I sat beside my mother and cradled her with my weak left arm as well as I could. She cried on my shoulder, and I cried with her, both of us feeling some shame and disgust for the way we had been forced to act in front of one another. Yet, there was a surge of accomplishment, over-riding the tragedy, and I began to smirk at the absurdity of the whole situation. We crouched on the floor like two war orphans, seeking comfort from each other.

"We're okay now, Ma. He's gone. I saw him run down the back stairs. We'll never see that son-of-a. . . gun again."

My mother tilted my head so that I was looking into her eyes.

Her voice returned. "Kelly, you're a good boy and I appreciate how good you try to be. But, Kelly, Dan Phillips is not a son-of-a-gun." I couldn't grasp her meaning.

Then she added, "He's a son-of-a-bitch! Now say it, Kelly!"

She was sincere. In an authoritative voice, I yelled, "Dan Phillips is a son-of-a-bitch!"

"Louder!" she commanded. So I did.

"One more time, both of us!"

In perfect harmony, we screamed, "Dan Phillips is a son-of-a-bitch!"

Then we started laughing like two inmates in an asylum. My arm was dislocated, my nose was broken, and my mother's face was severely bruised. We were laughing and crying and had nearly been killed, but the trial was over, and we had survived.

Police never came; neighbors never opened their doors, even from curiosity. We went to the emergency room of St. Joseph's. Nothing was physically broken, except my nose, but I almost passed-out when the doctor popped my shoulder back into its socket. We didn't press charges. Doing so would have brought Dan Phillips into our lives again. Charges, reports, indictments, testimonies, witnesses, and the whole barrage of bureaucracy would have thrown the adversaries together for at least another six months. It wasn't worth the price. We could at least cling to the fairly certain hope that he would never reappear. If he did . . . we had defeated him once.

It was nine o'clock by the time we got home. The door to the apartment was still ajar, but nothing had been touched. Brighton Park Code – never steal from a neighbor.

Without asking, Ma went to the kitchen and made two highballs. I sat stiffly on the couch, my arm in a sling and my nose covered with a bandage. I tried not to act surprised when she gave me the drink, which seemed much lighter in color than her drink, and I took it gratefully. Thoughts of the previous night's alcoholic reaction did not deter me, and I found the drink to have a soothing effect. My vow to never drink again had lasted eight hours, but I realized that there might be an appropriate time for consuming, and this moment was one of them.

Ma curled into the corner of the couch and draped her arm over the back. She studied me, making me uncomfortable, but her smile was serene. We were silent for several minutes as she let the drinks work their magic.

"Kelly, did you really have a girl up here?"

Really? I could not believe that with everything that had happened, my relationship with Linda Martinsen would take precedence. But she was a mother – my mother. She hadn't asked it maliciously. For once I was able to look her in the eyes as I spoke the truth.

"Yes, Ma. I did."

She showed no reaction. She had known before she asked. "Did you have sex with her?"

"Ma!" I became alarmed. Nobody but the guys in the locker room asked questions like that. I didn't want her to think that I had broken an unspoken trust, but I did not know how to answer such a forthright question. Her tone had asked for a simple truth with no animosity or threat of punishment, but I was no longer able to hold eye contact.

"No, Ma. Honestly, I didn't."

"Kelly." She waited acknowledgment, and I could tell that she was going to ask the question I feared most, about my changing moods and long nights. I forced myself to look back at her.

"You don't have to answer this if you don't want to, but I'd like to know. You're growing up too fast, and it's difficult for me to keep up. I should say I have a difficult time accepting you as a young man. If you're getting older, so am I."

There was a long pause and she seemed to leave the room while her memories carried her elsewhere, to a time before me. She broke her reverie and spoke softly.

"Last Friday, when you said that you were out all night at Jerry's, he called here and asked for you. I told him that you were supposed to be at his house. He became flustered and said that he had forgotten and that you hadn't arrived yet. You didn't spend the night at Jerry's, did you?"

I wanted to tell her everything – she had earned it. But I felt she already knew and only wanted confirmation. She really didn't want details. Perhaps she wasn't ready to know that her son had befriended a discarded, old stripper and had spent the night with her in a flea-bag hotel on Van Buren Street. Maybe she preferred to think I was still in the exploratory stages, that there was something left of her boy, her son.

"No, Ma. I wasn't at Jerry's."

There was no need to say more. She nodded and smiled. She was satisfied. She had always known everything about me, and I hoped that she would not force me to shatter the shards of boyhood images that remained.

That angelic smile never ceased, and she was satisfied. Her eyes were glassy as memories raced through her mind.

"Would you like to go to Crandall's again for dinner tomorrow? It's a holiday. I'll cut your meat the way I did when you were just a little boy."

Tears reformed in my eyes, and I hugged her. We laughed the nervous laughter of life's milestones, of mutual understanding.

"I love you, Kelly."

"I love you, Ma."

They were words that hadn't passed between us since I was child enough to be tucked into bed. We held each other for a few minutes, as we grew closer with our ever-widening distance.

CHAPTER 13

Year's End

As people do, my mother and I survived our weekend brawl and became stronger and closer because of it. Our fear of menace lessened as time passed, and in a few weeks we were almost able to laugh about our adventure, though the sensation of that fork piercing Dan Phillips' skin never completely left my memories.

Graduation was approaching rapidly, two weeks away, and the spirit of the school was light and anticipatory. Keeping faithful to our truth pact, I told Linda about the skirmish with Dan Phillips and how he had dislocated my arm and broken my nose. She was extremely sympathetic and cringed at what might have been. Of course, I never told her about Mary Harker – we had agreed to tell the truth, but there was nothing in our pact about telling the whole truth. She seemed more than satisfied to hear about just one conflict.

Memories of Mary Harker briefly subsided with the Dan Phillips affair, but it took very little to surface them again. Somebody bragging in the locker room about a trip to the Follies Theatre or a crude comment about a street hooker would enrage me, but I fought to control it. I looked at her picture almost every day, like an obsessed stalker.

Ironically, my brief fling with Mary had an adverse effect on my relationship with Linda. Mary had shown me kindness to assure me of my abilities and to teach me my responsibilities, but I guess it matured me more than she had intended. Linda was a nice girl, but Mary had whetted my appetite for a more mature woman who knew more about life. I wanted to skip the next five years of life, and get to the real stuff. I didn't want "to go" with anyone or try to become part of a new social group or worry about college or the job market. I just wanted to be there. But, of course, that was impossible. Linda was a sweet, kind, and sensitive girl, and she did not push our relationship to the next level. I was lucky to have Linda in my life and grateful for her patience. I relived that first kiss at the bus stop when I was hit with a "Wow!" bolt, that I hadn't felt since, but I sure wouldn't forget.

Bates taught us a poem by Oliver Wendall Holmes titled "The Chambered Nautilus." It was about a snail that would build a new and bigger chamber each year to house its more fully grown body. It would seal off the old chamber, but it had to carry it the rest of its life, though it could never return to its past chambers. The creature built a spiral shell, each chamber larger than the last, until it died with its past still attached to its body. I was never so impressed with a poem in my young life.

Linda was not the only person to make an issue over my battle scars from Dan Phillips. Swedarsky immediately claimed credit for my injured arm, despite the fact that it appeared ten days after our altercation. He vowed that my arm had suffered a hairline fracture during our fight, which did not immediately appear. The absence of a cast did not deter his pretentious bragging. I could have called him a liar behind his back and tried to make the truth be known, but I chose to ignore his boasts. It was his attempt to save face, and it meant more to him than to me. Besides, everyone probably knew the truth but tolerated the windbag, realizing that in a couple weeks they would not have to see him again.

Apparently trying to relieve her guilty conscience again, her shallowness being thwarted the last time, Laura LeDuc asked me what had happened. I told her that I had dislocated my arm falling down some stairs. There was a time when I would have created a fantastic adventure, probably saving an old lady about to be crushed by a city

239

garbage truck, in an attempt to impress her, but I no longer cared if she thought I was a gullible loser.

Whether it was from my recent growth or from the rumors circulating throughout the school I began to feel a tiny bit sorry for Laura. I no longer barked at her and often returned her smile. Word was out that her college boyfriend had left her after using her up, and with her recent disheveled appearance, she began to look like a young Ginny Dare. Further stories told that she had become a real slut and was making it with all her ex-boyfriend's buddies, just for spite and to get even with him. I found it impossible to accept that one person could affect another in so short a time, until I stopped to ponder the effect that Mary Harker had had on me.

Fair or not, Laura had dropped from queen of the school to back alley tramp, while I had soared from pimpled whipping boy to accepted individual. Once I would have fought anyone over a callous remark about Laura, but that time had passed into another sealed chamber, and I felt more pity for her than anything else. Times had changed – I used to pity only myself. Eventually I began to pity so many others – Swedarsky, Mary Harker, Laura LeDuc, and even my own mother.

Ma no longer questioned my every move. Nor did she nag me to help her. I did it all on my own – cleaned house, made supper three days a week before she got home, and simply took care of her. She seemed genuinely at peace. Baldy Smith, the guidance counselor, sent home some brochures on college costs, and Ma and I spent evenings studying them. My scholarship would pay my tuition, and Ma had enough money saved for a year and a half toward room and board and textbooks. I hoped to get a part-time job on campus to earn spending money. Ma wanted me to do well in college and I wanted to do well for the both of us. There were some major changes coming.

Jerry Hogan would not settle for a story about falling down some stairs. He eventually decided that I had broken it when I fell drunk into his bathtub the night of Paul's stag party. He spread the tale throughout the school about his wild party, where "Kelly Elliott was so drunk that he broke his arm falling into my bathtub." He didn't mention the stag films, because he never knew that they were shown. Ironically, Jerry Hogan had slept through what he had labeled, "the wildest party ever at Talbot High School," despite the fact that it had been attended by only two high school students.

As we counted to ten school days, word leaked to the students that Shipstead and Winegarden had "voluntarily" resigned, not that it mattered anyway. Supposedly, our unidentified source claimed to having seen them register at a "shake-and-bake" hotel in Cicero, where he was a busboy. This story revived the once dying term "Shipstead-Winegardening," and soon so-and-so were Shipstead-Winegardening when their parents were gone for the weekend. None of the rumors were verified, but nobody disputed them, making the story plausible to anyone who really cared. I never saw either of them again.

It was during lunch that I first heard the fate of the faculty's Romeo and Juliet. It was also during lunch that Jerry Hogan approached me with news I did not want to hear.

"Great news, Elliott. I got accepted at Northern. Maybe you and I can be roommates."

That revelation made my hot plate of creamed chipped beef on toast and mashed potatoes seem palatable. I tried to dismiss the misery of four more years of Jerry Hogan as my shadow.

"That's great, Jer. When did you get your letter?"

"Yesterday. I had to wait for final class rankings before I knew if I was in the top half of the class, but I made it. I was 275th."

There were 560 in our graduating class, so he made it by five people. I had been ranked 111th, which did not overwhelm me with pride. To brag about just making the top half was inconceivable, even to a cretin.

"Well, maybe we'll be roommates. Did you send in your dorm application yet?" Jerry continued.

"Yes," I lied. He may have been my best friend at one time, but I could hardly tolerate Jerry Hogan any longer.

"Too bad, but maybe we'll luck out anyway. Besides, I'm going to rush my brother's fraternity my freshman year. Then I'll be able to live in the frat house, free of dorm supervisors."

I muttered a rapid, silent prayer that he would be quickly accepted into the fraternity. Maybe his brother could pull some strings. The comradery we used to share was gone and would never return. Perhaps the day would come when he would change, but I envisioned little hope for our future relationship. I confirmed my conviction as I watched him mold his mashed potatoes into a mound and cover the tops with chipped beef – the artists' rendition of a female breast. Jerry tried to talk me into going to the party at his brother's frat house Saturday, but I was able to ignore his whining and begging. It felt good to say no, get up and walk away.

It turned out to be a beautiful, pre-summer night. I spent it walking my favorite Chicago streets. As I strolled down State Street, the Schubert Theatre was releasing its patrons from the Saturday night performance of *The Odd Couple*. Laughter, contentment, ease were all present. God, I loved Chicago and felt good. I was only three blocks from the Swan Hotel, but I had no desire to see it or even walk past it. I caught the el back to Brighton Park and briefly debated whether to spend the night at the theatre or head for home.

As I walked past the Brighton Theatre, I saw Jorge in the ticket office window, selling tickets to the all-night William Castle film festival. That would have been good, but I was going home. I walked up to say "hello" and he automatically started to punch the ticket dispenser button.

"No, no, Jorge. I'm not going in tonight. I'm heading home."

He let the message sink in a little, then smiled broadly.

"Home?" he asked to assure himself.

"Yes, Jorge. Home. As much as I have appreciated your help and kindness over the years, I don't think I'll ever be back for your all-night marathons."

He understood completely and continued his smile.

"Good for you, Kelly Elliott. And good luck after graduation. But you are always welcome at the Brighton Theatre. Vaya con Dios," he concluded with a little wave. It was the first time I had ever heard him speak Spanish. It struck me as odd.

Ten minutes later I tried to slide the key silently into the lock so I wouldn't wake Ma. No need to worry. She was curled on the couch, covered with an afghan, watching some old movie starring Betty Davis.

"Hi, Kelly. Want to watch some mindless late night movie with me?"

"Thanks, Ma, but I'm really whipped. I think I'll just go to bed. Night."

"Night, Kelly. Hey, you want to go to church tomorrow to see Father Pavlis? It's been a long time."

I thought for a few seconds, "Can I tell him a dirty joke?"

My mother laughed. "Sure, why not?"

"What time?"

"Seven o'clock mass?"

"Is there a later showing?"

"Pavlis is on at seven. If you want to see the headliner, you have to be there early. But the stand-by's have shows at 9:00 and 11:30."

I thought again. "Do I get ice cream after?"

"How about breakfast instead?"

"Wake me at 10:30?"

"God, you're a spoiled rotten kid," she joked. "Okay, Kelly. Good night."

"Night, Ma."

I slept like a morgue occupant and was startled out of a deep, pleasant sleep by my mother, who was already dressed for church. Fate played its hand and Father Pavlis served the 11:30 mass. I semi-listened, which was a huge improvement from my usual church-time thoughts. He even gave a special blessing to all the high school seniors who would finish school next week, and ironically gave an Irish blessing about some road rising up to meet us.

Father Pavlis stood at the door and shook hands with the parish as they left. When it was my turn, he covered my hands for a moment, looked at my mother with his stern Lithuanian smile, and said, "We did a good job with this one, Doris. Good luck, Kelly." Ma nodded her head in agreement, put her hand on my back, and herded me toward breakfast.

The final week of school was its usual pressure of final exams and the constant urge to escape and start the summer. In the case of seniors all we could think about was closing the door on high school and beginning the next phase, whatever that might be. They only held us a half day on Friday, and the atmosphere was carnival-like.

We all stood by our open lockers, waiting for a teacher to check us off the list of clean lockers, the last item before book returns and paying fines. Large, industrial size trash barrels were scattered throughout the halls, as most kids just threw away everything, not bothering to sort or keep anything.

My luck, our hall had Bates the English teacher going down the rows. At least he was fast with his checking, probably more eager than his students to get out of jail. Bates gave my locker a perfunctory check and crossed me off the list.

"Thanks, Mr. Bates. Have a good summer."

"Kelly, do you have a minute, please?"

Now what did I do? "Sure."

"Kelly, I really mean it when I say that you have come a long way this year. I know about the Laura LeDuc incident. That was as low as she could go, but she sure elevated you in my eyes. Sorry, but teachers make mistakes, too. Not many, but a few. You're going to Northern next year?"

"Yes, sir," I replied, stunned.

"Well, good luck, Kelly. You'll do just fine." He shook my

hand. The last day and Bates tells me that I'm a good guy. I think he meant it.

I started down the hallway, heading toward the girls' locker room. Suddenly someone grabbed my arm. It was Swedarsky.

"Hey, Kelly. Talk to ya' a minute? I want to ask you something."

Hey Kelly? Not Elliott. Not pizza face. I wasn't about to become his victim on my last day, especially half way out the door.

"What do you want, Swedarsky?" Who's in charge here with the halls full of teachers? I wondered.

"Relax, Kelly. I just want to ask you about college."

"College?" I yelled like it was a nasty joke.

"Calm down. Here's the deal. I got accepted to Northern State on a football scholarship, and I was thinking maybe you and I could be roommates."

Did someone just perform a lobotomy on me and I didn't know it? I could not be hearing this.

Without hesitation, "No."

"Think about it, Kelly. We're both from Talbot High, I could probably get some good football tickets for all the games. Maybe you could even help me with some of my homework. We'd have each other to talk to."

"No, absolutely not!"

He grabbed my arm tighter, as though not ready to take "No" for an answer. I forcefully removed his hand from my arm, and he did not resist.

"Why not?"

I stared at him in disbelief. "Do you really want to know, Swedarsky?"

"Yeah, I really do."

I didn't care if he was going to punch me. I'd live.

"First of all, you're a bully. Secondly, you have the manners of a neutered pig. And you are dumber than anyone I know, and you smell like a barnyard." I paused to see his reaction. He stood like an Easter Island stone face.

"I could change. High school is over."

"And would you like to hear the most important reason?" No reaction.

I grasped his forearms and spoke distinctly. "I don't like you, Swedarsky."

I paused to let that sink into his thick skull. "Good luck with that football thing of yours." And I continued my journey toward the girls' locker room, never glancing back.

Linda Martinsen was standing in front of her locker, her arms folded, patiently waiting for me. I walked up to her and we kissed.

"Ready?" she asked hesitantly.

"Absolutely! Let's get out of here."

"You know, Kelly, we're not coming back."

"Of course, I know. Let's go."

She grabbed my arm as I started walking toward the door. "Won't you miss it?"

"High school? Never. Why, what will you miss? Our friends are all in the neighborhood."

"Yeah, but it's not the same. You don't eat lunch with them every day. We had some good teachers. Going to games won't be the same. Passing notes. Gossip. The whole package. You won't ever walk me to class again, then race down the driveway to get to Bates' class. Our quick hallway kisses. I'll miss all that, Kelly. It's gone for good."

She almost looked like her eyes were getting misty. She was sensitive and made some good points.

I carefully phrased my reply, drawing on every graduation speech ever given. "Yeah, but we'll start a new part of our lives. Come on, maybe things get even better."

A few tears crept down her cheeks and Linda hugged me, then firmly grasped my hand and confidently led me to the exit.

"Kelly, we need to celebrate our last day. I'm going to buy you a coke at Birdie's."

"What?" I was puzzled.

"You heard me. You always pay for our dates, and only

take me to the most exotic night traffic courts. So why can't I buy you a lousy coke? We'll start a whole new feminist movement."

She pulled me through the exit door for some reason determined to buy me a coke.

And she did.

CPSIA information can be obtained
at www.ICGtesting.com
Printed in the USA
LVHW03s1750220618
581593LV00002B/415/P